A small disturbance

The lunatic with the knife, whom Nicholas now realized was nothing more than a girl, struggled mightily.

"Get yer filthy 'ands off of me, you murderin' lout!" she screamed.

"My dear," Nicholas addressed Dr. Gladstone. "Perhaps you'd better go with the other ladies." He nodded his head toward the ballroom, where the ladies were being led by two or three gentlemen.

Dr. Gladstone ignored him and shouted another command to the serving staff. At precisely the same moment another string of obscenities issued forth from the girl on the floor, along with another punch of her knee, which doubled Nicholas over.

"You'd better sit down, sir," the rose-silked woman said.

Nicholas tried to answer her, to keep his dignity and lie to her that he was all right, but pain had robbed him of his voice. It was several seconds before Nicholas was able to stand and then to walk, slightly bent, back to his chair at the table. By now, the other women had all been safely dispersed to the ballroom and the men were settling at the table again, ready for their port. Even a madwoman would not deter an English gentleman from the tradition of port and cigars after dinner.

"Sorry, bloody sorry." Eddie brushed at Nicholas's sleeves and straightened his jacket. "One never knows what one is getting in kitchen help these days."

Symptoms
of Death

Paula Paul

BERKLEY PRIME CRIME, NEW YORK

SYMPTOMS OF DEATH

A Berkley Prime Crime Book / published by arrangement with the author

PRINTING HISTORY
Berkley Prime Crime mass-market edition / May 2002

ISBN: 0-425-18429-3

Berkley Prime Crime Books are published
by The Berkley Publishing Group,
a division of Penguin Putnam Inc.,
375 Hudson Street, New York, New York 10014.
The name BERKLEY PRIME CRIME and the BERKLEY PRIME CRIME
design are trademarks belonging to Penguin Putnam Inc.

PRINTED IN THE UNITED STATES OF AMERICA

10 9 8 7 6 5 4 3 2 1

1

The dinner party was singularly unremarkable until the lu-
natic arrived.

And then, it was not the lunatic whom Nicholas Forsythe
remembered so much as the woman who had been at the
other end of the table. She was the one who stopped
the poor demented creature and saved them all from whatever it is lunatics do when they burst into a dining room
screaming and waving a machete. Mass murder?

Until that unfortunate incident, Nicholas had paid little
more attention to the woman at the end of the long table
than he had the white linen that covered the table or the
gleaming silver with which he brought the rare roast beef
to his mouth. He had only a vague memory of having been
introduced to her by Edward Boswick, fifth earl of Dunsford, his host. He had made the introduction earlier when
she first arrived at Montmarsh, the earl's country estate. The
memory was of rose-colored silk and a bit of décolletage.
Not particularly remarkable décolletage at that, if his memory served him.

The dinner had progressed beyond the roast beef to pud-
ding and cheese, and Nicholas was amusing himself in a bit

of flirtatious conversation with Mrs. Isabel Atewater, his arm resting on the back of her chair and dangerously close to her bare shoulder. He had just moved his forefinger close enough to caress the satiny skin of that very inviting shoulder in a manner discreet enough that her husband, Jeremy Atewater, would not notice. That is precisely when the crazy woman burst into the dining room.

Her hair was loose and flying wildly about her head, her eyes bright with passion. She carried a long knife in her right hand, and she waved it carelessly, crying, " 'E won't get by with it, 'e won't! I'll see to it meself! And you bloody well watch yer selves, all o' ye swells!"

"Come back here, girl! Come back here, I say! For God's sake, girl!" It was the cook calling out to the lunatic while she stood in the doorway that led to the kitchens. The cook wrung her hands in the voluminous brown muslin skirt that covered her more than ample hips. Behind her was a bevy of servants looking over her shoulder, mouths agape and eyes stunned.

Cook would not enter the dining room, however. Instead, she turned away, her face buried in her hands while the madwoman wrecked havoc in the dining room.

" 'Tis your fault, 'tis so!" The lunatic woman pointed the long knife at Edward, the host, before she swung it in an arc to indicate the entire table and then turned back to Edward. "I'll kill ye, Lord Dunsford! Ye bloody nob! And all yer nobbie friends. I'll kill ye for what ye done to Georgie. And none of yer bloody money nor yer bloody houses here in Essex nor in London will save ye!"

She swung the blade again, well off her mark but narrowly missing the top of Jeremy Atewater's head. In the same instant Nicholas sprang to his feet and held the mad woman's arms, restraining her.

The lunatic, whom Nicholas now realized was nothing more than a girl, struggled mightily. "Get yer filthy 'ands off of me, you murderin' lout!" she screamed.

She managed to wrench herself free of Nicholas's grasp and had raised the knife to do God knows what when the

woman in the rose-colored silk grasped the demented girl's
wrist and spoke to her.

Nicholas could scarce hear what she said, but he knew
the voice was soft, almost hypnotic, and at the same time
firm. In spite of the soothing voice, the girl continued to
struggle, and Nicholas, along with Atewater, Lord Dunsford, and Lord Winningham, tried to restrain her again.
They wrestled her to the floor, and Nicholas was aware of
the rose-silked woman shouting for the servants to fetch
something.

"It's with my wrap in the cloakroom. Hurry!" Then she
turned her attention back to the girl who, though she had
dropped the knife, was now kicking on the floor and
screaming obscenities. "Not too rough on her, gentlemen.
She's not going to hurt you," Miss Rose Silk said.

"My dear," Nicholas said, addressing Miss Rose Silk in
a voice that sounded choked because the lunatic girl had
just pushed her knee with considerable force into his stomach, "perhaps you'd better go with the ladies." Nicholas
nodded his head toward the ballroom where the other ladies
were being led by two or three of the gentlemen.

The woman ignored him and shouted another command
to the serving staff. At precisely the same moment another
string of obscenities issued forth from the girl on the floor,
along with another punch of her knee. This time the jab
landed several inches below Nicholas's stomach. Tendrils
of fire radiated from his groin to his buttocks and down his
legs. It doubled him over and brought bile to his throat. He
struggled to swallow it and to keep his balance.

"You'd better sit down, sir," the rose-silked woman said.

Nicholas tried to answer her, to keep his dignity and lie
to her that he was all right, but pain had robbed him of his
voice. He could do nothing except back away weakly and
obey her command.

The rest was a blur to Nicholas. He was vaguely aware
of a servant appearing with a large bag in his hand and the
woman removing a vial of something from the bag, then
mixing the contents with water and forcing the screaming
girl to drink. He also had a hazy memory of the silk-clad

woman leading the subdued girl away toward the kitchen.

It was several seconds before Nicholas was able to stand and then to walk, slightly bent, back to his chair at the table. By now, the other women had all been safely dispersed to the ballroom, and the men were settling at the table again ready for their port. Even a madwoman would not deter an English gentleman from the tradition of port and cigars after dinner.

"Sorry, bloody sorry." Eddie brushed at his sleeves and straightened his jacket. "One never knows what one is getting in kitchen help these days."

"I thought all we'd have to worry about is that band of robbers roaming the countryside," one of the gentlemen said. "Had no idea there would be madwomen. What was that all about anyway?"

"God knows," Eddie said, distracted now by a servant serving the port.

"Accusing you of murder?" Lord Winningham said. "Good God, man, what was she talking about?"

"I have no idea," Eddie said. "I've seen the wench only a few times, and the only time I've spoken to her was last year when Cook hired her and brought her to me for introductions."

"Then you don't know the poor dead bugger she was talking about?" Winningham asked. "Georgie, wasn't it?"

"Georgie?" Eddie shook his head. "I have no idea who the poor bloke could be. She made no sense at all. I suspect she'd been helping herself to the wine cellar."

All of the gentlemen laughed. "Then she must have had bloody good time, Eddie," one of them said, raising his glass. "The port is exceptional."

"Here! Here!" another said, and raised his glass—a signal to all to raise their own.

"The woman who ministered to her," Nicholas said as he selected one of the Havana cigars being offered to him by a servant, "who was she?"

"Oh, you mean Miss Gladstone?" Eddie said. "Didn't I introduce you?"

"Well, yes, you did, but I'm afraid I paid little attention to—"

"Gladstone?" one of the guests said with a certain amount of disgust in his voice. "Don't think I caught the name either. Not related to that bloody William Gladstone in Parliament is she?"

Eddie laughed. "No relation."

"Mark my word," the gentleman said. "The bastard will be prime minister again and what will that do to Disraeli and his foreign policy?"

The topic then turned to politics, and in spite of the fact that Nicholas had learned nothing more about Miss Gladstone, whose looks, he had decided, were far superior than he'd first thought, he did not change the subject. He aspired to a career in politics and took every opportunity he could to learn the political pulse of his class.

As the conversation continued, he downed several glasses of port, so that, by the time it was necessary to join the ladies in the ballroom, the pain in his groin had disappeared completely.

Once in the ballroom, he scanned the room for the woman who had aroused his curiosity in the dining room. Besides her slender form, lovely ginger-colored hair, and sparkling golden eyes, he'd been intrigued by her confident manner with the lunatic. The woman he sought was nowhere in sight. Isabel, however, caught his eye and gave him a coy smile as she wiggled her fingers at him from across the room. Nicholas knew full well what those wiggling fingers meant, but he had by now lost interest in Mrs. Atewater. He was beginning to regret his flirtation, since he would be confined with her and the rest of the guests at Montmarsh for a few days. It was Eddie's habit to invite the liveliest of his London friends out for an extended stay at his country estate in the summer. Nicholas, being the younger son of a viscount with no title to inherit since the family estate and title went to his older brother, had no country estate of his own. He preferred his London town house anyway, for entertaining as well as for living.

"Nicky, old boy! Enjoying yourself, I hope? In spite of

the bloody scene in the dining room." Eddie gave him a hardy slap on the back. Lord Edward had been his classmate at Eton, a handsome man in his early thirties with a stocky build and thick, flax-colored hair and hazel eyes.

"Enjoying myself? Of course, Eddie. Smashing party, as always." He noticed then how pale Eddie looked and how profusely he was sweating. "I say, Eddie, you're not in any danger, are you?"

Eddie laughed. "Danger? Why would you suggest that?"

"After all, that scullery maid did threaten you."

"Oh, that." Eddie pulled a handkerchief from his pocket and smiled. "I told you she must have been drinking. Or perhaps she's a bit touched in the head." He laughed again as he patted the perspiration from his forehead.

Nicholas laughed with him, but he didn't miss the worried look that Eddie tried to mask with his offhanded manner. "And that woman who led her away. What did you say her name is?"

"Oh yes, Alexandra Gladstone. You asked about her before, didn't you?"

"Yes, I think I did, but—"

"Odd woman, that one. But I was obliged to invite her just for the evening. She's the daughter of the late Dr. Huntington Gladstone, you know."

"No, I didn't know—"

"Odd bird in his own right, so it's no wonder his daughter is odd as well. A physician. No title. His brother inherited. No family of distinction, really. But so well respected in our little parish that one doesn't dare slight his offspring if one is to have a party."

Nicholas nodded. "Ah, the daughter of a physician, you say. Then that explains the potion she poured down the poor lunatic's throat with such efficiency. And all without even the slightest mussing of that lovely rose silk she was wearing."

Eddie cocked an eyebrow in a knowing gesture. "Oh, come now, Nicky, don't be going gaga over that one. Won't you have your hands full tonight with Mrs. Atewater? Oh, now don't deny you were flirting with her."

"Well, certainly I tried to be courteous, but—"

"Her room is next to her husband's, so take care when you steal your way across the hall tonight." He winked at Nicholas.

"Always thinking of my welfare, aren't you, Eddie?"

His old classmate grinned and gave him a friendly pat on the back. "If that's the case, then heed my advice. Miss Gladstone is not your type. Rather coarse, if you know what I mean."

"Really? She didn't seem at all coarse."

"Ah, yes, but listen to this: She's actually taken over her late father's practice. Trained well by the old boy, I'll grant you, and all the locals look to her for their doctoring same as they did her father. Knows all about autopsies and any number of ghastly surgical procedures." Eddie pretended to shudder. "Coarse, wouldn't you say? And unwomanly? No amount of silk can remedy that, I think you'll agree."

"Hmmm," Nicholas said, managing to sound noncommittal, in spite of the fact that his curiosity was aroused more than ever.

Eddie might have gone on with more about the woman, but he was distracted by another guest, who pulled him into a little knot of people by insisting that he settle a playful argument concerning the merit of a rather bawdy theater production they'd all seen recently in London.

Free of Eddie, Nicholas scanned the room again, looking for Alexandra Gladstone. He could not spot her, and he was still searching when he felt a hand fall ever so lightly on his arm.

"Isabel!"

"You were expecting someone else?"

A servant walked by with a tray of drinks. Nicholas took one quickly. "Someone else?"

"Who are you looking for, Nicky?"

"No one in particular." He took a sip from the glass and kept his eyes scanning the room.

"Are you going to dance with me?"

He looked down at her, as if he'd only just seen her. "Dance with you? Of course." He placed the glass on a

table, took her in his arms, and led her across the floor to
the strains of the Viennese waltz the orchestra played, making sure he twirled her around so that he had a view of the
door, just in case the mysterious Alexandra entered.

The poor scullery maid's moment of drama was the perfect
excuse for Alexandra to leave the party unnoticed. It was a
party she had attended only because she felt obligated. So
as soon as she was certain the girl—she'd learned her name
was Elsie O'Riley—was calm and in her bed, Alexandra
was on her way home to her own bed.

It had taken a little while, however, to determine what
had gotten the poor child into such a state. Alexandra had
finally pieced together the information she could get from
Elsie, along with the testament of the kitchen staff. The girl
was quite simply distraught over the death of her lover,
George Stirling. George, the cook said, was one of the boys
from town. He'd been found in an alley near the waterfront
that morning, dead of apparent strangulation. Elsie, it
seemed, had seen the body and was still distraught.

"We all feared young George would come to a no-good
end," the cook had said. "Keeping company with the wrong
sort, that one! No family that we know of, and not the sharp-
est wit, either. 'E was up to no good, that one."

All suspicion for George's death pointed to the band of
young thugs with whom George had been associating, according to the cook. She said the constable was questioning
them, and they had, in fact, claimed his body for burial.
Perhaps, the wise cook had surmised, young George had
learned something about the young thieves' trade that he
should not have known, and it cost him his life.

Elsie would have none of it, though. She believed, irra-
tionally it would appear, that Edward Boswick, fifth earl of
Dunsford, was to blame for George's death. It was not at
all clear to Alexandra why the child would think such a
thing, and it was her hope to straighten out the matter in
the morning when she returned to check on the girl's well-
being.

All of that had taken some time, so by the time she re-turned to her house on the outskirts of the village, fed and watered Zachariah, her dog, and helped Nancy, her maid-of-all-work, secure the house, it was quite late before she went to bed.

She had not been up long the next morning when she heard a knock on her door. Nancy was busy in the kitchen, so Alexandra answered the door herself. She was surprised to see one of the guests from the previous night's party at Montmarsh standing in front of her.

She could not remember his name. She could remember, however, that he had taken Elsie's knee in his groin the night before. He stood before her now, dressed in the casual attire of a gentleman, but so impeccably and elegantly out-fitted that he did not appear English. He could have been mistaken for a Frenchman, especially with his dark hair and swarthy, handsome face. Only his diamondlike blue eyes betrayed his true heritage.

He looked momentarily confused, as if he had expected someone else, a servant probably, to answer his knock. But he recovered quickly. "Miss Gladstone, I hope you will par-don my intrusion. I am Nicholas Forsythe. Perhaps you re-member me. We were introduced last night at Montmarsh."

"Of course, Mr. Forsythe," Alexandra said, relieved at having been given his name. "Please come in." She stepped aside to allow him to enter. He seemed reluctant at first, but she urged him in with a sweep of her arm. "Please . . ." Of course he would be reluctant. He would, no doubt, be find-ing it difficult to discuss whatever repercussions he might imagine himself to have as a result of the blow to his pri-vates the previous evening.

Zachariah had roused himself from his spot in front of the fire and was now standing beside her, nuzzling at her skirts. It was only then that Alexandra realized the true rea-son for Mr. Forsythe's reluctance. Zachariah was a 150-pound Newfoundland dog who had belonged to her father, and his bearlike looks could be intimidating. Alexandra couldn't bring herself to get rid of the creature, though, because he had been such a constant companion to her late father.

"Never mind Zack," Alexandra said. "He won't hurt you."

"Quite so." Mr. Forsythe stepped inside, and as soon as he did, Zack lost interest and returned to the fire. Mr. Forsythe, however, kept a wary eye on Zack until he was certain the dog was safely lying down and not preparing to pounce.

"If you would like to come back to the surgery, Mr. Forsythe," Alexandra said, pointing the way, "you can describe your symptoms."

"Symptoms?"

Alexandra was on her way to the surgery, but she turned back to her guest. "Please, sir, don't be embarrassed. You must think of me not as a woman, but as a physician."

"Physician?"

Alexandra took a deep breath. Perhaps this was going to be more difficult than she thought. Either he was terribly nervous and embarrassed or he was a bit daft. "I am a physician, Mr. Forsythe." She spoke slowly, softly, so as not to unnerve him further. "It is true that I was not allowed to study medicine in the traditional way. I was allowed into most of the lectures but, I'll admit, none of the surgeries and autopsies, because those in authority deemed it improper for one of my sex. But my father has trained me well in all that I missed because of our society's ridiculous reasoning concerning my gender, and I have secured a license. I am sure your friend, Lord Dunsford, will attest to my ability."

Mr. Forsythe laughed suddenly and so uproariously that Alexandra was taken aback. Zack raised his head to stare at the braying creature and let out an alarmed yelp. "Ah, forgive me, please," Mr. Forsythe said, sobering quickly and with a wary eye on the dog. "I can see how you misunderstood, but I didn't come as a patient. I came to discuss the lunatic."

"The lunatic, Mr. Forsythe? I don't understand."

"The girl who came roaring into the dining room last night, threatening our host."

"Oh, you mean Elsie. But she's no lunatic, I assure you." By now, Nancy had appeared with a tray bearing tea and scones. She'd no doubt heard the guest enter and had anticipated the need for tea without being told. "Thank you, Nancy. Sugar, Mr. Forsythe?"

"Yes, please, and a spot of milk. Not a lunatic, you say?"

"She was upset. Understandably. A friend of hers had been brutally murdered. Apparently by a gang of thugs."

"Upset?" Mr. Forsythe gave her an incredulous look. "That's an understatement, certainly. I can assure you that none of us would have slept soundly last night had you not sedated her with your potion. We would have all expected to have been butchered with that . . . that machete."

Nancy was taking an inordinately long time arranging the tea.

"That was not a machete, Mr. Forsythe. It was a carving knife. And as for the potion I gave her, it was nothing more than a placebo. Sugar water, to be exact."

"My God, we could have all been—"

"You were in no danger. The poor girl needed nothing more than a shoulder to cry on. I let her talk until she was exhausted. She has some irrational idea that Lord Dunsford killed her lover, although she couldn't, or wouldn't, say why she believes that. Interestingly enough, all of the other servants swear that the earl could not possibly have done such a thing because he was at Montmarsh when the poor fellow died. Some of them think his death wasn't a result of foul play at all, but that he died of a disease. Consumption, I would say, judging by the symptoms they described. Nevertheless, the girl was distraught and irrational, so I instructed Cook to look after her, and I will look in on her from time to time."

"I see."

"I had planned to ride to Montmarsh today to speak with Lord Dunsford about her. He may want to rid himself of her, of course, but I wanted to plead leniency for her."

"Hmmm."

Nancy lingered, dusting the mantel.

"I'm sorry you were frightened, Mr. Forsythe."

"Frightened?"

He took on an odd expression, and Alexandra couldn't tell whether she had offended him or merely surprised him. "By the girl's outburst, I mean. All of that bluster, those threats. It could have been very unsettling, but I should think one could see that she was frightened herself, that she was nothing more than an overwrought girl with a knife."

"Precisely."

Alexandra put down her teacup carefully and studied her guest's face. "Mr. Forsythe, you seem to be quite adept at the art of one-word conversation, but perhaps you could depart from that enough to tell me the real reason you're here this morning. Nancy, you may be excused."

"The real reason? Why, it was just as I said. I wished to discuss the luna—er, the scullery maid. I simply wanted to make certain that she was no danger to anyone or to herself."

"Hmmm."

Mr. Forsythe cleared his throat and looked decidedly uncomfortable. "Ah, perhaps, since you say you want to speak with Lord Dunsford this morning about the girl, I could offer you a ride. I took the liberty of purloining his carriage and driver this morning, since no one was out of bed when I left. I'm an early riser, you see."

Alexandra poured the last of the tea into his cup and doubted very much that Nicholas Forsythe was in the habit of rising early. He was after something. "That's very kind of you, Mr. Forsythe, but I'm afraid I'll have to decline. I've several patients to see before I reach Montmarsh."

"Then please allow me to take you on your rounds."

"I wouldn't want to trouble you, I—"

"No trouble at all. It would be my pleasure."

"But Lord Dunsford's carriage, he would certainly not want you to have it all day."

He pondered it briefly. "Perhaps I could drive your carriage for you, then."

"I have no carriage, Mr. Forsythe. I make my rounds as

my father did, on horseback. And when the weather is bad or when I am obliged to attend a social function I hire a carriage and driver."

"I see."

Alexandra was surprised to see how crestfallen he looked. It had never occurred to her until then that he had been pursuing her. She almost laughed aloud. The beautiful woman she'd seen him flirting with last night must have spurned him, and now he was casting about for another conquest to amuse himself until he returned to London.

"Perhaps I'll see you at Montmarsh," she said as Nancy reappeared to clear away the tea tray.

"Certainly." He stood, and Nancy put down the tray and went to fetch his hat and cloak. He pulled the cloak around him with a careless fling, took his hat, and picked up his brass-tipped cane, which he'd left by the door. He gave her a slight bow. "Until later, Dr. Gladstone."

Both Alexandra and Nancy watched as he turned and made his exit.

"Who was that dandy?" Nancy asked when the door was closed.

"One of Lord Dunsford's guests from London. I should have thought you'd picked up that much with your eaves-dropping."

"Eavesdropping? What do you mean, miss?"

Alexandra ignored her pretense of innocence. "I believe he said his name was Nicholas Forsythe." She was search-ing for her medical bag, which she thought she had placed on the floor next to the sofa. Zack must have pushed it underneath with his nose.

"I think he fancies you, Miss Alex."

"Nonsense." Alexandra was on her knees trying to reach the bag, which was, indeed, under the sofa. "He's bored, that's all. Once he returns to the city, he'll forget all about me."

"Say what you like, but he didn't come here concerned about a scullery maid. It was you that got him here. You and that gown you wore last night. I knew it would work if you cut it low enough in the front."

"Nancy! For goodness sake!" Alexandra tried to remain serious, but she couldn't stop the laugh that bubbled forth when she saw Nancy sputtering as she tried to keep her own laughter at bay. Nancy was only two years older than Alexandra, and she had been with Alexandra and the late Dr. Gladstone since she was ten and Alexandra eight. She was the closest thing to a sister Alexandra would ever have, in spite of the difference in their social classes.

Alexandra was still in a light mood when she let Freddie, her somewhat unreliable stable boy, help her into the side-saddle. Her mood stayed bright as she visited her two patients on the way to Montmarsh.

When she arrived at the mansion, however, an unexplained foreboding crept over her, darkening her mood. As she dismounted and started up the walk, Mr. Forsythe came quickly down the front steps of the house to meet her on the walkway. It was as if he had been watching for her.

He grasped her shoulders and looked into her face. That was when she saw the terror in his eyes.

"It's Eddie," he said. "He was murdered in his bed last night. Someone stabbed him in the heart. And Elsie's disappeared."

2

"Lord Dunsford? Dead?" Alexandra could hardly believe she was asking such a question. Edward Boswick, fifth earl of Dunsford, had become an institution in the countryside as well as in the nearby village of Newton-Upon-Sea, just as his father before him and, Alexandra was certain, his grandfather and great-grandfather and all the way back to the first earl of Dunsford. Much of the economic base of the area was grounded in the Dunsford lands and its tenants, and there was always a certain festive feel to the air when Parliament and the London social season ended and the earl came home to the country, bringing his aristocratic friends with all their finery, hunting excursions, and gay parties. It allowed the country folk and villagers a kind of voyeuristic pleasure, not unlike witnessing a parade, or perhaps a circus.

"I'm afraid it's true, my dear." Mr. Forsythe had taken her arm and was leading her inside to the great hall. "We're all as shocked as you are. None of us can believe Eddie is dead."

Alexandra realized that Mr. Forsythe did, indeed, look as if he was in shock. She popped open her medical bag and rummaged through it looking for smelling salts in the event he might need them. Perhaps she should suggest he lie down for a moment.

"But you mustn't let the rest of them make you feel you're at fault for not properly sedating that girl." He spoke before she could propose any remedy at all. "Of course you had no way of knowing she was a murderess."

Alexandra's hand remained suspended over her bag, and she turned to look at him. "Everyone is certain Elsie O'Riley is a murderess?"

He looked surprised. "Well, of course, she—"

"There is proof?"

"Surely you will agree that she—"

"Proof, Mr. Forsythe. Beyond reasonable doubt."

The look he gave her now was a bit condescending. "Proof, of course, must be left to the local authorities and to the courts, but you witnessed her threats with a knife, and the poor fellow was stabbed in the heart. The evidence certainly points to the young maid's guilt."

"I cannot believe it." Alexandra's tone was firm. "Elsie O'Riley is no murderess."

"And you have proof she is not?"

She faltered only a moment, but it was enough to cause a triumphant gleam in Forsythe's eye—a barrister who had outsmarted a witness. In spite of everything, she found herself intrigued, in fact, delighted to be challenged.

"I have no proof, Mr. Forsythe, which is to say, there is no proof for either her guilt or her innocence. My assessment is based upon intuition, which, I dare say, is exactly the same thing those who assess her guilty are using."

"Your point is well taken," he said. "But you must admit, circumstantial evidence—"

"I will admit nothing, Mr. Forsythe. And I assume, sir, that the constable has been notified."

"Of course. I dispatched a servant this morning, and he has returned. The constable will follow shortly." His expression changed. "As I was saying, I hope you will not be too upset, Dr. Gladstone, that the other guests may express their anger at you for not properly sedating the girl."

She held his eyes a moment and was surprised to see true

discomfort there over her supposed plight. "Upset? Of course not. I did what I thought was best. If I was wrong and did indeed help bring about Lord Dunsford's death by my negligence, then I shall be sorry. As for the assumptions of others, erroneous or otherwise, I cannot be responsible for that."

For the first time since she had seen him today, Nicholas Forsythe smiled. "Are you always so restrained and detached? It's a pity you weren't born a man. You would make an excellent barrister."

"The pity lies in the fact that one must be born a man."

He raised an eyebrow, but before he could comment, he was distracted by the sound of a knock against the hard birch of the front door.

The butler appeared as if from thin air to open it. Alexandra watched as the man she knew as Constable Robert Snow stepped in. She heard Snow give his name to the butler while he looked over the man's shoulder at her and Mr. Forsythe, where they both stood at the foot of the grand staircase. Snow immediately caught her eye, and she read in that glance that he had been told, by the servant who was sent to fetch him, no doubt, that she was considered, in part, culpable for what happened to Lord Dunsford.

The butler approached them with the constable in tow and spoke to Forsythe.

"Mr. Forsythe, the constable, Robert Snow, is here." The butler's head was slightly bowed and his voice hushed in deference to the death of his master.

Forsythe, it appeared, had taken charge in the absence of his host. He shook Snow's hand and then turned to Alexandra. "Dr. Gladstone, may I present Constable Snow."

"I have known Dr. Gladstone since she was a child," the constable said.

"I hope you are well," Alexandra said to the tall, thin, somewhat ethereal-looking man. She had, indeed, known Robert Snow all her life. Before he became the constable, he had been a schoolmaster. He went about his duties as constable as he had when he was a teacher—with an air of quiet, detached self-confidence.

"Of course." The constable glanced at the stairs. "I should like to see the body now," he said. "And of course, no one should leave the house until I've had a chance to question everyone." His eyes went to Forsythe again. "You will show me where the body is, and you, Dr. Gladstone," he said, turning to her, "will examine the body and provide me with the medical report."

He turned away and headed up the stairs. Alexandra exchanged a look with Forsythe, who raised his eyebrows, and she responded with a slight shrug. Along with Forsythe, she followed the constable up the stairs.

*Isabel Atewater watched the goings-on from a front-facing win-*dow in her bedroom. She had seen the Gladstone woman ride up to Montmarsh and watched Nicholas run down the steps to meet her and lead her into the house.

Eddie had said the woman was some sort of physician, so she must be coming back to check on that ranting kitchen maid. Well, she wouldn't find her. The wretched creature had disappeared. Everyone was saying the previous night's tragedy was partly the Gladstone woman's fault, that if she had properly sedated that horrible girl she could not have murdered poor Eddie. Everyone, that is, except Nick.

As for Nick, well, he was only living up to his reputation as a Don Juan and flirting with her, although the Gladstone woman didn't seem to be his type. Not flashy enough. Perhaps in the country, one gets desperate. Perhaps that's what she herself had been—desperate—when she was flirting last night with Nick.

If any of her recent actions were acts of desperation, it had to be Eddie's fault, didn't it? How utterly cruel and unfeeling he had been. How dare he break off their relationship in such an abrupt and uncaring way.

It's been amusing, Izzy, but I've outgrown you. I'm sure you'll agree it's time we both moved on.

Outgrown you, he had said. As if he had thought of her as a silly child. Well, she was no child, and she wasn't about to allow him to embarrass her by ending the relationship and then moving on to some trollop with whom he could laugh about his previous romps with Isabel Atewater.

She had been flattered that Edward, Lord Dunsford had been attracted to her. An earl! And she only the daughter of a baronet. She had begun to think that perhaps she'd been too hasty in accepting Jeremy Atewater's marriage proposal after all. But then her feelings for Eddie had gone beyond flattery. She'd loved him. And she'd thought he loved her.

She'd set out to make him jealous by flirting with Nick Forsythe. In truth, though, that wasn't completely born of desperation. She had to admit to herself that she well might have flirted with Nick under any circumstances. He was one of the most in-demand bachelors in London, and, if Lady Beeton was correct, one of the most exciting lovers.

Isabel could do with a little excitement. Six years with Jeremy Atewater had brought her to that. Jerry was far too busy with his money and his banks to have time for her. Not that he had ever been an exciting lover anyway. In spite of that, Isabel would never have considered leaving him for anyone except Eddie. She'd have liked the chance at being the countess, Lady Dunsford, in spite of the scandal a divorce from Jeremy might have caused. But Eddie had embarrassed her by spurning her, and no man who embarrassed her would live to get away with it.

And now that Eddie was dead, she was beginning to realize that she had a lot to be thankful for in Jeremy. After all, he provided her with a fashionable London town house and a grand estate in the Midlands—purchased, of course, rather than inherited.

True, he had no title, and true, his ancestors had been common merchants. His great-great-grandfather had been a shoe cobbler, to be exact, who had built his business to such a level of prosperity that he had begun loaning money to fellow merchants. His son had been the first to leave the cobbler's bench and establish a small bank. Succeeding generations had built the bank with shrewd investments until they had become one of the wealthiest families in London, able to afford luxuries equal to anything the aristocracy might have, including the finest public schools for Jeremy, which had made him a classmate of Eddie Boswick and Nick Forsythe and where he had met the distinguished alumnus Lord Winningham, among others.

Isabel, whose baronet father was of considerably diminished fortunes, knew there was more to life than a title, unless it brought money with it. And who was to say she might not be Lady Atewater someday anyway, since there was talk of knighthood for Jerry. For his contribution to the economy, of course. The queen was no fool. She understood the importance of money as well as Isabel.

But, Isabel thought, even if she did appreciate Jeremy, she still felt justified for anything she had done to Eddie. Even if he was dead now. She'd never felt sentimental about the dead anyway.

She'd openly flirted with Nick last night and made sure Eddie knew about it. Yet Eddie had not seemed in the least troubled by it. All the more reason for her love for him to seethe and simmer and come to a boil in the form of hate.

She'd fallen asleep waiting for Nick to come to her room, but he never showed up. Perhaps she would have to find a way to get even with him as well for that little embarrassment.

All the time she was awake waiting for Nick she'd had to listen, through her open door, to the other guests making their disgusting night noises, none of which a lady could even mention, except, perhaps, Eddie's coughing.

She recognized that cough. She'd awakened to it more than once in the sunny bedroom of his London house. This time she'd lain in bed for a while, listening, and finally, she'd gotten out of bed and padded silently down the hall to his room. No one had seen her, she was sure of it, so there was no need to mention it when the constable, who had been sent for, came asking questions. Everyone was convinced it was that dotty kitchen maid who had stabbed him anyway, so why make things confusing for anyone?

Isabel was sure that all the guests felt as she did, as if they couldn't wait to get away from Montmarsh and back to London. In fact, she would have been gone already except that Nick and Jerry and Lord Winningham and all of

the others had said it would not be good form to leave
before the constable arrived. Isabel could not, for the life
of her, see what difference it made whether or not they
stayed to talk to the constable when everyone thought they
knew who the killer was, but her attempts to convince anyone else of that had been in vain.

She saw a shabby carriage approaching the house. It was
the constable in his equally shabby uniform.

Isabel watched as the officer alighted from the carriage,
brushed at his uniform, squared his shoulders as if he had
just been ordered to attention, and marched toward the entry
to Montmarsh.

It would be over soon then, and she and Jeremy could be
on their way back to London. They could leave the constable to worry about the fact that everyone assumed there was
a murderess running loose in the area, as a result of the
Gladstone woman's negligence.

Isabel turned away from the window and was about to
ring the bell to summon a maid to help her pack for the
journey home when she thought she heard footsteps in the
hall, and then voices. When she went to her door to peek
out, she saw that the constable, along with Nick and the
Gladstone woman, were in the hallway, and they all seemed
headed for the bedroom where Eddie's dead body lay.

It was out of the question that she should wait in her
room and not know what was being said in Eddie's room.
She realized that it was not likely that any of the other
guests would see her, since they were all still in the drawing
room where they had gathered after breakfast to express
their individual horror and to mourn poor dead Eddie after
the chambermaid found him this morning.

When she stuck her head out into the hallway again, there
was no one in sight. Removing her slippers quickly, she
walked down the hall with such stealth and lightness she
imagined that she might appear to be an apparition.

The door to Eddie's room was slightly ajar, and she found
that if she pressed herself close to the wall in the dark hallway several feet back from the door, she could see everyone
in the room reflected in the mirror across from Eddie's bed.

A spot the size of a small melon on Eddie's sheet had turned an ugly dark crimson, and Isabel could see that his face was a ghastly shade of white. For a moment she thought she might lose her breakfast because of the horrible sight. His eyes bulged, and his tongue protruded slightly. She had never actually seen what happened to a body after it had been dead for a while. Never realized how truly undignified death was and how *improper* the human body was in such a state.

But she forced herself to remain where she was. It was important that she know what they would say.

Miss Gladstone appeared intent upon her examination and oblivious to the indecency of death. The constable, with tail feathers spread, stood with his notepad and pen poised, waiting for her to speak, while Nick, fool that he was, stood back with an expression of such admiration on his face that one might have thought he was waiting for the Gladstone woman to raise Eddie from the dead.

*Alexandra removed her hands from the cool, pale body of Ed-*ward Boswick and wiped them on a towel. She glanced at the constable, who waited expectantly, and when she spoke, her voice was low and confident. "It is my opinion that the earl died of strangulation."

The constable's eyebrows went up in surprise. "Strangulation, you say?" There was a condescending chuckle. "Certainly, my dear woman, you did not miss the blood or the obvious wound on his chest."

"And neither did I miss the mark on his throat nor the fact that his eyes bulge and his tongue protrudes. He was strangled, sir, with a ligature of some sort, and he was stabbed later."

Constable Snow eyed her with a questioning look. "Would you mind explaining, Dr. Gladstone?"

She did her best to keep her voice even and not to allow her impatience to show. "I've formed my opinion about the cause of death based on a few facts. First, there is relatively little blood, which suggests that by the time Lord Dunsford's chest was stabbed, his heart had stopped pumping and that some of the blood, following the laws of gravity, had begun to pool in the bottom of the body, which indicates that he was already dead when his chest was stabbed. Second, there is a mark at his neck suggesting strangulation, and, as I mentioned, the protrusion of the eyes and tongue. It is logical to assume, then, that death came by strangulation and he was stabbed, perhaps sometime later, as an afterthought. Not in the heart, as Mr. Forsythe assumed, but slightly below the heart."

The constable frowned. "Are you suggesting, Dr. Gladstone, that the killer came back into the room to stab Lord Dunsford after he was already dead?" Constable Snow had measured his words in such a way as to make it sound as if he thought that idea was preposterous.

"It is possible," Alexandra said. "Or it is possible that someone else came in and stabbed him after the first intruder had strangled him."

"Hmmm," Forsythe said.

The constable frowned and shook his head as if to dismiss her hypothesis altogether. "I see no reason anyone would commit such an act."

She scarcely gave the constable time to finish his sentence. "In the first instance, to make it look as if someone else had killed the earl, or in the second instance, because the second intruder did not know the earl was already dead."

The constable's eyes widened in surprise. "What?"

"Hmmm," said Forsythe again. "In your first example, someone might have wanted to make it look as if the scullery maid had killed him."

Alexandra nodded silently, and the constable immediately protested. "My good woman, you can't be serious."

Forsythe was still ruminating. "The poor lunatic could be the perfect pawn."

Constable Snow raised a hand and shook his head as if to ward off any more of Forsythe's words. "It is my understanding that Elsie O'Riley, a kitchen maid, threatened to kill Lord Dunsford and others with a knife last night at dinner, and that she has now disappeared. That was the message conveyed to me by the servant who was sent to fetch me. If the servant got his information wrong, then I must know immediately."

"The servant was correct," Alexandra said, "but—"

"Then we have a suspect," Snow said.

She shook her head. "I'm not so sure. It could be that the girl fled simply because she was frightened that she *would* be accused, which may be precisely what the real killer wanted."

Constable Snow considered her remarks for a moment with a finger to his pursed lips. "Very well," he said at last. "I shall question each of the guests as well as the servants. No one is to leave the premises until I give permission."

The constable then pulled the sheet up to cover Lord Dunsford's body, which was clad in an elaborate red silk nightshirt, and gave instructions that Alexandra and Forsythe were to wait for him in the library downstairs and that everyone else, guests and servants, was to be instructed to be there as well.

Alexandra gathered up her medical bag and stepped into the hall, along with Forsythe and Constable Snow, just in time to see Isabel Atewater hurrying away. The constable called out to her.

"Madam! Madam, could I have a moment, please?"

Isabel kept walking, and Alexandra sensed that she was only pretending not to hear. In the next second Forsythe called out to her as well.

"Isabel, my dear."

Isabel stopped walking and slowly turned around with both hands over her heart as if she were trying to hold in some emotion.

"Isabel," Forsythe said again as he walked toward her. "I'm afraid the constable has a favor to ask of all of us."

"I'm sorry, but I'm not feeling well." There was a tremble in her voice that Alexandra was certain was not artificial. "I was just going to my room to lie down."

"You're quite pale." Forsythe's tone was solicitous.

Alexandra saw that she was, indeed, very pale. "Perhaps I can help."

Isabel's eyes darted toward her. "Oh no, it's nothing. I'm just a little tired. No, what I mean is . . . I, well, I'm . . ."

She continued to stammer until the constable stepped forward. "Forgive me, madam, but I must ask you to forego your rest a bit in the interest of police business."

Isabel's eyes widened. "Well, I . . ."

"I can understand how distraught you all must be, especially the more delicate among you," the constable continued. "And I'm certain you'd like to see this matter resolved as quickly as possible. I beg your cooperation to facilitate the matter."

Isabel hesitated a moment, then spoke in a voice that had lost its tremble and had become cooing. "Well, if it won't take long. You see, I really am distraught, and I must get back to London as soon as possible. My physician, a man of true skill, is there"—she gave Alexandra an accusing glance—"and I simply wouldn't trust anyone else to attend me. My condition is really quite delicate."

"Oh, I'm certain it is, madam." The constable offered her his arm and led her toward the grand stairway. "And you can be sure I will keep that in mind, and that I will complete the investigation as soon as possible."

Alexandra watched as Isabel breathed what seemed to be a sigh of relief. She gazed into Constable Snow's eyes and gave him a demure, yet flirtatious smile.

3

Lord Henry Charles Scargrave, fourth earl of Winningham,
watched as the guests gathered in the library while he held
the hand of his whimpering wife, seated next to him.
Around them, the air was golden, gilded with sunlight
streaming through the long windows that overlooked the
front gardens.

He had an almost uncontrollable longing to be outdoors,
to allow that golden light to engulf him and baptize him
with its splendor. If he could, he would run among the trees
shouting and singing, disturbing their silent green medita-
tion on this fine morning.

But he could not. He must follow the holy ritual of De-
corum. He had been with the other guests earlier when they
gathered en masse in the drawing room, each of them
shocked and bewildered by the horror of what had happened. He had commiserated with each of them, being solicitous to his wife and the other ladies, expressing his own
shock in low, murmured tones with the gentlemen, and being equally vocal about the culpability of Miss Gladstone,
who, of course, should have had the good sense to sedate
the kitchen wench appropriately until she could be properly

dealt with this morning. That was, after all, what they all thought she'd done.

He could not admit to anyone, least of all his wife, that he was, in truth, immensely grateful that Elsie O'Riley's temperament had displayed itself in the very public and threatening way that it had, and that Miss Gladstone had not sedated her. Because of those events, the matter of Eddie's death was sure to be put to rest quickly, and that alone made him want to shout like a Nonconformist zealot.

Of course there would be the formality of questioning by the constable, but that would most certainly be over in short order. The constable would not seriously suspect any of the guests.

So here he sat in the library, watching as the other gentlemen lead the ladies in, everyone looking appropriately shocked and sorrowful. Young Forsythe entered, deep in conversation with that odd Gladstone woman, to whom he seemed to have taken a liking. Atewater entered alone, grief cutting deep grooves in his paler-than-usual face. His wife, presumably, was too ill to accompany him, since she had excused herself early from the assembly in the drawing room this morning.

Ah, but he was wrong, here she came now on the arm of the constable, looking anything but grieved. She appeared to have mesmerized the poor bloke. But that didn't surprise Winningham. He knew her reputation among the aristocracy. Eddie had not been exactly discreet in his descriptions of their affair, and Winningham had witnessed her shameless flirtations with others many times before. He had even thought he might have a go at her himself one of these days, in spite of the fact that he was a good twenty years her senior. She seemed to be rather undiscriminating so long as the fellow had a few pounds in the bank and possessed a title. It did surprise him, however, that she would flirt with someone of the constable's class who had neither title nor money. For the moment, though, he had other interests and concerns. He wanted to get this little formality of talking with the constable behind him.

As he continued to watch and to pat Lady Winningham's

well-cushioned hand, the golden light, communing with
dark clouds, faded to blue and lurked in the curtains. The
new gloomy light made him think again of Eddie. Foolish,
cruel Eddie.

Winningham had known him since he was a child, long
before the boy's father, the fourth earl of Dunsford, died
and Eddie inherited his title. Their families were, in fact,
connected by a common ancestor several generations back.
Winningham himself had made some discreet contacts on
behalf of the young Boswick when it appeared he could not
pass the entrance exam to Eton. As his association with the
future earl of Dunsford increased and their friendship deep-
ened, Winningham quickly saw that the boy was no dunce.
True, he had no intellectual bent, but he possessed a sharp,
quick mind and a level of cunning that rendered him both
attractive and formidable.

Winningham had fallen prey to both traits. Edward Boswick's knack for increasing his already sizable fortune by
shrewd investments was indeed attractive. Winningham had
invested some money of his own more than once at Eddie's
behest and had benefited handsomely.

He had even seen something of his younger self in the
man—his daring, his willingness to experiment, his una-
bashed eagerness to indulge himself. What Winningham
lacked that Eddie had, however, was a level of narcissistic
cruelty.

Winningham would never have guessed that his own
self-indulgent willingness to experiment would bring him
face-to-face with Edward Boswick's formidable, cruel op-
portunism. The astonishing unfairness of what Eddie had
done to him had been a bitter surprise. Gentlemen simply
did not do to their peers what Eddie had done. It was clear
the younger generation had no sense of honor.

Winningham prided himself on the fact that his fifty-two
years did not show on either his face or physique. He looked
to be, he was told, and so he believed, a good ten years
younger. Even the degree of corpulence he had attained had
done nothing but improve his bearing, he believed.

Yet, in spite of that, one did have to keep in mind one's

mortality. There could be, perhaps, fewer than ten years left. There was so much of life to live, so many experiences to partake of, and so little time to do it. Winningham thought that what he felt was a certain healthy joie de vivre, and that what he had done was nothing more than an attempt to add one more worldly experience to his ever shortening life.

What was damnably unfortunate was that Eddie had caught him and the rather pretty young man in the act, and what was even more unfortunate was that even before Eddie had arrived, Winningham had determined that the experience was not particularly to his liking, and that he would not be likely to repeat it.

How Eddie had known the address of their tryst or how he managed to obtain a key to the room would forever remain hidden from him now. He could only attribute it to Eddie's cunning. Blackmail he attributed to his cruelty. It had done no good to try to explain to Eddie that it had been only an experiment, that it was not likely to become a habit. It certainly did no good to speculate that it was something Eddie might have tried himself at one time or another.

It was very expensive blackmail, already wiping out all of the investment gains he'd made as a result of his alliance with Eddie. But he had to pay, didn't he? He had to pay or lose his seat in the House of Lords, the respect of his peers and his family. He had to pay or lose himself. The only other alternative was to get rid of Boswick.

He had planned it so many different ways, none of them satisfactory. And then Boswick had invited him to his country estate for no other reason than to embarrass him and to goad him further, he was certain. But he couldn't refuse the invitation could he? His wife would certainly be unhappy about a refusal and would demand an explanation, and what excuse could he give? He'd felt trapped. At first. And now that it was over he wanted nothing more than to run through the meadows shouting his joy of salvation. Or perhaps to collapse into tears at his relief for having been saved.

But he could do neither now. He must play the role of Lord Winningham with his mask of shock and grief, and he must wait, quietly, patiently.

The constable cleared his throat and began. "Ladies and gentlemen . . ."

The man had assumed a Napoleon-like stance, one hand tucked into his coat, the other resting on the table. Winningham was fascinated. He studied the man, his scuffed boots, badly in need of a blackening, the fabric of his uniform, grown shiny with wear and frayed at the cuffs, his full head of hair, slightly too shaggy to be fashionable, and a large, pitted nose that domineered his countenance like a boatswain.

". . . the servants' accounts of the kitchen maid, Elsie O'Riley, and her threats last night with a large knife . . ."

The constable—hadn't he said his name was Snow?— had a voice that was too nasal, giving it a whining quality as if he'd been caught in a blizzard and come down with a good case of the grippe. The voice was irritating, the kind of voice that Winningham found difficult to listen to. His own hot and distracted thoughts melted the substance of the man's words.

What if Snow proved to be too clever? An in-depth investigation, in which he looked for motives, could prove devastating. But if he too quickly blamed that wretched kitchen maid without a thorough enough investigation, some bloody reformer might claim he swept evidence under the rug, and that could cause a scandal, or worse, open up the case to even more scrutiny. There was plenty to worry about no matter which way the situation went.

"I asked Dr. Gladstone to assist me in . . ."

Several of the ladies had grown quite pale, Winningham noticed, and his wife's plump hand convulsed against his palm, obviously at something Snow had said. Isabel Atewater, however, remained composed with a look as self-satisfied as the Mona Lisa. The Gladstone woman was equally composed, but there was a hint of a troubled frown on her pretty forehead. Jeremy Atewater frowned as well, but with less of a troubled look than of concentration. Nicholas Forsythe, however, simply listened, his visage revealing nothing except that he undoubtedly possessed a barrister's objectivity that bordered on the amoral.

". . . the obvious conclusion, given the girl's threats and her disappearance. However, the investigation . . ."

Winningham listened but heard nothing as Snow's words piled up, covering them all with mind-numbing facts. He began to think he might fall asleep. But he was lulled out of his drowsiness by a sudden outburst from Isabel, and he quickly realized that he was alone in his distraction. The others, he saw, were becoming equally as agitated as she.

"It's simply out of the question for me to stay here until you complete the investigation. I have to get back to London. Tell him, Jeremy!" Isabel's pretty face had grown quite red, and Winningham could see a dewy ring beginning to develop around her hairline.

"The lady is quite right to protest," one of the gentlemen said over the din of voices. "You can't expect that of us, Snow. I, too, have appointments in London."

"Please, please . . . ladies and gentlemen, I beg of you . . ." Snow tried in vain to calm the rabble.

"None of this would have happened if Miss Gladstone had done her duty and sedated that kitchen maid." Winningham was surprised to see that it was his own Lady Winningham standing and shouting to make her protest heard while she made lacy threats with her handkerchief. "We are all innocent, and she has brought on all the trouble!"

Winningham heard Miss Gladstone's name shouted in more than one angry voice, and by this time young Forsythe was standing, trying, along with Snow, to quiet the angry crowd, but one protesting gentleman grew even louder.

"She should be ashamed to call herself 'doctor.' Why, the woman shouldn't be trusted to administer even to dumb animals. She should have—"

"Please, sir, please," Nick pleaded. "Let us give the good doctor a chance to explain her—"

"Explain? She can't explain. All she can do is make excuses for the deranged murderess she failed to protect us from. The girl should have been taken away to an asylum immediately, and any doctor worth his salt would have known—"

"Of course she should have known!" Isabel interrupted over the gentleman's tirade and Nick's continuing efforts to calm the group. "And yes, she *is* making excuses to cover her mistake, claiming he died of strangulation instead of that stab in the heart that kitchen girl gave him! Indeed! She only wants to make it look as if the girl is innocent. But the girl's run away, hasn't she? Innocent people don't run away!"

"Here! Here!" Lady Winningham once again accentuated her fury with a wave of lace.

"Quiet, please!" This time Nick's voice had such a loud commanding tone that everyone fell into a stunned silence. Snow took advantage of the calm to speak again.

"The investigation has just begun, and it is my responsibility to look at all possibilities. The good doctor and I will confer further, and all of you, along with the servants, will most likely be interviewed by me individually, but I assure you, I will inconvenience you as little as possible. I know that all of you are anxious to leave the primitive countryside and return to London, but you must understand that even in the hinterlands, the queen's laws must be followed to the letter. I will do my best to see to it that you can all leave as quickly as possible. But do keep in mind, some or all of you could be called as witnesses later."

Winningham did not miss the resentment in Snow's attitude, and he could not help but smile. He was not so much amused by Snow's defensive jibe at his superiors as he was relieved to see that the situation was deteriorating into pandemonium. Confusion could slow the investigation. Confusion could protect him.

"Have the carriage readied for me? Oh no, that won't be necessary, Mr. Forsythe." Alexandra was pulling on her riding gloves, preparing to leave Montmarsh. She had already been questioned by the constable. She gave her testimony regarding Elsie, and it had been established that she had left the house while Lord Dunsford was still in the ballroom, and therefore, before the murder took place. She had, how-

ever, been instructed not to leave the village.

"Oh no, I insist upon the carriage for you," Mr. Forsythe
said. "I'm sure Eddie would have wanted it, especially after
what you've been through."

"All I've been through?"

"It has to be uncomfortable to have all of those misin-
formed people acting as if this is somehow your fault." Forsythe reached quickly for the door to open it for her, since
the butler, along with all the other servants, was waiting to
be questioned by Constable Snow.

"Uncomfortable? Of course not." She was not being entirely truthful. It *had* been disconcerting to hear their com-
plaints and accusations. For the briefest moment it stirred
fears that she had been wrong about Elsie O'Riley. Could
the girl really have been distraught enough to kill? Alexandra had nothing but instinct to go on when she left Elsie,
who by that time was already asleep, even without a seda-
tive. But the cause of Lord Dunsford's death had reinforced
her instincts. He had been strangled, there was no doubt
about that, and the stab wound had come later.

"Ah, wonderful, the carriage is ready," Forsythe said. She
glanced at the driveway and saw that he was right. The
carriage and driver were waiting for her, and Lucy, her
horse, was tied to the back. Forsythe must have summoned
it much earlier than she thought.

"This really isn't necessary, Mr. Forsythe," she said.

"Of course it is. Quite necessary." He lightly grasped her
elbow and led her toward the carriage.

"But . . ."

"No need to protest. It is done now." He helped her in
and, to her surprise, went around to climb into the other
side.

"Really, sir. To accompany me as well is asking too
much, and besides, didn't the constable say none of you
were to leave the premises? Neither you nor the driver?"

"The driver was not on the premises last night. He was,
in fact, seen by the constable himself in the local pub, so
he has the perfect alibi. As for me, I would be less than a
gentleman if I didn't accompany you, and that duty out-

weighs any edict from the local constabulary."

"I find your attitude rather overly protective, not to mention cavalier."

Forsythe signaled for the driver to leave. "Please keep in mind, Dr. Gladstone, that there is a murderer loose. I fail to see how you find my concern for you either overly protective or cavalier."

She glanced at him, wondering if he was only pretending to be obtuse. "When I said you were cavalier, I was referring to your attitude toward the law."

"There is a murderer loose," he said, again with the kind of emphasis one might use for a particularly slow child.

She raised an eyebrow. "Then you are convinced that Elsie is guilty, since all the other suspects are confined to Montmarsh and she is the only one who is *loose*?"

Forsythe spoke cautiously after a brief silence. "Not necessarily, but you must admit the evidence raises suspicions."

She turned toward him suddenly, defensively. "What evidence?"

"Why the fact that she threatened Eddie, and the fact that she then fled."

Alexandra shook her head. "I believe that is called circumstantial evidence. You must take into account that he was not killed with a knife. He died of strangulation."

"That doesn't clear Elsie, does it?" Forsythe said. "She could have strangled him, couldn't she? And then used the knife?"

Alexandra glanced at him again. "But why would she do that?"

Forsythe shrugged. "Who knows why anyone kills, really, but obviously she thought Eddie was somehow responsible for her lover's death."

Alexandra frowned. "Oh, I know none of you wants to think one of you could have done this," she said. "But it actually could have been one of you. Or one of the other servants."

"And with what motive?" he asked.

Alexandra pulled her shawl a little tighter around her. "I

don't know. You knew Lord Dunsford better than I. Perhaps you can think of a possible motive. Perhaps you even had one yourself."

She expected him to claim insult. Instead, he seemed to consider the premises for a moment. "Well, Eddie did like the ladies, that was quite well known, and he wasn't always discreet about his liaisons, but I know of no reason for a jealous husband among the guests."

"Are you sure?

"Well, I'm reasonably sure, although I'll admit, I didn't know everything about Eddie's escapades, and I certainly hadn't seen as much of him recently as I once did. And as for me, I'm afraid I have no motive." He gave her a broad smile.

"So it could have been a jealous husband?"

"Well, anything's possible, but . . ." Forsythe shrugged as if he was dismissing the idea.

"How about gambling debts?"

"None that I know of. Eddie was quite wealthy, you know. Not likely to be in debt to anyone."

"Suppose someone was deeply in debt to him."

"I suppose that's possible," he said. "But it's not likely to be anyone at the house, is it? One isn't likely to invite someone who owes one money, is he? And even if Eddie did such a thing, anyone deeply in debt would be embarrassed to come."

"Unless he thought to get revenge."

"My word, Dr. Gladstone, I don't know whether to think you diabolical or merely analytical."

By now the carriage had reached her house. "I shall leave that for you to decide, Mr. Forsythe."

He got down from the carriage and walked around to offer his hand to help her alight while the driver untied Lucy's rope. "If you are so certain that Elsie O'Riley isn't guilty, I should like to help you investigate that possibility."

"I try to leave police business to the police," she said as he walked her to her front door.

His eyes held hers for a moment, then he tipped his hat and bowed slightly. "Very well. Good day, Dr. Gladstone."

She watched him walk away and then, in spite of herself, called out his name.

"Mr. Forsythe . . ."

He turned to look at her.

"How, exactly, would you go about doing that? Investigating possibilities?"

He smiled in a manner that seemed to her to be triumphant and took a step toward her. "I could question the other guests. Discreetly, of course."

"To what end?"

"Why, looking for motives, of course."

"But you just said you know of no motives."

"I don't, but who is to say we ever really know the heart of even our closest friend? I shall report back to you with what I learn." He tipped his hat and stepped into the carriage again, and, in spite of herself, Alexandra found herself wishing she could join him in that "discreet" investigation.

4

"Irish, she is, that kitchen maid up at Montmarsh, and the way I sees it, 'tis always the Irish at the bottom of things when it comes to trouble. Me husband feels the same, 'e does."

Nell Stillwell's head bobbed as she spouted her opinion, making it difficult for Alexandra to examine her infected eye. She had earlier given the butcher's wife a solution of St.-John's-wort and hyssop leaves to wash the eye that had become inflamed from a bit of straw from the pigsty. It was apparent to Alexandra, however, that Nell had not followed her instructions, judging from the almost full bottle of solution that remained on the woman's shelf, not to mention the condition of her eye.

"Why have you not washed your eye, Nell?" Alexandra dabbed at the oozing pus with a bit of cloth.

"Well, there isn't time, is there, Dr. Gladstone? What with all the extra work when the earl is back at Montmarsh, along with all of them guests and their fine appetites for beef and pork. It keeps me husband busy, it does, and me-self along with 'im."

"But you could lose your sight in that eye. It has gotten

much worse. You must be careful." Alexandra dropped some of the solution into her patient's eye, then placed a large bandage over the infected area and wound the gauze around her head to secure it. She glanced at Zack, who usually accompanied her on her rounds. He was pacing back and forth, agitated by the smell of fresh meat.

"Lose me sight you say? 'Twould be better than this watery glob o' oozing pus, the way I sees it, and all the time causing me the pain of Hades in that socket."

"But, Nell . . ."

"Aye, if some things would but die, 'twould end our troubles, wouldn't it?"

Alexandra finished the bandaging and took a large bottle from her bag. "You mustn't think like that, Nell. There's still a chance we can save your eye. I'm going to leave you with more solution, fresher and more potent. I want you to use it daily."

"And was that what the kitchen maid was thinking, was it?"

Alexandra glanced at her patient, confused. "I beg your pardon?"

"The kitchen maid. Elsie O'Riley's her name. The one what killed the earl. I guess she thought if someone would but die, 'twould end her trouble."

"What makes you think Elsie O'Riley killed the earl?"

Nell gave her a sly look. "Why, Dr. Gladstone, you was there yerself when she made the threats, so I hear. Why, the whole village has talked of nothing else since it happened the night before this last."

"Threats don't make her guilty." Alexandra spoke as she packed her supplies back into her bag, marveling at how quickly the news had spread.

Nell gave her a wave of her hand. "Go on, now. She had her reasons."

"You're referring to young George's death."

Nell's one eye brightened. "Aye, so you know, and did you know young George was a ne'er-do-well? Spent his time with other young thugs when he wasn't with Elsie, 'e did. And young men with naught to do will make trouble, the way I sees it."

"I've heard about George and his less than desirable friends, but that still doesn't make—"

"And did you know that some blame Lord Dunsford for George's death?"

Alexandra's facade disappeared. She glanced at the woman, suddenly alarmed. "Nell!"

"Aye, I sees that you know."

"I know nothing of the kind, Nell Stillwell. Who, exactly, blames Lord Dunsford for George's death?"

"Them that knows." The Cyclops eye bore into Alexandra.

"Knows what? What are you talking about, Nell? That's only a rumor started by a frightened young girl."

Nell turned her eye away from Alexandra and stared at the window. She spoke only one word. "Aye."

"What do you mean, 'aye'?"

Nell faced her again, briefly. "I knows what I knows." Once again she turned her glance away to stare out the window. "It's like I said, Miss Alex. Some things is best left to die." She stood and made her way to the stairs as if to return to the butcher shop below. "Your father would know what I mean."

With that she was gone, leaving Alexandra to finish gathering up her medicines and make her way down the stairs. She had not missed Nell's point in making reference to her father, nor the fact that she had called her "Miss Alex," rather than "Dr. Gladstone." It had been a long struggle to get a certain few of the villagers, Nell among them, to stop thinking of her as little Miss Alex. When she was uncertain about a diagnosis, or they felt for any reason that she was particularly obtuse or inept, they often gave her the edict "Your father would know." It was something she might never live down.

She had one more patient to see before noon, and then she would return home for a quick lunch before she opened the surgery to see patients in the afternoon. She secretly hoped there would not be many on this particular afternoon, and that she would have time to steal away to Montmarsh and perhaps meet with Nicholas Forsythe. She was eager to learn if he had, in fact, been able to discern any more from his surreptitious investigations.

Her next patient, John Beaty, known to most as Old Beaty, was well into his seventies and, because of his rheumatism, now left all of the work to his son, who was known as Young Beaty. Young Beaty, like his father before him, was an oyster man. Old Beaty spent his time either warming his aching joints at his daughter-in-law's hearth or, on a good day, among other old farmers and fishermen at the Blue Ram.

Old Beaty greeted Alexandra with a toothless grin when he saw her approach through the open door. "Aye, the good doctor!" he cried out.

Alexandra stepped inside. Zack followed and made himself comfortable next to the hearth. "Hello, Mr. Beaty. You're feeling better it seems."

"It's yer medicine what done the trick."

Alexandra glanced at the empty bottle she had left with him—a mixture of poke root, blue flag root, prickly ash bark, black cohosh root, and bitterroot mixed in two quarts of whisky. "Mr. Beaty, what has happened to your medicine? I gave this to you only two days ago, and you were supposed to take only three tablespoons a day!"

"Aye, but it made me feel so good, I takes me a little more each day."

Alexandra raised an eyebrow. "Along with the whisky you take with your cronies at the Blue Ram, I suppose."

"Medicinal it is. You said so yerself."

Alexandra tried to suppress a smile. "Too much will make your rheumatism worse, Mr. Beaty."

"And now you sounds like yer father, you does. Would never let me have me dram of whisky. Don't be going back to his old-fashioned ways, girl."

"You've done your vapor baths faithfully?" she asked, ignoring his scolding.

He shook his head. "Makes me sweat too much, they does."

"The purpose is to make you sweat, Mr. Beaty." Alexandra spoke as she gently manipulated one of his gnarled hands. "The theory is that it will sweat out some of the poison in your body that causes the rheumatism."

" 'Tis a pity it won't sweat the evil out of some."

Alexandra gave him a wary look. "I suppose you're referring to the awful thing that happened at Montmarsh."

" 'Twas awful all right. And the story's on everybody's lips, it is."

"Apparently."

"And she done it all for that no-count George Stirling. He'll never return the favor, I'll tell ye that much."

"I suppose not, since he's dead."

"There's more than one corpse that walks among the living."

Alexandra gave Old Beaty a quick skeptical glance while she continued to massage the twisted knot that was his hand. "I never knew you to be superstitious, Mr. Beaty, nor to judge another quickly. Elsie's not proven guilty yet."

"Never said she was guilty, now did I, Dr. Gladstone? But I say this: If you wants to help the lass, ye'll find that bloody corpse."

Alexandra stopped the massage, but still held his knot of a hand. "What are you saying, Mr. Beaty?"

"The Blue Ram speaks, you know, with a hundred voices." He removed his hand from her grasp, carefully. "What one says, the other says the opposite, but it adds up to one thing."

"Which is?"

"Which is, ye best be careful, Dr. Gladstone. If ye wants to help Elsie, ye best be careful. Ye best not be seen together."

"Mr. Beaty!" She took his frail shoulders in each of her hands and forced him to look at her. "I'm not certain what you're attempting to say, but if you know where Elsie is, tell me."

Old Beaty shook his head. "I knows but naught."

"But you don't think she killed Lord Dunsford, do you?"

"I don't know the lass, so how could I make a judgment?

And I told ye, I knows but naught, so ye mustn't let on that
I told you but naught." He got up from his chair, creaking
and groaning, and walked toward his bed, leaning heavily
on his cane. He stopped once and spoke over his shoulder.
"I'll be needin' more of yer fine medicine, Dr. Gladstone."

Alexandra watched him silently for a moment, then,
knowing it would be futile to push him further, she picked
up her bag. "I'll bring it when I visit tomorrow."

She bid him good-bye, signaled to Zack to follow her,
and rode Lucy back to her house. When she arrived, the
surgery, which could be entered by a side door, was already
beginning to fill with patients, and Nancy was doing her
best to keep order. It was almost time for tea when the last
patient left. She was very tired indeed, but a good strong
cup of tea and one of Nancy's delightful chocolate biscuits
would revive her, and then she would ride over to Montmarsh to confer with Mr. Forsythe.

She was about to summon Nancy for the tea when there
was a knock at her door. It opened slightly, and Nancy stuck
her head around the edge.

"There's one more, Miss Alex." Nancy, who had been
her playmate when they were younger, had never been able
to develop the habit of addressing her as Dr. Gladstone.
Alexandra did nothing to discourage her chosen form of
address. Truth was, she would have felt a certain loss of
closeness to Nancy if she'd used the more formal title. Besides, to both of them, Dr. Gladstone would always be her
father, Dr. Huntington Gladstone.

"One more?" Alexandra could not keep the weariness
from her voice.

"I'm afraid so," Nancy whispered. "He's been waiting for
over an hour now."

"Very well. Show him in." Alexandra picked up a medical volume from her desk and went to the bookshelf to put
it away while she tried to shore up her energy for one more
consultation and examination, knowing that it would make
her too late to ride all the way to Montmarsh to visit with
Nicholas Forsythe.

She heard Nancy's voice from outside her door. "The

doctor will see you now, sir." Her back was turned to the door while she shelved yet another volume when she heard the patient enter.

"Loosen your clothes, please, and have a seat on the table. I'll be with you short—" She stopped with the word unfinished as she turned around and saw that the "patient" was none other than Nicholas Forsythe.

"Loosen my clothes? An interesting suggestion," he said.

"Mr. Forsythe! I . . ."

"Perhaps you should call me Nicholas, given the fact that our relationship has so quickly evolved."

Alexandra felt her face grow warm, and she knew she was blushing—something that rarely happened. She had thought her profession had made her immune to it, but his remark was extremely impertinent. She did her best to recover.

"Are you ill, Mr. Forsythe?"

"And why would you think I was ill, Dr. Gladstone?"

"This is a surgery after all," she said, her voice cold.

"Of course, but didn't we agree that I would report back to you after I'd had a chance to learn something from the other guests?"

"You do have something to report, then." An eager excitement had crept into her voice in spite of her attempts to sound cool and detached.

"Something rather interesting, I think. It seems that Eddie . . ." Mr. Forsythe stopped speaking, and his eyes grew wary as Zack ambled into the room and sniffed his feet, growling.

Alexandra knew what that growl meant, and she spoke the dog's name in a tone that was quiet but urgent, but she was too late. Zack had already pounced. His two front paws were on Mr. Forsythe's shoulders. He fell back against the examination table and might have tried to push the dog away, except that he had to use both hands, placed behind him, to steady himself against the table. Zack, in the meantime, was licking Nicholas's face enthusiastically with his enormous tongue.

Zack, Alexandra knew, loved almost everyone, and the

only thing intimidating about him was his size and his low growl, which was more like a soft grumbling and was meant to be friendly.

She spoke the dog's name again, sharper this time, and the animal turned around and settled himself at her feet, still grumbling. She glanced at Mr. Forsythe, who kept his wary eyes on the enormous black-and-white dog. "I was just about to ask Nancy to bring tea to the parlor," she said. "Perhaps you'd like to join me."

"What? Oh, yes, of course." Mr. Forsythe never took his eyes off of Zack as he spoke, and he made sure Alexandra and Zack left the room ahead of him.

Nancy, in fact, was waiting just inside the parlor, as if she expected Alexandra to bring her guest there. "Shall I prepare tea, Miss Alex?" Nancy asked before Alexandra could speak.

"Yes, please." Alexandra tried to ignore Nancy's little smile and raised eyebrows as, behind Mr. Forsythe's back, she glanced first at him and then back to Alexandra, as if to say *I told you so.*

Only when Zack was comfortably settled once again at Alexandra's feet and Mr. Forsythe had seated himself a safe distance away did he relax a little. "I say, interesting animal." He nodded a little stiffly at Zack. "Rather like a bear, wouldn't you say?"

"He's large, certainly, but it's only his appearance that is intimidating." Alexandra stroked the dog's head. "Actually, he's as friendly as a puppy."

"Indeed."

"He seems to like you. You noticed how he licked your face."

"Indeed," he said again, stiffly.

"You were about to tell me, sir, about your conversations with the other guests."

"Oh yes, of course." Mr. Forsythe took his eyes off of Zack at last. "Odd thing is, I'm not certain that everyone is sincerely mourning poor Eddie's passing."

"Oh?"

"Yes, it seems the chap had his own way of intimidating

people." Mr. Forsythe leaned forward eagerly. "Several people, in fact."

Alexandra's interest was piqued. "What do you mean, exactly?"

"Eddie was something of a bully when we were in school, but I assumed he'd outgrown that." Mr. Forsythe settled back into his chair. "Of course I don't see him as often as I once did, in spite of the fact that we are distant cousins. I was busy reading law for several years, you see, and then as a barrister I find myself quite busy."

"Of course." There was an expectancy to her tone that was an invitation for him to go on speaking.

"Perhaps bully is not quite the right word." He frowned, thinking about it. "Eddie was always more of a manipulator. He used people, you might say. And that, apparently, made a few people rather cross with him."

"And some of the guests were among those who were cross?"

"Yes, Isabel Atewater for one. According to some of the other ladies, whom I just happened to hear gossiping while I lurked outside the east-wing parlor, Isabel and Eddie had been having an affair."

Mr. Forsythe paused as if to gauge whether or not the subject was too indelicate, but Alexandra kept her countenance and did not comment. She waited for him to continue.

"And it seems that Eddie had broken it off." He appeared decidedly uncomfortable.

"I can understand that she might have been chagrined, but that hardly seems a reason to kill him. One would think it would be enough just to make him . . ." Alexandra suddenly understood the reason for Mr. Forsythe's discomfort, and it had nothing to do with the indelicacy of the subject. Isabel had obviously been using him to get back at Lord Dunsford, which was, no doubt, a blow to his ego.

"To make him jealous?" Mr. Forsythe sighed as he finished her thought for her. "One would hope that would be enough, but Isabel was seen going into Eddie's room the night he died."

"Really? By whom?"

"Lady Winningham. It seems she couldn't sleep, and she had just stepped in the hallway on her way down to the library to fetch something to read when she saw Isabel going into Eddie's room. She claims she was so shocked she simply ducked back into her room and never made it down to find a book."

"You overheard all of this while you were lurking, as you say, outside the east-wing parlor?"

Mr. Forsythe nodded.

She paused a moment, collecting her thoughts. "Did Lady Winningham see Isabel leave Eddie's room?"

"Apparently not."

"And did she say whether or not she carried anything? A long scarf, for example, or a knife?"

"She didn't mention it."

"So Isabel could have been going to his room for a lover's tryst."

Mr. Forsythe shrugged. "I suppose that's possible."

"And Isabel," Alexandra said. "Has she said anything?"

Mr. Forsythe was about to answer when Nancy entered, carrying a tray of sandwiches, tea, and chocolate biscuits. She placed the items on the table and took a long time arranging them, then she stepped back a few steps, waiting.

"That will be all, Nancy. Thank you." Alexandra watched as Nancy bowed slightly and walked away, but she sensed an unmistakable reluctance on Nancy's part. Nancy loved a good story, and the recent goings-on at Montmarsh would likely be the best one she'd hear in some time.

Mr. Forsythe waited until the girl was gone, and then said in a low voice, "Isabel took to her bed immediately after Constable Snow questioned her, and since no one will be allowed to leave for a while, she has sent for her London physician to be fetched to Montmarsh."

Alexandra nodded, remembering Isabel's remarks about her lack of trust in any physician other than her own personal one. "And no one has spoken to her since?"

"I tried, but . . ." Mr. Forsythe cleared his throat nervously.

"But what?"

"Well, you see, I thought I would steal away to her room and interview her since she and I are . . . or rather, that is, we have been . . ." Mr. Forsythe stretched his neck as if his collar was too tight, and Alexandra noticed a film of perspiration on his upper lip. "What I'm trying to say is that we have been . . ."

"I know what you're trying to say, sir. That you and Mrs. Atewater have been considerably more than friends. That you have been lovers, perhaps." Alexandra watched as his face went from white to crimson.

"My dear Dr. Gladstone, I assure you that nothing could be further—"

"No need to assure me of anything, Mr. Forsythe. I have no interest in your personal affairs. Why weren't you able to interview Mrs. Atewater as you had planned?"

In spite of Alexandra's well-practiced detached tone, he still appeared immensely uncomfortable. "Well, it was rather awkward you see, since Jeremy never left her side."

"Jeremy? Mr. Atewater, you mean?"

"Precisely."

"Do you have any reason to believe that Mr. Atewater had knowledge of his wife's affair with Lord Dunsford?"

Mr. Forsythe took out his handkerchief and mopped his brow. "I think that's possible. Apparently everyone else knew."

"Except you, of course."

He sighed again, then after a pause said, "I see what you're getting at. If Jeremy did know, then he had a motive to kill Eddie. The jealous husband, as you postulated earlier. And I have to admit Jeremy has been rather gloomy lately. Even before Eddie's death, I mean."

"And how is he now?"

"Gloomier than ever. As we all are." There was a pause as Mr. Forsythe seemed deep in thought. "Well, almost all of us."

"Almost?" Alexandra felt as if she was trying to diagnose the illness of a particularly reticent patient.

"Winningham," Mr. Forsythe said. "For some reason I got the feeling he could hardly contain his joy. Oh, of course he tried to put on a sad face, but there was a certain—well, gleefulness he couldn't seem to hide."

"Interesting."

Another silence while Mr. Forsythe considered it.

"Any particular reason that you know of why he would be happy that Lord Dunsford is dead?" Alexandra asked.

"Of course not," Mr. Forsythe said, but he didn't sound convincing.

Alexandra tried to prompt him. "He didn't owe Lord Dunsford money, for example?"

Mr. Forsythe shook his head, still wearing a thoughtful expression. "Not likely. Winningham is quite wealthy in his own right."

"Something else then. Blackmail, perhaps."

Mr. Forsythe frowned with surprise. "Good lord, no. Winnie is the epitome of propriety."

"I see."

Mr. Forsythe turned his distracted gaze suddenly to focus on her. "I know what you're thinking. The epitome of propriety is precisely the type to worry about his reputation and be vulnerable to blackmail."

Alexandra thought it best not to acknowledge that was exactly what she was thinking. She simply sat and waited for him to continue his musing, which she hoped would reveal more.

"As I said, Eddie could, certainly, be manipulative." He seemed to be speaking to no one in particular, or perhaps to himself. "And those things I overheard. . . ."

"In the east parlor, you mean." Alexandra said when the pause had stretched long enough that she feared he might lose his train of thought.

"Oh no. I also lurked where the gentlemen were congregated."

"Of course."

"It seems there have been rumors that Eddie—well, that Eddie wasn't above blackmail."

"Interesting."

"I never paid attention to rumors in the past, of course. But now I must admit . . ." There was another long pause, the kind a person might make when he or she is making a particularly difficult confession to a priest. "One might say that . . ." Mr. Forsythe cleared his throat. "Well, that I myself was a near victim of blackmail at his hands."

"A near victim? I don't understand."

He gave a dismissive wave of his hand. "Oh, it happened a long time ago. We were both quite young."

There was another long pause during which Zack, who still slept at Alexandra's feet, began to snore loudly. She feared the noise might distract Mr. Forsythe, so she nudged the dog with her toe, which only served to make him snore even louder. Mr. Forsythe, however, seemed not to notice. He merely cleared his throat again, uneasily.

"I was much younger, you see. Fresh out of Eton, and I had just begun to read law at Oxford, but I took a holiday and traveled to London. I happened to see Eddie, who, by then, had inherited the earldom, and he had just returned from surveying his estates."

Alexandra nodded, encouraging him to continue.

"I suppose we were both somewhat exhausted by our new duties, and we meant only to have a relaxing evening."

"Of course."

"It was perhaps a bit too relaxing."

"How so?"

"Well . . ." Mr. Forsythe hesitated, clearly uncomfortable. "I don't know quite how to put this. . . ."

"You spent a night in debauchery, perhaps?" Alexandra's voice was quiet and unemotional.

Mr. Forsythe's expression was a mixture of discomfort and denial. "I wouldn't go so far as to call it . . ." He breathed another uneasy sigh. "Well, perhaps you've chosen the right word after all."

She tried prompting him once again. "And for this, Lord Dunsford threatened to blackmail you?"

"He threatened to report my activity to my father unless I paid a tidy sum. I couldn't have my father know, of course. He was not a well man, and, well, I'm sure you can see my position."

"Indeed."

"Well . . ." Mr. Forsythe mopped his brow again. "Nothing came of it, of course, because Eddie realized he couldn't implicate me without implicating himself. As I said, it was a long time ago, and I assumed Eddie would outgrow such tricks. But I dare say, at the time it showed a ruthless side of the old boy that surprised me."

Alexandra took her last sip of tea and set her cup down carefully. "And if he hadn't outgrown it . . ."

"Then I suppose it's possible, according to what the other gentlemen were implying, that at one time or another, practically all of us could have a motive to do the old boy in."

5

The knock at the door came early while Alexandra was still having her breakfast. Nancy went to see who it was, then left the visitor in the front hall while she stepped into the dining room to tell Alexandra what was needed.

"It's Jamie, one of the stable boys from Montmarsh, Miss Alex. He says Cook has need of you. It's her nerves, the boy says."

Alexandra made a quick gesture of touching her napkin to her mouth and stood. "Tell him I'll leave as soon as I can get Lucy saddled. I'll just get my bag and—"

"Oh no, they sent a carriage for you, miss. He says you're to come right away." Nancy's eyes were large and round with excitement.

Alexandra hesitated only a moment, wondering who would have the authority to send a carriage now that Lord Dunsford was dead. The steward, no doubt. After all, the estate always had run quite efficiently during Lord Dunsford's long absences in the past.

She hurried to the surgery and picked up her bag, checking to make sure she had a supply of laudanum to provide for the cook. It was only natural that the woman would be distraught and complaining of a case of nerves, considering all that had happened at Montmarsh—a kitchen maid gone berserk, the earl murdered in his bed, and a house full of unhappy guests who were being forced to stay during what could be a protracted investigation.

Zack gave her a sharp bark and an eager anticipatory look as she walked toward the door. Alexandra rubbed his head. "Not this time, Zack."

He walked away in a sulking pout, and Alexandra stepped outside and allowed Jamie to help her into the carriage. The boy seemed nervous. His hands shook, and he appeared to be on the edge of tears. The events at Montmarsh had taken their toll on everyone.

When they reached Montmarsh, Alexandra entered through the servants' entrance, which would give her quicker access to her patient. Jamie led her downstairs to the cook's room, then backed away shyly.

The scent of cooking spices—nutmeg, ginger, and cinnamon—mixed with smells of rancid fat and boiled meat greeted her when she opened the door. It was as if the smells of the kitchen had attached themselves permanently to the cook.

Hester Pickwick, known to the household as Cook, lay on her narrow bed with a damp, folded cloth across her forehead while she cried. Occasional twitches, which looked a bit like convulsions, made the bed shake. They were not convulsions though, of that Alexandra was sure. It was only the tension in her body, which the laudanum, and perhaps a soothing, caring voice, would soon alleviate.

Since the cook didn't seem to realize Alexandra had entered, she knelt at her bedside and spoke quietly. "Mrs. Pickwick, Dr. Gladstone here."

Cook opened her eyes, let out a long sigh, and then sobbed harder.

"Mrs. Pickwick, please. I know you're distraught, as well you might be. Perhaps you could talk to me about it." Alexandra's father had taught her long ago that a case of so-called "nerves" could sometimes be cured simply allowing the patient to verbalize his or her fears. He had cautioned,

Symptoms of Death   53

however, that the talks could be as addictive as laudanum.

"Talk? What is there to say except the devil will have his way with us, he will! Lord Dunsford murdered in his bed! And me the one to blame." Mrs. Pickwick sputtered her words amid choking sobs.

"I don't understand. How are you to blame?" Alexandra kept her voice low and soothing.

"Didn't I tell the housekeeper to hire the girl? The poor Irish lass what killed him?" Mrs. Pickwick covered her face with her hands and shook her head.

"That doesn't place the blame on your shoulders." Alexandra's voice was more forceful this time.

Mrs. Pickwick sniffled and spread her fingers to peer at Alexandra. "You think not?"

"Certainly not." Alexandra picked up one of her plump hands and held it. They felt like warm, moist dough. "In the first place, there is no proof that Elsie killed Lord Dunsford, and secondly, even if she did, how could you possibly have known that she would?"

Mrs. Pickwick pulled her hand away and straightened herself into a sitting position. "Well, I couldn't have, could I? She seemed such a sweet thing. Even Mrs. Chapman, the housekeeper, will say that she was. It was that scofflaw George Stirling what led her astray, as I told you the night of Lord Dunsford's party. Fancied herself in love with him, she did. Well, she's better off that he's dead, I say. She could easily find herself a nicer young man." Mrs. Pickwick shook her head. "She was a sweet girl, all right. A bit high-strung, I'll grant you that, but wouldn't hurt a fly."

"Am I to take that to mean you don't believe she actually did it," Alexandra said. "Killed Lord Dunsford, I mean."

At that, Mrs. Pickwick broke into sobs again. "Well, they're saying she did, are they not? And her swinging that knife around. Saw her yourself, you did. So what am I to think? Oh that poor, poor girl." She sobbed harder still and amidst her sobs muttered, "I'm hoping she'll get away, I am." She stopped crying suddenly. Her face was as colorless as flour. "I didn't mean that, Dr. Gladstone. You believe that, don't you? I'm out of my head with grief. Over Lord

Dunsford, you see. I didn't mean a word of it."

Alexandra reached a hand to pat her on the shoulder. "Of course you didn't, Mrs. Pickwick," she said, in spite of the fact that she believed she meant every word. Hester Pickwick did not think Elsie was guilty any more than she herself did, and her grief was not for Lord Dunsford, but for Elsie.

"There's something else I've got to tell you," Mrs. Pickwick said, grappling at the bedcovers.

Alexandra put a soothing hand on her shoulder. "Try to calm yourself, Mrs. Pickwick. You're not to blame for anything that has happened."

"It's not the blame I'm thinking of, Dr. Gladstone." She wadded the edge of the sheet in her fists. "It's the master. Lord Dunsford hisself."

"Lord Dunsford?"

Mrs. Pickwick spoke to her in a hoarse whisper. "Yes, the earl hisself. Had I not seen his body carried out by the constable and the undertaker with my own eyes, I would not believe he was dead."

"I don't understand . . ."

"He's here, he is." Her whispering voice was salted with terror. "Walking the halls of Montmarsh, he is. I heard him. More than once. And that cough of his that he gets when he stays too long in that foul London air, I heard that, too." Mrs. Pickwick's ample bosom heaved, and a black fear engulfed her like a thick soup.

"Now, now, dear. You mustn't fret." Alexandra spoke once again in her soothing voice. "Sometimes when a person is under a great deal of strain—"

"You think I've grown daft, but I know what I hear, and I know what I see." Mrs. Pickwick's eyes were large and frightened. "And see him I did. Wearing his tweeds! And that brown jacket he always wears in the country! Saw him this morning, I did, when I went up to fire the ovens."

There's more than one corpse that walks among the living. Alexandra shivered as she remembered Old Beaty's words.

"I *have* gone round the bend, haven't I? I'll end my days in the asylum." She was wailing again.

Alexandra once again forced herself to speak with calm. "You haven't gone around the bend; you've simply been under a great deal of strain."

Mrs. Pickwick only shook her head and cried harder.

"Please, Mrs. Pickwick, calm yourself. Hallucinations under these circumstances are not uncommon. People often think they see the deceased, or hear them speak."

Mrs. Pickwick stopped crying long enough to look at her. "They do?"

"Of course. You mustn't let it frighten you. It will pass." She took the vial of laudanum out of her bag. "I'm going to leave this with you. Take a few drops in water now, and another few drops this evening before you go to bed. It will help you rest, but you must be careful. My late father had begun to believe the opium in it is addictive. There's no proof, mind you, but it's best not to take chances."

"I'm not one to take chances, Dr. Gladstone, I'll tell you that." Mrs. Pickwick's voice was strained, but she was trying to calm herself.

Alexandra gave her a smile and a pat on the arm. "Send for me if you need anything more. She started to take her leave, feeling uneasy. What she had told her patient earlier wasn't entirely the truth. While it was true that it was somewhat common for a person to believe he or she had seen the deceased, it was almost always a loved one they saw. A symptom of grief. And Mrs. Pickwick's grief was clearly for Elsie, not Lord Dunsford.

Just as she reached the door, Mrs. Pickwick called out to her. "Dr. Gladstone, there is one thing you must do for me." Alexandra turned around to face her. "You've got to find Elsie before it's too late."

"Mrs. Pickwick—"

"No! Hear me out!" There was desperation in her voice. "You've got to find her before they hang her for something I know in my heart she could never do. You must help her, Dr. Gladstone! Please! Please!" She was on the verge of hysterics. "You must help the poor lass! It's what your father would have done."

"Please try to rest." Alexandra spoke quietly, then left the room and climbed the stairs, feeling drained of all her energy. She did not know Hester Pickwick terribly well, but she had treated her once or twice for small things—a superficial burn she'd gotten during the course of her cooking or, once or twice, a case of the grippe. It was enough for Alexandra to form an opinion that she was a woman possessed of a great deal of common sense and practical knowledge, not one given to hallucinations or hysteria. Yet, her fervor about wanting Alexandra to find Elsie had certainly bordered on the hysterical, which possibly, but not likely, could give rise to the hallucinations. Whatever was going on, the woman was truly worried about Elsie and was convinced she had not killed Lord Dunsford.

On the other hand, Nell Stillwell and much of the rest of the town, as well as the guests at Montmarsh, seemed convinced that Elsie was guilty.

When Alexandra reached the top of the stairs, she took a deep breath, deciding she needed a few minutes alone to clear her head and collect her thoughts before she began her rounds and opened the surgery. She stepped outside, using the servants' entrance, and was about to ask for the carriage to take her home again. She stopped, however, long before she reached the stables.

Constable Snow was standing just outside the paddock gate speaking with Jamie. She turned away, not wanting to talk to the constable, or to anyone else, at the moment. But neither did she want to reenter Montmarsh Hall for the time being. It seemed to want to suffocate her with its atmosphere of gloom and fear.

Perhaps a short walk in the fresh air would do her good. She'd spied a copse of trees and brush just outside the formal gardens, well away from the stable. The constable's back was turned to her as she walked, and, with enough good fortune, she would be well into the thicket before he turned around.

The day had begun to warm already, though it was not

yet noon, so she slipped her shawl from her shoulders and loosened the top button of her frock. By the time she reached the stand of trees, she had begun to relax a little, and her head seemed to clear.

As she drew closer and allowed herself to be swallowed by the thicket, she became entranced by the landscape. So much of the timber had been cut away from the English countryside that she had come not to expect much more than a smattering of trees. She had never been this deep into the grounds of Montmarsh, however, and had never realized the wooded area was there redolent with the scent of moss, damp earth, and the scaly-fingered leaves of trees.

She began to enjoy the novelty of it and to drink in the scent of the oak and beech and to listen to the pipits singing to each other as they flitted from tree to tree. The copse, however, did prove to be quite narrow after all, and in a short time she could see the edge of the thicket. Near the edge, but still hidden in the trees, were the ruins of a stone cottage. Dry branches lay across the top, a dead sacrifice to the long-gone thatched roof. A malignancy of lichen spread over the walls. Yet they still stood in a slowly dissolving rectangle. It had most likely been a worker's cottage several hundred years ago, perhaps the lodging of Montmarsh's woodcutter or swineherd or some other laborer.

While Alexandra watched, a dark form passed one of the open square slots that had once been a window. She was startled at first, because the form looked human. But she told herself she must have been mistaken. The light was not good because of the tree shadows, and it would be far more likely to be an animal of some sort that she had seen—a good-sized animal to be sure, perhaps a sheep or a calf, or even a deer.

She walked closer to the building to have a look, and that's when she saw the very human eyes staring back at her. The eyes were at once frightened and menacing, and the mouth gaped open with teeth bared as if emitting a silent scream.

Alexandra wanted to flee back into the woods, or at the very least to turn her eyes away from the creature in the dirty, blood-soaked dress. She did neither. Instead, heart pounding, she took a cautious step forward and managed to speak in a quiet, but trembling voice.

"Elsie . . ."

"Go away! I warn ye, don't come near." The girl had found her voice at last, and she backed away as she spoke. Alexandra could see her dirt-streaked hands quivering like something dying.

"I'm not going to hurt you, Elsie. Please, let me help." Alexandra tried to keep her voice low so as not to frighten the girl.

"I don't need none of yer help, and I warned ye once. . . ." Her voice trailed off, and she was shaking with sobs.

Alexandra took another step forward, and Elsie backed away even more until she was in a cowering squat in a corner, still crying. Alexandra moved to what was left of the doorway. She had to duck her head to step inside onto the earthen floor, and she advanced toward Elsie slowly.

"Elsie, I know you're in trouble, but I want to help you. Do you remember me? I took you to your room that night at Montmarsh. I helped you then, and now I want to—"

"Ye'll bring the others here. I know ye will! Them what wants to hang me." She croaked the words amid sobs, and Alexandra bent down and reached out to touch her frail shoulder. To her surprise, the girl didn't flinch. Alexandra put her arms around the slender shape, and the girl collapsed against her.

"Tell me what happened," Alexandra said, bringing her to her feet. "Tell me what you know, so I can help you."

Elsie's surrender was short-lived. "I know nothin', and ye'll not make me say I do!" Her voice had become a hoarse, frightened whisper as she pulled away from Alexandra's embrace and turned her back to her. "And ye'll never find the bloody knife either!"

"The knife? The one used against Lord Dunsford? You know where it is?"

Elsie's answer was a scream that drove hot needles into Alexandra's spine. At the same moment she saw what had frightened Elsie. Constable Snow was only a few feet away from the ruined cottage. With him were Jamie, Nicholas Forsythe, and Jeremy Atewater. The constable carried in his hand the kitchen knife Elsie had brandished the night of the dinner at Montmarsh. It was now coated with darkened and dried blood and gore mixed with damp earth.

Elsie suddenly flailed Alexandra with her fists. "Ye led them to me, ye bloody wench. Betrayed me, ye did. Yer no better than the rest of the bloody nobs."

"Elsie, please . . ." Alexandra grabbed the girl's wrists and did her best to calm her, but she was interrupted as Constable Snow ducked his head to step into the doorway.

"Step back, please, Dr. Gladstone. I'll handle this." The constable handed the knife to Atewater and then quickly reached for the heavy wrist irons the stable boy carried. With remarkable swiftness, he fastened them on Elsie's thin wrists. A keening sound came from her, a long, thin streak of something sharp and painful.

The constable spoke as he fastened the wrist irons. "Elsie O'Riley, you're under arrest for the murder of Lord Edward Boswick, earl of Dunsford."

Elsie collapsed. Constable Snow caught her just before she reached the dirt floor and jerked her against his side.

"On what grounds are you accusing this girl of murder?" Alexandra struggled to keep her voice calm.

Constable Snow glanced quickly at Alexandra. A dark frown furrowed his brow, and a muscle worked in his jaw. Alexandra read his anger in that expression, and she thought for a moment that he would refuse to answer her.

"On the grounds that the murder weapon was known to be in her possession in the early morning hours after Lord Dunsford's murder, and, further, that she was seen trying to hide it," he said finally.

"Murder weapon?" Alexandra's voice was tight. She glanced at Mr. Forsythe. His face was grim, and he shook his head slightly as if to warn her not to push the matter further.

In the same instant, Jeremy Atewater thrust the gory knife toward her. "This!" He held the hilt of the knife by his fingertips, as if he was loath to touch it. "The knife that was thrust into Lord Dunsford's body."

"But how can you be sure?" Alexandra knew her question to be futile. She recognized the knife Jeremy Atewater held as the same knife Elsie had brandished in the dining room of Montmarsh Hall.

"All of the guests have identified the weapon as the same one Elsie O'Riley threatened Lord Dunsford with." Snow's voice was tight and strained. For a moment, Alexandra thought it was because he resented having to explain anything to her, but it occurred to her that he could possibly be as uncomfortable with the situation as she was.

"And beyond that—" Atewater began, but Snow interrupted him, quietly.

"There is the fact that she was seen burying the weapon in the early hours of the morning after the murder."

"Yer lyin', ye are!" Elsie cried, suddenly coming to life again.

"It's your word against Jamie's." Snow motioned with his head toward the stable boy. "He says he saw you burying it."

Jamie ducked his head and seemed to want to shrink inside himself, as if he wanted to deny what the constable was saying.

"Jamie . . ." Alexandra began with first a glance toward Mr. Forsythe, who still looked as troubled as Jamie. She remembered how upset Jamie had seemed when he came for her that morning. Obviously he was frightened by what he claimed to have witnessed.

"I seen her, Dr. Gladstone." Jamie didn't look up as he spoke, and his voice was barely audible.

"And we found the weapon in precisely the spot where young Jamie told us to dig." Atewater, who now held the knife firmly by the hilt, had a slight nervous quiver to his voice, as well one might expect, Alexandra thought. The whole affair was more than a little upsetting. When she glanced at Mr. Forsythe again, he nodded sadly, as if to agree with what Atewater had said.

"But why?" Alexandra spoke in a whisper as she glanced at Elsie.

"I never done it!" Elsie cried. "I never killed no bloody earl. Even if I did bury the knife, 'twas only because I knew I'd get the blame. But I never done it. If Georgie was here, 'e would tell ye who done it. 'E knew all about them murderin' nobs, 'e did!"

Constable Snow took Elsie's arm and led her away, a grim expression on his face. He spoke in crisp, curt tones to Mr. Forsythe and Atewater, telling them they, and the other guests, would be free to leave as soon as a hearing before the justice of the peace could be arranged, at which time they would be called as witnesses. He assured them the hearing would be scheduled as quickly as possible.

Alexandra was left with a feeling of helplessness and with Old Beaty's words echoing in her head.

If you wants to help the lass, ye'll find that bloody corpse.

6

Jeremy Atewater stood slightly behind the woman known as Dr. Gladstone and, along with the others, watched as the wretched kitchen maid was hoisted, wrist irons and all, into the constable's shabby carriage.

Atewater was as interested in the doctor as he was the prisoner. He had a vague recollection that Eddie had said the woman's Christian name was Alexandra. He had thought at the time the Greek derivative must have been an affectation on the part of the woman's parents—an attempt to show off a middle-class education. The more he saw of the woman, however, the more he thought it was no affectation at all. She had the demeanor of educated aristocracy, in spite of the fact she had no title.

Over the years, Atewater had developed a nose for that particular quality. He suspected a person was born with it, in much the same way one is born with blue or brown eyes. It could not successfully be acquired, he believed, because a person's true colors would always show. He was particularly sensitive to that because he suspected others could see through his own veneer of education and material acquisitions to the true working-class core of his being.

In fact, that theory had been proven to him more than once in his school days when certain bloody young nobs who already held titles or would someday inherit them mocked him for his working-class roots. For that very reason, he had felt a certain resentment toward most of the guests, including Alexandra Gladstone. He tried to suppress his resentment. After all, at least in this case, what did it matter now? He would not likely ever see her again, since Constable Snow had said all the guests could leave after the hearing this afternoon.

He had noticed the little silent exchange between the Gladstone woman and Nick Forsythe when the constable confronted Elsie, and he had wondered what it meant. He was reasonably sure it was more than Nick's standard flirtatious exchange. He'd sensed it was something about Elsie. Something dangerous, he feared. Could it be that the gossip was true, and the two of them really were convinced the girl wasn't guilty? He would not allow himself to think of that. He would take comfort in the fact that someone had been arrested for the murder of dear old Eddie and as soon as the trial was over, he would never have to think of it again.

Isabel, he knew, would be happy to hear the news of the arrest, but he would enjoy keeping it from her just a bit longer. She had not been downstairs when the constable brought the knife to be identified and so didn't know the case was as good as solved. Let her suffer a bit longer in her room where she had closeted herself to wait for that expensive doctor she'd sent for out of London.

Atewater was not inclined to feel kindly toward her. He knew she had been in love with Lord Dunsford, knew, in fact, that he had been cuckolded. His greatest fear had been that others might know about it as well, and he would appear foolish in their eyes. He would throw the wench out, except that he couldn't afford the scandal of a divorce. It simply wasn't good for business.

As the carriage bearing the unlucky Elsie pulled away from the grounds, Atewater noticed Nick standing next to him. "Is this hearing likely to last long, Nick, old boy?" Atewater asked.

"I'm afraid not. The hearing is only for the purpose of determining if there's enough evidence for her to be bound over for trial. It will be little more than a formality. It seems quite obvious the evidence is there."

"So we should be able to leave by tomorrow." Atewater spoke more to himself than to Nicholas.

"Are you quite sure it's really over, Mr. Forsythe?" Alexandra said.

Atewater didn't wait for any further discussion of the matter. He took his leave by murmuring that he'd best go check on his dear wife.

In reality, he had no intention at all of seeing about Isabel, but as he made his way upstairs to his room, hoping to send a servant for a basin of water with which to refresh himself, and a glass of whisky to help him relax, he passed by Isabel's room. The door was open, and he saw that instead of keeping to her bed, she was up, fully dressed, and talking with animation to a maid, who appeared to be packing a trunk. He stopped for a moment, staring out of curiosity, and Isabel saw him.

"Oh, Jerry! Have you heard? There's wonderful news." A pair of underdrawers were draped over her arm, and she waved a stocking at him.

"News?" he said, in spite of himself.

"They've arrested that horrible girl, and we can go home! As soon as a hearing of some sort is over."

Atewater stared at her, stunned that the news had reached her so quickly, and at least slightly disappointed that she wasn't still suffering over the bugger's death. "How did you know?" he asked when he found his voice.

"Why, the servants, of course. They were all shown that awful knife and asked to confirm it was the one that creature used to threaten everyone before the constable went off to find her. The servants said some stable boy knew where she was." She threw the drawers at the maid and glanced back at Atewater. "And they said you were there to help dig up

the knife. You're my hero, Jerry." She gave him a coquettish smile.

Atewater pulled a cheroot from his breast pocket and
struck a match against the gleaming mahogany chest. Giving all his attention for several seconds to drawing in the
flame, he finally exhaled a fetid cloud that made both Isabel
and the maid cough. When he spoke, his voice was cold.

"Well, I must say your mourning for the poor bastard
seems to have been short-lived. Are you always so cavalier
about your lovers?"

Isabel's face turned the color of tallow, and she stared at
him speechless for a moment before she shooed the maid
away with an angry abruptness. "Leave us! Go! Go!"

As the maid hurried out, Atewater leaned against the wall,
smoking and happily polluting the room with the cheroot's
dead-rodent odor while he watched, amused. When Isabel
turned back to him, anger had brought the blood back to
her face, turning it a lurid crimson.

"How dare you speak to me in such a way in front of a
servant! How dare you speak to me that way at all!" Her
words were a hot steam of hisses.

Atewater gave her an amused, condescending smile, still
leaning against the wall, never taking his eyes off of her.
"Don't pretend you're the wrongly accused, faithful wife,
Izzy. Self-righteous anger doesn't become you. You're
nothing but a fool, my dear, for allowing Eddie to use you.
If you had even a drop of sense, you'd have known he'd
simply dispose of you when he was finished. He jilted you,
didn't he? You must have despised him for that. Enough to
kill him?"

She stared at him, red-faced and speechless for a moment.
He knew she was surprised that he knew about her lover,
and the surprise gave him a rush of excitement. Now, he
expected another sputtering denial. Instead, he saw something flicker in her eyes, some dangerous cold wisdom. That
extrasensory hint that she might not be the vapid fool he'd
come to think she was both alarmed and excited him.

"I'm not the only fool standing here." Her voice had lost
all of its heat and was now like cold stone. "What about

those business ventures you were in with Eddie? You're angry because he was more clever than you, aren't you? Were *you* angry enough to kill him?"

Jeremy jerked his cigar from his mouth and grabbed her arm. "What are you talking about, whore? What do you know of business ventures?" He felt his blood roaring in his ears as he envisioned Eddie talking of their joint business dealings in some cozy postcoital moment.

"Stop! You're hurting me." She tried to wrest her arm free, but he held fast.

"What did he tell you?"

"Nothing!" She still sounded defiant. "You told me yourself that Eddie was a cheat. You said you'd never do business with him again."

He let her go with a shove that sent her crashing against the bureau. "You're right, the bastard was a cheat. But I got even in spades. No one cheats me and gets away with it."

"Is that a confession, Jerry?"

She was egging him on, which still frightened and aroused him. He had never known her to be this way. Had Eddie's death somehow changed her?

"When did you learn to be so clever, Izzy?" he asked.

She laughed. "Me? Clever?"

The coldness was still there, in her eyes. He could almost believe she *was* capable of murder.

He gave her a disdainful look and left, slamming the door behind him. He made his way down the hall, wondering if he had ever really known his wife, wondering, too, what she actually knew about his business association with Eddie. It was true, he had ranted about Eddie's underhanded tricks involving an investment, and he had confessed that he'd lost a little money. Did she know, though, that it was more than a little? Did she know that the reason he'd lost was because her lover, the illustrious Edward, earl of Dunsford, had taken more than his share? It was true, he could not prove it, but he knew Eddie had pocketed a nice profit while claiming the venture lost money. He could almost see Eddie laughing at him while he rolled in bed with his wife.

Atewater knew Lord Dunsford often enjoyed other peo-

ple's misfortunes, especially if he caused them. He'd revel
in them, in fact. It could be that he'd told Isabel just for the
pleasure of making her uncomfortable—if Isabel was, in
fact, capable of feeling discomfort over her husband's problems.

Nevertheless, he could imagine Eddie doing just such a
thing. He knew for a fact more than one of his guests had
reason of one sort or another to hate Eddie, but Eddie had
invited them here just to enjoy their discomfort. And the
guests had accepted, of course, because they couldn't afford,
either for social or business reasons, to risk being dropped
from Eddie's guest list by shunning one of his gatherings.

By the time he reached the drawing room downstairs, all
the other guests were gathered, and the butler had brought
sherry. A celebratory mood bubbled just under the surface.
However, everyone was trying to remain discreetly serious
and quiet and to appear to be in mourning. Nicholas, who
was involved in an animated and serious conversation with
Dr. Gladstone, seemed oblivious to the general mood of the
room.

"Smashing job you and the constable did, Atewater, old
boy!" One gentlemen gave him a slap on the back as he
spoke in an appropriately hushed voice. The slap, however,
was hearty, almost enough to cause him to drop his cheroot.
He stubbed it out quickly in an ashtray, which had appeared
fortuitously in a servant's hand. It wouldn't do to offend
the ladies with his smoke, and thus endanger his social
standing.

"Yes, yes," he said, looking around for a glass of sherry.
"Nasty business. Best to get it over with quickly."

"A toast!" Lord Winningham shouted as he held his glass
high. Winningham's mood was uncommonly and inappro-
priately jovial. "To Atewater and Forsythe! You saved the
day, chaps, by helping the constable bring in the murderer."
He looked around, suddenly embarrassed at his outburst,
cleared his throat nervously, and added, "In memory of
Dunsford, of course."

There was a quiet and hesitant chorus of "Here! Here!"
Atewater bowed slightly, showing just the proper amount

of humility. Out of the corner of his eye, he saw that Nick was looking quite uncomfortably embarrassed.

"I would remind you, ladies and gentlemen, that the girl has not yet been proven guilty." Dr. Gladstone's voice, rising above the others, stunned everyone to silence.

"Surely you're not still defending her," one of the ladies said. "After all, she was found with the knife, she voiced her motive, and she had the opportunity."

"Is it possible that she wasn't the only one with motive and opportunity?" Dr. Gladstone asked.

There was a nervous rumbling in the crowd. "What, exactly, do you mean?" Winningham blurted.

"That the evidence against Elsie is . . ." She turned to Nick as if to seek confirmation. "I believe the term is *circumstantial*," she said.

Nick seemed unable to speak for a moment, as if he was as stunned as the others. He quickly collected himself, however, and nodded. "Yes, yes, of course. Circumstantial," he said in an odd voice.

Winningham, red-faced and flustered, spoke up. "It sounded, Miss Gladstone, as if you were implying that one of us could have committed the crime. I think I speak for all of us when I say that I find it insulting that you would suggest—"

"No insult was intended, sir, and I implied nothing of the kind. I, too, find it difficult to believe that any of us here could have murdered Lord Dunsford, but I find it equally as difficult to believe that Elsie O'Riley committed the crime." Dr. Gladstone spoke with an air of authority and self-confidence that Atewater found shocking in a woman. Yet it was somehow appealing.

"How so?" Lord Winningham persisted. "We've just pointed out that the girl made threats and—"

"I am aware that she made threats and that she was seen burying the knife, but it was not a knife that killed Lord Dunsford. He was strangled, and I might point out a girl the size of Elsie would not have had the strength to do that, since, of course, Lord Dunsford would have resisted."

An excited murmur rippled through the crowd, and Atewater leaned closer to hear what else this woman had to say.

"If he was strangled in his sleep, he couldn't resist," Winningham said.

"It would have awakened him, and he would have struggled," Dr. Gladstone countered.

"If it wasn't a knife, then how do you explain the stab wound?" a man's voice asked. Atewater, who kept his eyes on Dr. Gladstone, could not tell who it was.

"He was stabbed after he died." Dr. Gladstone remained calm and unflappable, which Atewater found fascinating. He had never seen a woman quite like this one, and she might have gone on longer, giving him more opportunity to observe her if Isabel hadn't burst into the room suddenly and collapsed on the floor in a swoon.

Dr. Gladstone rushed to her as a crowd gathered around her prone body. "Give her some air," the doctor pleaded and knelt beside her. Atewater watched as she took Isabel's wrist to check for a pulse and loosened the top button of her dress, then passed some smelling salts under her nose. Isabel's eyes fluttered and opened, and as soon as she saw Dr. Gladstone, she pushed her away as if she were some offensive animal.

"Jeremy! Where is Jeremy?" Isabel screeched.

Jeremy pushed his way through the crowd to stand beside her, because it seemed the only thing he could do under the circumstances, although her dramatics were proving embarrassing.

By this time Isabel had brought herself up to a sitting position and was allowing some of the gentlemen to help her to her feet. As soon as she saw Jeremy, she began to cry. "Oh, Jeremy, you've got to get me out of here. I've seen him! Seen him with my own eyes!"

"Hush, my dear. You're not feeling well; you must be quiet." Atewater hoped his words would calm her and minimize the embarrassment, but she went on ranting.

"It was Eddie! Walking in the shadows outside the house. But he's dead! I saw him myself, being carried out by the coroner! How can a corpse be walking? I saw him! Saw

him with my own eyes, and then he disappeared like a vapor!"

Atewater had to clench his fists to keep from slapping
her. She was making a complete fool of herself, and, by
association, of him as well. He tried to think of something
to say to diffuse the moment, but he feared that to speak
would only make it worse.

He needn't have worried. It was that fool Winningham
who saved the day. By now Atewater had become convinced the old fool was more than a little tipsy, and what
he said only confirmed it.

"My God! I saw him, too. Thought I was losing my mind,
but if the lady saw him as well . . ."

Another excited murmur went up from the crowd, and
Atewater saw his opportunity. "Please! Please, everyone.
Calm yourselves, please." The crowd obeyed as if they were
sheep, and Atewater continued. "We're all quite understandably upset by the events of the past few days, but we must
keep our heads about us and remain strong."

"Of course, Atewater's right," the gentleman who had
complimented him earlier said. "You've got a head on your
shoulders, old boy." He slapped him on the back again.

Atewater followed through with his advantage. "I suggest
we go to our rooms to prepare for departure. We'll all meet
in London again for Lord Dunsford's funeral, of course, but
perhaps by then we'll have had time to cope with this tragedy."

He very gently took Isabel's arm and led her out of the
room, thinking that the entire messy situation had worked
to his advantage after all.

"They're all daft," Mr. Forsythe whispered as he took Alexandra's arm to escort her out of the room. When Alexandra didn't reply, he stopped suddenly and let go of her.
"Surely you don't believe what those two were saying. A
ghost?" He gave an indignant snort. "An old man in his
cups and a hysterical woman are hardly credible witnesses."

Alexandra was mulling the so-called ghost sightings over

in her mind, and she knew she'd once again taken a little too long to reply. "Perhaps not, but . . ."

Mr. Forsythe raised his eyebrows and cocked his head, wearing a skeptical expression. "My dear, you are a woman of science. I find it difficult to believe you would even consider the possibility of a ghost."

Alexandra turned away from him and resumed walking toward the door. She had already asked a servant to see that a carriage was ready. "I find it interesting that three people claim to have seen the ghost of Lord Dunsford."

"Three?" Mr. Forsythe sounded surprised as he hurried to catch up with her.

"Yes, Cook told me this morning she has seen Lord Dunsford, or what she insists is his ghost. I dare say sightings by three different people is interesting."

"Mmmm," Mr. Forsythe said, pausing before he opened the door for her. He seemed lost in thought for a moment, but he quickly gathered his wits. "I say, why don't we discuss this over luncheon? We could have the staff prepare something, and we could take it in one of the private sitting rooms perhaps."

"That's very kind of you, but I still have my rounds to do, and I must open the surgery by one, and, since I am sure to be called as a witness at the hearing, I must make myself available for the justice." Alexandra regretted the stiff, formal sound of her statement. In truth, she would like to discuss the odd situation with someone who showed signs of intelligence. Besides that, she was hungry, but what she had said was true; she was running out of time to make her rounds.

"Very well then." In spite of his smile, Mr. Forsythe did not hide the disappointment in his voice or in his face. "Perhaps I'll see you at the hearing." He raised an arm to signal one of the stable boys. "The carriage for Dr. Gladstone, please."

"You're welcome to call," Alexandra said, "but I assumed you would be returning to London with the others."

"London?" He sounded for a moment as if he'd never heard of the place. "Oh, yes. Yes, of course, London."

"It was a pleasure meeting you, sir. Perhaps we will indeed meet again sometime."

"Yes, of course." He seemed oddly distracted. Perhaps the death of his friend was finally taking its toll.

He helped Alexandra into the carriage, and when she looked back, long after the carriage was on its way, he was still standing on the path, watching her departure.

Alexandra was tired by the time she finished her rounds, and by the time she returned to receive patients in her surgery, a message was waiting for her, summoning her to appear at a hearing for Elsie O'Riley later that day. The hearing obviously had been hastily arranged so Elsie could be properly charged in time for trial when the assizes convened. She had to close her surgery early in order to be at the Blue Ram, where all such hearings, as well as the courts of the assizes, were always held, since there was no public building large enough.

Just as Mr. Forsythe had forewarned, the hearing was a mere formality, and it became even more obvious as she answered the questions of Squire Thomas Trowbridge, a local landowner who acted as justice of the peace, that Elsie would indeed be bound over for trial. Poor Elsie appeared frightened and confused. She could not afford a barrister to represent her. Although she had the right to cross-examine the witnesses herself, she did not know how to exercise that right. She asked no questions, but sat with her head bowed, awaiting her fate. If only Mr. Forsythe could have volunteered his time, but, since he was a witness himself, that was out of the question.

As it turned out, she did not see Mr. Forsythe at the hearing. He, like all the other witnesses, had given their testimony and their depositions and had been dismissed.

She was looking forward to a light supper and bed, but before Nancy had finished preparing the meal, someone pounded at the door. Alexandra opened it to a man dressed as a farm laborer who introduced himself as Seth Blackburn.

"It's me wife," he said, his face gone white and his big, roughened hands twisting a dirty cap. "The baby's comin', but 'tis turned bottom first, and me wife is dreadful screamin'. You must come with me, doctor, and we best hurry."

Alexandra left her supper untouched. She had to saddle Lucy herself, since Freddie went home to his mother at night. It cost her some time, but finally she raced alongside Seth on his Percheron to the cottage at the edge of town. Alexandra had never met Seth Blackburn nor his wife. Mrs. Blackburn, whose name she learned was Priscilla, like most of the working-class women Alexandra served, never came to her during pregnancy or childbirth unless a problem developed. Alexandra's efforts to encourage regular visits of all women with child had so far been to no avail. She couldn't help thinking that if she had seen Priscilla Blackburn sooner, she might have detected the breech position of the baby and been able to effectively turn the fetus. Now, she could only pray that she was not too late to help the woman and her child.

The Blackburn's cottage smelled of boiled cabbage and consisted of only one room furnished with a crude wooden table and chairs, a few shelves, and a cupboard, all on a hard-packed earthen floor. The deep-set windows were hung with white muslin curtains, however, and the pots above the fireplace were gleaming, giving the place a warm, cozy look. A boy of about two years sat on the floor with a yellow dog of mixed ancestry. At one end of the room were more curtains used to partition a bedroom. Priscilla, her face drained of blood, lay on the straw bed. Her dark red hair was plastered to her face with perspiration.

A hoarse moan escaped her throat when she saw Alexandra. It was hard to tell whether the moan signified relief or despair, but the hoarseness told Alexandra she had spent a long time screaming in pain.

The baby's buttocks were already presenting themselves, and Alexandra had to wash quickly and get to work. She was not able to turn the baby, and the most she could do was aid the birth by slipping her hands into the canal to manipulate the small body a little. Priscilla's body tore hideously as the buttocks emerged, and she screamed in agony. Seth, accustomed only to his own daily, less arduous labor, turned away, frightened. Alexandra, however, worked hard, stopping only occasionally to wipe the sweat from her brow with the sleeve of her dress, wishing she could offer her patient the luxury of ether, as women in the cities used now. It had become quite popular since the queen had sanctioned it by being the first in England to use it when her son was born. But Alexandra could only offer soothing words and a leather strap for Priscilla to clamp her teeth into when the pain was at its pinnacle.

It was tiring and painful labor Priscilla endured, and it cost her a large quantity of her life's blood. After several hours, the baby, a boy, was born, and Alexandra knew the reason for the breech presentation. There was a twin. The second boy was stillborn a few minutes later.

Seth, who had excused himself twice to step outside to vomit, now stood by the bed with trembling hands and was even more white-faced than his wife. He did not yet know the second baby was not breathing. "Twins, by God! She's give me twins!" he cried, and for a moment Alexandra thought he might faint with ecstasy, or at least wake the boy who had now fallen asleep on the floor, using the yellow dog as a pillow.

"The second one does not live," she said quietly. Seth's face drained of its color again, and he fell to his knees weeping. Priscilla's glassy stare showed no emotion. She turned to Seth and spoke only two words in a weak voice. "Bury it."

While Seth took the lifeless form in his arms to oblige, Alexandra wrapped Priscilla's abdomen with tight bandages to provide support for the loosened tissue and gave her citrate of iron and quinia, along with a generous cup of beef broth, then helped her put the surviving baby to breast.

"Take a little of the powders each day," she said, referring to the iron and quinia, "and I will provide more when that is gone."

Priscilla shook her head, too weak to speak, but Alexandra knew she was most likely concerned about the cost.

"You must," she said, "to restore the blood you've lost, else you'll not live to see the babe walking."

Priscilla's eyes grew wide with fright, and Alexandra knew she would take the powders. She knew, too, that it would not likely ever be paid for, but the worst of her knowledge was that even if she took the medicine faithfully, she still might not live more than a few weeks.

She left Seth with instructions to see that Priscilla continue the medication, along with rest. She did not waste her time giving her the usual instructions for a two-week lying-in period. Working-class women, even the sickest, did not have the luxury of giving up two weeks for recovery from childbirth. Most doctors said lower-class women survived without the lying-in because they lacked the delicate constitutions of the upper class. Recently, though, Alexandra had begun to wonder if all women, except for the very sick such as Priscilla, would benefit by leaving their beds sooner.

She was too tired to contemplate that now, though. She wanted only to get back to her home and fall into bed for at least four hours of sleep before she had to begin another day.

Lucy found the way home with no guidance, for which Alexandra was thankful. She found she had to use all of her powers of concentration to keep from falling out of her side-saddle in her sleep.

The light Nancy left burning in the parlor was a welcome and comforting sight, and as Alexandra slipped from the saddle, she could think of nothing but getting Lucy put away and getting into her own warm bed.

She had the saddle in her arms and was on her way to the barn to put it up when she felt a human arm circle her neck tight enough to cut off her breath so that she couldn't cry out. Then the arm moved, and a hand, cold and damp with sweat, clamped her mouth just as the tip of something cold and sharp touched her throat. A quick, sharp pain, and then warm blood ran down her throat and between her breasts, soaking into her dress to mingle with Priscilla's blood.

7

Alexandra tried to twist her neck so that the assailant would not puncture her jugular vein, but the strength of the heavy hand on her mouth and around her throat prohibited any movement. She knew she was about to die.

It could have been death that jumped, dark and hulking, from the shadows, forcing her, along with her would-be killer, down to the ground. She knew, though, before she hit the ground, it was not death who attacked, but Zack. She could see her assailant next to her, a shadowy masculine form, struggling on the manure- and straw-strewn ground as he tried to escape Zack's lunge. Zack would have had the advantage, except that he smelled her blood, and his menacing growl changed to a frightened whine as he turned toward her and gently kissed her wound with his tongue.

It was just enough time for the man to scramble to his feet. For a moment Zack seemed confused as to whether he should run after the man or stay by Alexandra's side. He ran, his bark loud and ferocious in the darkness. He stopped a few yards out before he caught up with the predator and watched, as if to make sure he was not coming back, then he ran back to Alexandra.

By the time he reached her side, Nancy had a lamp lit and was standing at the door holding it and calling out into the night.

"Who's there? What is it, Zack? Zachariah!" She held her lamp high, peering into the darkness.

Zack gave one sharp bark, and Alexandra, her hand clasped to her throat, cried out. "Nancy. I'm here! Come help me."

"Miss Alex? Is that you?"

Before Alexandra could answer, Zack ran toward Nancy, grabbed the skirt of her nightgown in his teeth, and pulled her, dancing an awkward side step.

Nancy let him pull her while she tried to keep her balance and hold onto the lamp. As soon as she was close enough to see the blood-soaked front of Alexandra's dress and to see the blood pouring from her throat, she stopped and put a hand to her mouth to stifle a scream.

"Help me up, Nancy. I've got to get inside."

The sharp command brought Nancy out of her stupor. She set the lamp aside and pulled Alexandra to her feet. "What happened, miss? Who hurt you like this?"

"Someone with a knife. I don't know." Alexandra could hear the weariness in her own voice, and she was not certain her legs would carry her inside. She walked with her arm slung around Nancy's shoulders while Nancy held her tightly at the waist and Zack barked his encouragement.

Alexandra called out to the dog in her weak voice. "Good Zack. Good boy. You saved my life."

"If I hadn't just let him out for his nightly business, where would we be, miss? I ask you that." Nancy sounded half tearful, half angry as she helped Alexandra into the house. "You shouldn't be out at night, you know that."

It was an old argument to which Alexandra didn't bother to respond. She'd said too many times that she had no control over the time, day or night, her patients needed her.

"And I've told you dozens of times," Nancy continued. "You should have a boy who stays around at night. Not someone who goes home to his mum the way Freddie does."

That was an old argument as well, but now Alexandra's response had a new irony. "If Freddie had been here tonight, he'd most likely be dead now."

"Oh my, Miss Alex, don't talk that way." Nancy's voice trembled as she spoke. Her hand trembled as well when she reached to open the door and guide Alexandra inside.

"Take me to the surgery," Alexandra said, "and bring me a basin of hot water."

For a moment, Nancy didn't move. Instead, she stood looking at Alexandra shaking her head while tears rolled down her cheeks. "Who would do this, miss? And why?"

"Nancy, please. I've got to tend to this wound right away."

"Oh, yes." Nancy hurried away with the lamp, leaving Alexandra to light her own lamp and find her way to the surgery. Zack followed like a shadow.

She was standing at the mirror, trying to examine the wound when Nancy returned with the water and fresh bandages. She went to work immediately helping Alexandra clean the gash, but she was not the usual calm, efficient Nancy who so often helped Alexandra with medical emergencies.

"You must calm yourself, Nancy." Alexandra was once again examining the wound in the mirror. She had seen that, while it was a significant gash, it was not at the jugular vein, but it was in the tender area where the chin joins the throat. It was not so deep that it could not heal, and no vital muscles, tendons, or blood vessels had been affected. "I'm going to have to depend on you to help me close the wound."

Nancy's eyes grew wide. "Close the wound? Oh no, Miss Alex, I couldn't."

"Of course you can. You've helped me sew up dozens of wounds."

"But not on you, Miss Alex. Not on you." Zack growled, low in his throat, and Nancy jerked her head toward him. "Now don't you go telling me what to do as well. I've had enough of your bossiness."

"I'll need to mix a styptic before you close. Can you

bring me the ingredients, please, Nancy?" Alexandra held a piece of gauze to her wound as she spoke, and it quickly soaked with blood. Seeing the blood, Nancy turned white again, and for a moment Alexandra feared that she would faint. She turned away quickly and gathered the items.

Within a few seconds Nancy brought a mixture of gallic acid, powdered opium, sulfate of zinc, and alcohol. Alexandra mixed the ingredients, then soaked another piece of gauze in the mixture and applied it to her wound. Ribbons of fire radiated from her throat under her skin and through her tissue and nerves to her jaw, eyes, and head and down the back of her neck to her shoulders and back, but she kept applying the solution until the bleeding stemmed enough to finish the task.

"Now the sutures, please, Nancy." Alexandra had barely spoken the words when the room began to whirl around her, and there were dark spots interrupting her vision.

"Miss Alex!" Nancy's frightened voice and Zack's alarmed bark seemed to come from very far away, and then the dark spots consumed her.

She awakened to the sharp scent of ammonia and the sight of Nancy bending over her. She lay on the floor where she had slipped from her chair. Zack looked down into her eyes, doing his best to lick her face while Nancy swatted him away with one hand and waved the smelling salts under her nose with the other.

Alexandra's first reaction was acute and almost unbearable embarrassment. It wasn't unusual for her patients to faint from pain, especially when they had been deprived of rest, but she had not expected to succumb herself. She tried to get up, but Nancy pushed her down.

"Not yet, you don't," she said.

"But I'm all right, Nancy. I don't know what came over me. I'm sure I just—"

"I'm afraid you just found out you're mortal like all o' your patients."

"You must let me up from here, and you must understand there were extenuating circumstances that caused me to . . . to, well, slip for a moment, and—"

"You'll not be getting up until I'm sure the blood is back to your head where it belongs, and you didn't just slip, as you well know. You fainted. You needn't worry, though. Nothing's hurt but your pride." Nancy was dabbing at Alexandra's throat with another soaked bandage. Alexandra's moment of weakness had brought out Nancy's strength. She was fully in control now. Within a few minutes she had Alexandra up on the table, needle and sutures in hand.

"And how was the Blackburn baby?" Nancy asked as she took the first of her neat little stitches. It was a device Alexandra had used herself to distract patients. If she could keep them thinking of something other than the needle, the pain was not so noticeable. By the time Nancy had finished, Alexandra had told her the whole story of the birth of twins, the one who did not survive, and the condition of the mother. The distraction worked, at least to the extent that she didn't embarrass herself again by fainting. Zack, in the meantime, watched it all, wearing a concerned look and giving Nancy an occasional scolding growl. Within an hour, Nancy had finished her task and had helped Alexandra out of her bloody dress and into bed.

Alexandra was awakened the next morning by Zack's bark signaling that someone had approached the house. She was only half awake, however, until she heard the sound of voices downstairs—Nancy's voice, of course, but to whom did the other belong?

Alexandra glanced, bleary-eyed, at her clock on the bureau, and then her eyes sprung open wide when she realized it was after eight. She should have been up long ago to see after Priscilla Blackburn and her other patients.

The room spun crazily when she stood up, and she had to find the edge of the bed with her hands and sit down again. She must have lost more blood than she'd realized, and then there was the matter of healing. She'd often told her patients not to try to resume normal work after an injury, since, as her father had taught her, the body must use a great deal of its energy to heal. She'd also chided her patients when they told her they had no time to wait. Now it was she who could not wait. There was work to do.

The voices downstairs were louder now, and it sounded as if an argument was in full play. Nancy's voice rushed up to her on agitated waves.

"No, you cannot see her. Dr. Gladstone is not well this morning."

The words of the other voice, a male voice, were less distinguishable to her. She eased herself out of bed and went to her door and called out. "Tell the patient I'll be down in a moment."

She stepped back into her room, quickly changed her bloodied bandage, and dressed herself hurriedly. She'd chosen a simple dress, free of rushing and lace and extra petticoats. She tried to dress her hair, but was having trouble keeping the pins in, so she pulled them all out and let her hair flow freely about her shoulders. Perhaps it was not in the best of taste, but when a patient was waiting, one could not worry about meaningless rules of propriety.

Alexandra hurried out the door and to the stairway. Nancy was at the bottom, just starting up. "Why didn't you wake me, Nancy? I should never sleep so late. You know I don't like to keep patients waiting."

"Don't worry, miss. 'Tisn't a patient. 'Tis only—"

"Mr. Forsythe!"

He grinned at her, and she noticed he was wearing tweeds, not the more formal attire a gentleman would be expected to wear on a return trip to London. "The second time you've mistaken me for a . . . Good lord! You've been wounded!"

"No need to worry. It's not life threatening." She sounded more cavalier than she felt. In truth she had awakened several times during the night remembering with horror her encounter with the knife-wielding stranger and grateful for Zack snoring on the floor next to her bed. Even now, in the peaceful, rose-colored light of the summer morning, she still felt cold fear when she remembered. Nevertheless, she tried to sound unruffled. "I'm surprised to see you here, Mr. Forsythe. I thought you were to leave for London early."

"Never mind my leaving for London," he said, taking

both of her hands and leading her to the parlor. "Tell me what happened. Have you hurt yourself?"

"Hurt *herself*? I think not!" Nancy sat a tray of tea and scones on the table in front of the sofa just as Mr. Forsythe, still holding Alexandra's hands, sat with her. "A murderer, it was. Met her in the stable yard." Nancy, her eyes wide, nodded emphatically at Mr. Forsythe.

"A murderer?" Mr. Forsythe's eyes were as wide as Nancy's as he glanced from one to the other.

"I'm afraid Nancy's exaggerating a bit," Alexandra said. "In truth, I have no way of knowing—"

"Exaggerating am I?" Nancy put her hands on her hips. "Ask her to tell you the whole story, and we'll see if I'm exaggerating." With that she turned and left the room.

"Tea?" Alexandra asked, reaching for the pot.

Mr. Forsythe put a hand on hers to stop her from pouring. "Not until you tell me the whole story."

She sighed. "If I tell you the story, you'll be late leaving for London."

"I'm not going to London."

She gave him a surprised look. "Not going to London? But why?"

"Never mind why. I want to hear about your encounter and what made your Nancy mention a murderer."

"Oh, all right." She sounded impatient as she poured the tea, in spite of his protest. "But I can't bear to relive it without a bit of tea." She took her time stirring in the milk and sugar, then took her first swallow while Mr. Forsythe glared at her. But she was stalling for time, trying to remember whether she'd seen anything at all, whether she'd sensed anything.

Finally she told him, giving all the facts she remembered, finishing with, "and then Nancy helped me dress the wound, and I went to bed."

"And you have no idea who it was?"

"It was too dark. I couldn't see."

"Not even when your dog chased him away."

"Nothing except a shadowy form."

Mr. Forsythe was silent, a troubled frown making a deep furrow on his brow.

Alexandra picked up her cup carefully. "May I be so impertinent as to ask what you are thinking, sir?"

He glanced at her. "The same thing you're thinking."

She held his gaze for a moment, then shook her head slowly. "Oh no. I'm not thinking that at all."

"Of course you are."

"But what possible motive would Lord Dunsford's killer have to kill me?"

"I think you know the answer to that as well."

Again their gazes held while Alexandra's thoughts spun logic in her head. She sighed again and slumped back against the sofa. "I've been a bit too mouthy and free with my opinions, haven't I?"

"I'm afraid so," Mr. Forsythe said, helping himself to a scone. "Someone at Montmarsh yesterday heard you say someone other than Elsie killed Eddie, and that person became frightened that you knew too much and tried to do you in. I would wager it was a man, since it would obviously take some strength to hold you still with a knife at your throat."

"Perhaps it was a woman who hired a man to kill me."

"Perhaps." Mr. Forsythe brushed crumbs from his mouth with a napkin. "But you are in danger, nevertheless. I think it wise that you not take any chances by being out late at night alone, and you shouldn't go unescorted during the day, for a while at least."

Alexandra put her teacup down with a bit too much force. "That's impossible. I have my patients to see, and I have no way of knowing what time of day or night—"

"I'll be your escort."

"I have Zack."

He glared at her. "Why wasn't he with you last night?"

"He *was* with me. At the crucial moment at least." She was beginning to feel as if she was in the witness box defending herself.

He stood, towering over her. "I'm afraid that's not good

enough. You must understand, Dr. Gladstone, that your life is in danger. I will be your escort."

Alexandra stood as well and faced him with simmering anger. "I won't deny that I was frightened, Mr. Forsythe, and of course I understand the necessity for caution, but I don't need—"

"Ah, you're such a gentleman, Mr. Forsythe." Nancy had suddenly reappeared with another plate of scones. "These are troubled times, and a lady can't be too careful, so of course the good doctor will appreciate your assistance. Will that be all, miss?"

"That will be quite enough," Alexandra said.

Nancy made another little curtsey and left.

Mr. Forsythe turned to her. "So it's settled, then. What time will we leave for your rounds?"

"Of course it's not settled. Nancy doesn't make decisions for . . ." Alexandra saw the determined expression on his face. "Oh, very well, then. As soon as I've put up my hair." She turned quickly and walked toward the staircase.

"Your hair is lovely when it's loose," he said to her back.

She hesitated only slightly, glad that her back was turned, so that he could not see her face, and hurried up the stairs.

Mr. Forsythe drove her on her rounds in another one of the carriages he had purloined from Montmarsh. At each stop, he waited in the carriage like a hired man because Alexandra had insisted that she see her patients in privacy. The talk at each stop was of Elsie's arrest. As before, her patients, like the entire parish, were divided as to whether or not the girl's incarceration was warranted.

When they arrived at the Blackburnses at the edge of the parish, and their last stop, Seth Blackburn was outdoors chopping wood while his older son played with the dog a few feet away.

Seth removed his hat and wiped his brow with his arm when he saw the carriage. Alexandra saw immediately the pallor of his skin and the dark circles under his eyes and knew that he had not slept.

"Dr. Gladstone." Seth's voice sounded weary, and he gave Mr. Forsythe a quick, curious glance.

"Good morning, Seth. This is Nicholas Forsythe, a friend who is accompanying me on my rounds today."

Seth ignored the introduction and looked straight at Alexandra. "She doesn't fare well, my Priscilla. I fear for her, miss. You must help her!" Then he added as an afterthought, "You've met with an accident, miss."

"A clumsy fall," Alexandra said, reaching for her bag. That was the story she'd given all of her curious patients. "Does Priscilla eat?" she added, eager to change the subject.

Seth shook his head sadly. "A scarce mite, and she's weakening. She needs care, I know, but I ought to be in the fields. It's my labor that keeps us alive, miss. I know not what to do. Her mother and her sisters are fifty leagues away."

"Then we must find someone to care for her," Alexandra said as she moved quickly toward the house.

"I cannot pay, miss, I don't—"

"Payment will not be necessary." She spoke in curt tones, throwing the words over her shoulder.

Priscilla lay in bed, pale and drawn, holding the screaming baby to her breast. She spoke in a weak, lifeless voice. "He'll not suckle."

Alexandra took the baby from her arms and tried to quiet him. She suspected that the reason the baby would not suckle was because there was no milk. Priscilla was too weak. She would have to find a wet nurse for the baby, but there was little she could do for Priscilla. Her body would need time to rebuild itself, if she was not already too far gone.

After examining Priscilla and the baby, she left Seth with the instructions to continue the iron, quinia, and beef broth, then asked Mr. Forsythe to stop at a house in the village where Daisy Simmons lived. Alexandra gave her two pounds to nurse the Blackburn baby and care for the mother.

"I saw you pay that woman," Mr. Forsythe said after they had delivered Daisy to the Blackburns' home. "Do you always spend more to care for a patient than you are paid?"

"Of course not. Otherwise, how would I live in such luxury?"

Mr. Forsythe glanced at her, and a faint, knowing smile brushed his lips as he flicked the reins to urge the horse to move faster.

"Where are we going?" Alexandra asked when she saw they had passed the road to her house.

"We're going to the gaol."

She glanced at him. "To see Elsie." A statement, not a question.

"To report the attack last night to the constable," he said without looking at her.

"Are you sure it's necessary? I really don't think—"

"Of course it's necessary. You don't want whomever it was out attacking other women, do you?"

Alexandra hesitated. "Since you put it that way. . . . But still, I'm not sure—"

"And you're right." He seemed determined not to give her an opportunity to object. "I want to see Elsie, but if the constable is astute enough, neither of us will be allowed to see her, since we are both witnesses. Still, I'd like to know whether she knows anything about that attempt on your life." He frowned as he spoke, concentrating on driving the carriage.

"What makes you think she would?"

He shook his head. "I'm afraid I don't have a logical reason. It's just a feeling I have that Elsie isn't telling us everything she knows."

8

Constable Snow was the only police officer in the village of Newton-Upon-Sea. His office was located on the ground floor of the local gaol in a narrow wooden building, two stories high, which, over the past century had developed a decided tilt toward the street. Across the street was the Blue Ram, housed on the ground floor of the village inn that had been in the same location for three centuries.

The inn also leaned toward the street, forming a broken arch with the gaol, and giving the impression of two decrepit and impoverished courtiers bowing to each other.

Robert Snow was sitting at his desk, pouring over a mound of reports he was obliged to write when Mr. Forsythe opened the door for Alexandra to enter.

Alexandra read his face, which was suddenly punctuated with surprise. He stood awkwardly, knocking over a dry inkwell, but he quickly regained his composure. "Dr. Gladstone!" He gave her a slight bow while his long hand deftly set the inkwell upright. "Mr. Forsythe," he said. "A pleasant surprise." In contrast to his awkwardness a few seconds before, he moved with an odd grace around his desk to pull a chair forward for Alexandra. "Please be seated, Doctor. And may I offer you tea?"

"Thank you, but no," Alexandra said. "We've come to see Elsie."

Mr. Forsythe spoke at the same time. "We've come to report an incident."

"I see." Snow sat down at his desk, decidedly more at ease now, and picked up a pen. He glanced up at them. "What sort of an incident." Obviously he had chosen to ignore Alexandra's request for the moment, at least.

"An attempt on Dr. Gladstone's life," Mr. Forsythe said.

There was the slightest change in Snow's eyes. Was it surprise or alarm? "That explains the bandage at your throat, then." His tone was matter-of-fact.

Alexandra's right hand went inadvertently to her throat. She thought she had done a sufficient job of covering the bandage with the light shawl she'd wrapped around her neck.

"Explain, please," Snow said in his schoolmaster voice. He was looking directly at Alexandra.

"Someone attacked me in my stables as I was returning from delivering Priscilla Blackburn's baby last night. I'm afraid it was rather late."

Snow wrote something on a notepad. "Did you recognize your attacker?"

"Of course not."

"You saw his face?"

"I'm afraid I didn't. It was quite dark, as you might imagine."

"You were not seriously injured, I trust."

"No." Alexandra saw Mr. Forsythe start to protest, but she gave him a warning look, and he said nothing.

"A thief perhaps." Snow put down his pen and leaned back in his chair. "We've had a spate of burglaries recently. I suspect a gang of young toughs who seem to have come here from Chelmsford."

"You've actually seen these young toughs? Or are you only speculating?" Mr. Forsythe moved toward him with an air of confidence as he spoke, looking and sounding very much like a barrister.

Snow's answer was a short and curt "yes," leaving Alexandra and Mr. Forsythe to wonder which question he'd answered. He turned back to Alexandra. "I assume you were able to frighten the attacker away, Dr. Gladstone?"

"Zack, my dog, frightened him."

"Ah yes, the Newfoundland. I suggest you take him with you from now on when you find it necessary to be out late." He stood up and walked around his desk. "I shall do my best to apprehend the attacker, Dr. Gladstone, but you must understand that it will be difficult without a description of the suspect."

"Perhaps you could question the young toughs from Chelmsford." Mr. Forsythe's suggestion might have been innocuous except for the hard edge of sarcasm to his voice.

Snow's face reddened as he turned toward him, and Alexandra spoke quickly in an attempt to diffuse the situation. "We've another mission here, Constable. We've come to see Elsie."

Snow turned to her. "Ah yes." His head bobbed slightly while he clasped his hands behind his back, and fixed his eyes on a spot just below the ceiling. He rocked slightly, back and forth, on his heels. It was a stance Alexandra had seen many times before when, in those days when he was still a schoolmaster, he was either pondering a question his student had asked, or was waiting for the correct answer to a question he had asked. She had been his student because her father had hired him to come to the house regularly to tutor her, since, being female, she was not allowed to attend the local school. After Nancy came to live with them, she sat in on the lessons as well. Her father hired Snow because he recognized him as an intelligent man and a gifted teacher. And Snow had come daily, after working until midafternoon at the school, without ever once complaining of being tired.

He had taken the job as constable only a few years ago, presumably for higher wages. He had no family of his own, but, according to the gossips, he sent money regularly to a woman in London.

Snow dropped his gaze to Alexandra and then to Mr. Forsythe. "It would certainly be out of order for me to allow either of you to see her, since you are to be witnesses at her trial."

Mr. Forsythe approached him, slightly aggressive in his movements. "I understand that, of course, but since Dr. Gladstone is—"

Snow turned to Alexandra and spoke to her, interrupting Mr. Forsythe in midsentence. "She is—not well."

"Not well?" Alexandra was alarmed.

Snow frowned, a troubled expression. "I am referring to her mind. It is disturbed."

"She's hardly more than a child, and she's been accused of murder, I should think one *would* be disturbed." Mr. Forsythe said.

Snow ignored him again as he spoke to Alexandra. "She appears to be hallucinating."

"Indeed!" Alexandra was now both curious and alarmed.

"Yes. She seems to think young Stirling speaks to her from the grave."

Alexandra relaxed somewhat. "A common phenomenon when one is grieving."

"Yes, of course," Snow said, as if he'd been trying to coax the right answer from her all along. "Perhaps, under the circumstances, you, being a physician, should be allowed to see her." This time he turned to Mr. Forsythe, as if for confirmation that his questionable decision could pass the test of legality.

"Certainly," Mr. Forsythe said. "And I—"

"Will not be allowed to see her," Snow said.

"But . . ." Mr. Forsythe managed to make that one word sound indignant.

Alexandra put a hand gently on his arm. "Allow me to be alone with her for a few minutes."

"But . . ."

"This way, please, Dr. Gladstone." Snow led Alexandra toward the back of the building and unlocked a door to a large room with two small, narrow windows near the ceiling. It had the musty odor of rodent droppings mixed with the stench of human bodies. There were no individual cells in the country gaol. Instead, all prisoners who were awaiting trial were kept together in one room, where they slept on blankets on the floor. However, since it was mandatory that males and females not be kept together, Elsie was not with the three men who stared at Alexandra with hollow-eyed lechery as she passed through their cell to a narrow, heavy doorway. The short train of her skirts picked up black grime from the dirt floor as she walked.

Snow chose a key from a large ring he wore attached to his belt and unlocked the door. As soon as it was open, Alexandra saw a rat scurry across the small room and disappear into a crevice where the wall joined the floor. The window in this room was little more than a narrow hole midway up the wall.

Elsie, who had been lying on a blanket on the bare floor, suddenly sat upright and stared at the two of them with frightened, sleep-blurred eyes. She cringed and seemed to be trying to make herself disappear into the wall just as the rat had.

"Dr. Gladstone wants to talk to you a moment, Elsie," Snow said in a voice that was not unkind, that was, in fact, devoid of emotion. He stood aside for Alexandra to enter. "I shall wait outside while you examine her," he said. "But you must not speak of the charges against her. You need only to call out to me when you're finished."

When Snow left and the door was closed, Elsie stopped her cowering, and her eyes lost some of their fear, but she remained cautious. "What is it ye wants with me, miss?"

"I just want to talk to you, Elsie. I see no need for a physical examination."

"I got nothing to say."

"First of all, I want to assure you again I had nothing to do with your arrest. I did not lead the constable—"

Elsie interrupted her. "I know that, miss. I was scairt when I accused you of that. Too scairt to think straight." There was a long silence while Elsie stared at nothing. Alexandra could hear the sound of her own breathing, but Elsie hardly seemed to be breathing at all.

She dropped her head. "They'll be hanging me, won't they, miss?"

"I don't know," Alexandra said. She sat down beside Elsie on the blanket, manipulating her skirts with some difficulty, then unfastened her small ribbon-trimmed hat and leaned her back against the wall. She was mindful of Snow's warning about not discussing the case, but, she rationalized, she could not properly examine her mental state without discussing it.

Elsie turned her face toward her with a quick movement. "Ye'll ruin them fancy things yer wearin'."

"There's nothing fancy about them, so never mind." Alexandra had few frocks that could be labeled "fancy." Most of her dresses, which Nancy made for her, were of cotton for summer and wool for winter. However, in spite of the fact that Alexandra tried to discourage her for practical reasons, Nancy still insisted on trimming them with pleated or draped overskirts, sometimes gathered into a bustle at the back, and occasionally adding a bit of lace or lawn ruching at the neck or cuffs.

Elsie's eyes took in Alexandra's pale green cotton dress with its ivory, dirt-stained underskirt and straw bonnet, which Nancy had trimmed with matching ribbons. There was, for the briefest moment, a look of longing in her eyes.

"Are ye really a doctor, miss?" she asked, bringing her gaze back to meet Alexandra's eyes.

"Yes." Alexandra spoke quietly.

Elsie squinted her eyes and wrinkled her nose in a puzzled gesture. "How can that be? I mean, ye bein' a woman and all?"

"My father taught me."

"And have you not heard 'tis not proper for a lady like you to be doin' such things?"

"I've heard that, yes."

There was another long silence until Elsie spoke again, and this time there was a coldness in her voice. "Me own bleedin' father taught me nothing except the feel of the back of his hand across me jaw. Until I was grown. And then 'twas the feel of his bleedin' pecker bangin' away that he taught me."

Alexandra felt a tightness in her chest and a longing to take the poor child in her arms. In spite of her talk of being grown, she couldn't be more than fifteen. But she said nothing. She merely kept her eyes on Elsie's face, inviting her to say more. Elsie looked away.

"Elsie . . ."

She responded with a hate-hardened laugh, and there was something in her eyes that made her look older than her young, smooth face implied. "Don't pity me, miss. Ye think me the only one what got stuck by 'er old man? Well, I ain't. If ye've not learned already, it's time ye know. They's all alike, men is. Wouldn't give ye a farthing for a single one of 'em, I wouldn't."

"Except George Stirling."

Elsie jerked her head around to look at Alexandra. "What do ye know about Georgie?"

"I know nothing about him, except that he's dead. You said that yourself that night at Montmarsh."

Elsie dropped her eyes again. "Aye, 'e's dead all right." She spoke in a hoarse whisper. "Seen 'em take his body away with his face gone blue, I did." She raised her eyes to look at Alexandra. "But I heard 'im calling to me one night, just outside the window 'ere. It was Georgie's voice callin' to me from the grave, I'll tell you that! I'd know that voice if I was in the grave meself."

Alexandra reached to touch Elsie's hand, and to her surprise, Elsie didn't shrink away. "Elsie, sometimes when we're grieving—"

This time Elsie did jerk her hand away quickly. "I know what yer thinkin'. Yer thinkin' I've gone loony."

"I think nothing of the kind, Elsie. It's just that you should understand that when a person is grieving, she might—"

" 'E come back from the grave, 'e did. Come back to warn me." Elsie's voice trembled.

Alexandra stood and started to reach a hand toward her

again, but thought it best not to risk alarming her. "To warn you of what?"

"To warn me of my death."

The poor child was frightened by the prospect of hanging, along with grieving for her lover and trying to cope with the scars of her past. It was enough to make anyone slip into madness. Alexandra knew she was beyond any help she could pull from her medical bag.

"Would you like me to ask the parish priest to talk to you? Perhaps he could give you some comfort."

Elsie gave her a derisive laugh. "It's not a bloody priest I'm needin'. What can 'e do for me? No more than Quince, I say."

"Quince?"

"Aye. Quince. 'Quince can 'elp you,' Georgie says. 'Ye must tell 'im I sent ye,' 'e says. And 'ow do ye think I can talk to Quince,' says I. 'What with me in chokey.' " She glanced at Alexandra. "Sometimes Georgie can be a bit daft."

"Is this Quince someone you know?" Alexandra asked.

Elsie nodded. "Georgie's friend. One o' them no-counts what hangs around the pier. I never liked 'im meself."

"Then why do you think George would want you to talk to him?" Alexandra asked.

Elsie turned to face her, and some of her premature hardness had been replaced by a look of naiveté. "Why, because they swore a blood oath for one to watch out for the other. Like brothers, Georgie said." Some of the hardness came back into her eyes. "But I say Georgie was a fool to trust 'im. Never trusted 'im meself."

Alexandra nodded as if she understood. "But if you *could* talk to Quince, what do you think he would say to you?"

Elsie wrinkled her nose again. "And 'ow would I be knowin' that?" She fell silent again, then spoke quietly. "But if ye wants to know what I think Georgie would think, it would be that if anybody can get me out of 'ere, 'tis Quince."

Alexandra kept prodding. "And why do you think that?"

"Because Quince knows things," Elsie said, still edgy.

" 'E's the one what told me that it was the bloody earl what killed Georgie, and 'e knows who killed the earl, too."

Alexandra felt a jolt of surprise mixed with alarm. "Elsie, if you know anything about either of those two deaths, then you must tell Constable Snow."

"Knows anything?" Elsie looked suddenly alarmed. She backed away from Alexandra. "So that's what yer doing coming 'ere in yer fine clothes and yer soft voice. Trying to get me to say I done it, are ye? Get away from me!" she screamed.

"That's not what I meant at all. Please, Elsie."

"Get out!" Elsie's scream had reached a loud, high timbre. "Get out, I say. Ye ain't gettin' me to say I done something I never done!"

"Is everything all right?" It was Snow's voice calling from outside the door, and at the same time, Alexandra heard the key rattling in the lock. Then the door burst open and Snow stepped inside. He quickly grabbed Elsie, pinning her arms to her side with his long, sinewy hands, while he looked into her face. "Enough!" It sounded like a bark, and Elsie's screaming dissolved to a whimper, and then to a wide-eyed, white-faced stare. "I think you'd best leave, Doctor," Snow said over his shoulder to Alexandra.

Alexandra started to protest. If she could have just a little more time with Elsie, perhaps she could correct what she had said that got them off on the wrong footing. But she said nothing. Constable Snow was probably right. She should go. Still, it was with a large measure of reluctance that she picked up her bag, carrying it, along with her hat, in her hands.

Mr. Forsythe was waiting for her in the constable's office. He stood up as soon as he saw her. "What happened? You and the constable were gone for such a long time, I'd begun to think he'd locked *you* up."

"What? Oh, no. Of course not."

Mr. Forsythe gave her an odd look. "You sound distracted."

"Well . . ."

"Good lord! She told you something." He looked around

as if he was expecting Snow to return at any moment. "Let's get out of here, and you can tell me what she said."

"It was just a lot of gibberish, really," Alexandra said as he took her arm and led her out of the building. She stopped and turned to look at him. "And why were you so belligerent back there with Constable Snow? Didn't I tell you there was undoubtedly nothing he could do about the attack on me?"

Mr. Forsythe took her arm and started her walking again. "That excuse about the young toughs from Chelmsford was just too convenient. I can't help wondering if there's not another reason why he's not more aggressive about investigating the attack. And stop trying to change the subject. What did Elsie say?"

"Just as the constable said, she claims George Stirling speaks to her."

"About the murder?"

"She claims he told her to talk to someone named Quince, who apparently is one of those young men Constable Snow suspects may be thieves. I think she believes he can help her. She claims Quince knows who murdered Lord Dunsford and George Stirling both. In fact, she says Quince once told her it was Dunsford who murdered George."

Mr. Forsythe stopped and looked at her. "Good lord!" By this time they were standing beside the carriage. He helped her to her seat, then sat beside her. "So she's gone gaga, then?" he said as he took the reins.

"I'm not so sure."

He jerked his head around to look at her. "You think she's actually speaking to the dead?"

"Nooo." Alexandra pondered it. "I think there's a possibility she's hallucinating, but I think the whole story about this Quince is her way of saying *she* thinks Quince knows some answers. But she can't quite make herself believe he can help her."

Mr. Forsythe frowned. "Why not?"

"Because he is male, and the only male she ever felt she could trust is George Stirling."

"Rather odd, I should say."

Alexandra didn't respond to his remark. There was no easy way she could tell him why it wasn't at all odd that Elsie wouldn't trust men. "The trouble is, I botched the whole conversation with Elsie. I think she would have told me more if I hadn't been such a fool."

"You? A fool? Come now, Dr. Gladstone, what could you have possibly said to her that was foolish?"

"I should have continued to go along with her story that George had told her to contact that Quince fellow. Instead, when she made the claim that he knew the identity of both Lord Dunsford's and George's killers, I made the mistake of telling her that she should tell the constable if she knew who had done it. She immediately interpreted that to mean that I thought *she* was the killer and went into hysterics."

"And what *do* you think about it?" Mr. Forsythe asked.

"I think that I should like to talk to Quince."

"And how will you find him?" He had that barrister sound to his voice again.

"Why, I shall go down to the pier and ask about until I find him."

"I think not. It could be quite dangerous, you know."

"Mmmm," Alexandra said.

9

Alexandra was alarmed the following morning when she realized she had once again overslept by two hours. The
wound at her throat had obviously taken more of a toll than
she realized.

She dressed hurriedly and ran downstairs to demand of
Nancy why she had allowed her to sleep to such a late hour.
She found Nancy dusting the parlor, but before she could
confront her, Nancy handed her a cheap and somewhat
greasy envelope.

"Two messages for you, miss," she said.

"Two? But there's only one—"

"The other is from Seth Blackburn. He came himself,
earlier."

Alexandra saw the look on Nancy's face and felt a void
in her chest. "Priscilla?" Her voice was little more than a
whisper.

Nancy nodded and looked down at her hands. "She's
gone, miss. Passed away in the wee hours of the morning,
her husband said."

"You should have . . ." Alexandra didn't finish her sentence. It would do no good to scold Nancy for not waking

her. Not now, anyway. She felt stunned as she walked past
Nancy into her surgery. She closed the door and sat in one
of the chairs, staring out the window at nothing. She always
felt a keen sense of futility when she lost a patient, but never
more than now. She had done literally all she could for
Priscilla, knowing all along that it was not enough. She was
too weak, had lost too much blood, probably had become
severely anemic during the pregnancy as well. Perhaps if
she had come to her earlier, the iron and quinia would have
helped. But perhaps not. Perhaps there was, in the final anal-
ysis, nothing that could be done.

What Priscilla Blackburn had needed was, quite simply,
more blood in her body. Given time, iron might help build
it back in some patients, but not in patients such as Priscilla.
She needed blood immediately, and there was simply no
way to infuse blood into a human being. Doctors, including
her own father, had tried, but the patient almost always died.
Even sheep blood had been tried in at least one experiment.
Obviously there was something about the properties of
blood that no one understood. The practice of medicine was
a humbling experience. It served to illustrate with resound-
ing authority the frailties and weaknesses of both the patient
and the physician.

Alexandra sat alone, staring out the window for several
minutes more until Nancy knocked softly on the door and
stuck her head in. "Will you be wanting anything more before you start your rounds, miss?" It was Nancy's way of
seeing if she was all right and of making sure she got started
on her work. It was already almost noon, and she was three
hours late starting on her rounds.

"What? Oh no, I'll just get my bag and . . ." As she stood,
the crude envelope Nancy had handed her fell from her lap
to the floor. "Have Freddie saddle Lucy for me, please," she
said as she stooped to pick up the envelope.

"She's already saddled, Miss Alex. I did it myself. Freddie didn't show up this morning."

"Thank you, Nancy. I'm on my way." Alexandra tore at
the envelope hurriedly, fully back to herself and eager to
catch up on her work.

"Yes, miss." Nancy murmured and disappeared. Alexandra pulled a sheet of coarse paper from the envelope and held it up to the light of the window to read, grasping it in one hand while she reached for her bag with the other. She had only read a few words before she forgot about the bag and gripped the paper with both hands, startled as she read the entire brief message, scrawled in a crude, childish penmanship.

Docter Glad Ston, The gerl is rite. Quince nos who kilt the erl. Meet him at 10 tonite at the old peer. He will help you.

The note was not signed, and Alexandra felt a cold shiver creep down her spine. She had told no one except Mr. Forsythe about Elsie's mention of Quince, and no one else except Constable Snow knew of her visit to see Elsie. Neither Mr. Forsythe nor the constable would have written this crude note, of course.

"Nancy!" she called. "Nancy, come here please. Immediately!"

Within a few seconds, Nancy stuck her head in the doorway. "Yes, miss?"

"Who brought this note?"

"I don't know, Miss Alex." Her eyes widened as she noticed Alexandra's face. "Is something wrong?"

"You don't know? Someone must have handed it to you."

Nancy shook her head. "Oh no, I'm afraid not. 'Twas slipped under the door. I found it when I came to sweep the hall. There it was on the floor. I thought 'twas somebody paying his bill, or more likely giving you an excuse why he could not. It's done that way at times, miss, as you know."

Nancy was right. Patients did occasionally slip money or their excuses for late payment under the door.

"Is something wrong?" Nancy asked again.

"No. Of course not. I was just . . . curious." Alexandra folded the note and placed it in her medical bag. No point in alarming Nancy. She was as protective as a mother hen, as it were. "Has Mr. Forsythe been here this morning?"

"He has. Came by to escort you on your rounds, he did. But I told him you needed your rest, to which he quite agreed, I might add."

"You should have awakened me long ago, Nancy."

Nancy stiffened. "You needed to—"

"Never mind," Alexandra said. "It's always impossible to argue with you, and I don't have time anyway, but if Mr. Forsythe should stop by again, ask him to stay until I return. I need to speak with him." She kept her voice as calm and even as possible.

"Yes, miss." Alexandra saw an unspoken question flickering in her eyes, but not the slightest hint of regret for her impudence.

She closed her medical bag and headed for the door. Nancy hurried ahead of her to hand her a shawl and parasol. "Should I mention the note to Mr. Forsythe, miss? If he stops by again, that is." Nancy was too clever. She obviously had guessed there was something in the note Alexandra wanted to share with Mr. Forsythe.

"No, of course not," Alexandra said, hoping to put an end to it. But, knowing Nancy, who was smarter than most people she knew, there would be no end to it until her curiosity was satisfied. No doubt she would have Mr. Forsythe equally as curious within a few minutes after his arrival.

She left to see her patients, determining to stop by Montmarsh later, in case Mr. Forsythe was still there. She had planned to stop by anyway, to check on Mrs. Pickwick.

Alexandra's patients talked less about Elsie's arrest this time. It was as if they all simply accepted her imprisonment with a degree of complacency, whether they considered her guilty or not. Now the talk was of the wound at her neck, which she continued to try to explain away as a nasty fall, and of the earl's funeral, which was to be held at St. Paul's in London with the archbishop himself presiding. It would be grand, they said, attended by all the important members of the peerage and of the House of Commons as well as the queen herself. His funeral cortege would be spectacular, and his casket would ride on a gilded carriage pulled by eight

matching steeds. All of this had come to be known by the
residents of Newton through servants at Montmarsh who
had traveled to London with the body.

The funeral being planned at Seth Blackburn's home was
considerably less grand. Alexandra stopped by to give her
condolences and found Seth sitting alone in his dark little
cottage. The wet nurse she had hired had taken the children
to her own home for a few days until Seth could get his
wits about him. In truth, he had hardly thought at all about
the funeral and seemed at a loss as to what to do. His grief
had rendered him almost completely dysfunctional.

Alexandra spent some time talking to him. He was reluctant to talk himself, however, a characteristic of all levels
of English society Alexandra considered unhealthy, although she was well aware she possessed that very characteristic herself. When he did finally appear to want to talk,
all he could do was cry, and he was so consumed with his
grief, he forgot to be embarrassed.

When she left, she felt drained, but she took the time to
stop by the wet nurse's home to tell her she thought Seth
would be ready to see his children by morning. She also
made the financial arrangements for her to work as a full-
time nurse for the children for at least a few months.

By the time she finished, there was barely time to ride to
Montmarsh, but she felt an overwhelming need to talk to
Mr. Forsythe about the cryptic note she'd received. She
urged Lucy to a faster trot and rode to the estate. When she
arrived, the house and grounds looked deceptively tranquil,
as if nothing but the most pleasant of lawn parties or the
gayest of balls could have ever taken place there. Certainly
not murder.

She knocked at the door, hoping to leave a quick message
with the butler to have Mr. Forsythe join her for tea, have
a look at her patient, and then she could be on her way and
arrive at her surgery on time.

"I'm afraid Mr. Forsythe is no longer here," the butler
said in his most formal voice.

"I see."

"Mr. Forsythe has returned to London," the butler added.

"I don't believe he'll be back to Montmarsh."

Alexandra found herself speechless for a moment, but she collected herself quickly. "Very well. Then I shall just check on Mrs. Pickwick."

The butler moved aside to let her enter, and then escorted her to the kitchen where the cook was up and about. She refused to talk any more about the ghost she had claimed to have seen and dismissed Alexandra as soon as possible.

When she arrived home, she could smell the lamb stew Nancy was preparing for luncheon, and by the time she had hung up her hat and shawl, Nancy was moving toward her, drying her hands on her apron and announcing that lunch was ready in the kitchen. Alexandra always had her lunch in the kitchen and insisted that Nancy keep it as simple as possible so they could both be in the surgery by the time patients arrived.

"Any more messages for me, Nancy?" Alexandra kept her voice casual.

"No messages. Were you expecting one?" Nancy with her probing mind.

"Not especially." Alexandra spread her napkin on her lap. "Did Mr. Forsythe by any chance drop by?" Again, working at sounding casual.

Nancy set a plate of the stew and another plate of brown bread on the table. "Mr. Forsythe? Why, no, miss, I'm afraid not." Nancy's curiosity was palpable, but Alexandra didn't know how she would explain anything to Nancy when she was completely puzzled herself.

Alexandra sat in silence, trying to eat the stew, which, although it really was quite good, she was too preoccupied to enjoy.

Why would Mr. Forsythe leave for London so suddenly without telling her? He had been keen on the idea of helping her unravel the events surrounding the murder at Montmarsh. If he decided suddenly to return to London, then it must be very urgent business. But he seemed to be the responsible sort who would have left a message for her with Nancy, to explain what had taken him away.

"Do you suppose something has happened to Mr. Forsythe?" Nancy's question brought her out of her contemplation.

"Why would you ask that?"

Nancy gave her a shrewd look. "I really did think he'd come back to take you on your rounds, and when he never showed up, well . . . What with all that's been going on around here—people being murdered, attacked in their own stable yards—why, one becomes a bit edgy, don't you think?"

"I see your point, Nancy, but I'm sure Mr. Forsythe is all right. I suspect he's returned to London." Alexandra took another taste of the stew.

"Returned to London? Now why would he do that?" Nancy was clearly as puzzled as she.

"He's a busy barrister, Nancy. I'm sure he has more important matters to attend to than our provincial problems." Alexandra was not sure how convincing she sounded, and in the next few seconds, she realized that it was not at all.

Nancy turned away from whatever it was she was doing at the stove and put her hands on her hips. "I would say the murder of the earl of Dunsford is a bit more than a provincial problem." She sounded more than a little irritated at Alexandra's apparent obtuseness.

She was right, of course, but Alexandra was at a loss as to how to respond.

"Do you think it has something to do with the message you got this morning?" Nancy sat down across from her at the table and leaned forward eagerly, her chin on her hand. It was not the sort of liberty a servant would ordinarily take, but the relationship between the two of them was too long-standing and too grounded in childhood intimacies to withstand complete convention.

Nevertheless, Alexandra was a bit surprised at the question. "What makes you ask?"

Nancy cocked her head and looked at her accusingly. "Why, Miss Alex, you know you can't fool me. I saw how upset you were. That message had something to do with the murder, did it not? And you're wanting to talk to Mr. Forsythe about it. Or else you're afraid he's in danger."

Alexandra forced what she hoped was a casual laugh. "Your imagination is running away with you, Nancy." She ignored Nancy's continued accusing look. The truth was, she would have liked to share the contents of the note with her, along with the rest of the story, including Mr. Forsythe's sudden flight to London, but she knew how protective Nancy could be. She'd be on the verge of apoplexy if she knew Alexandra was thinking of going to the pier to find Quince.

Nancy was obviously about to probe her again when they both heard the bell on the surgery entrance ring, announcing that someone had entered, and Nancy was obliged to hurry away to greet them. Alexandra finished her lunch quickly and was on her way to the surgery herself when she met Nancy in the hallway.

"It's the Higgins boy with his mum. He looks as if he might have gotten a bit of poison ivy. I'll prepare the borax solution."

Nancy disappeared into the kitchen again, and Alexandra went to see her patient. She was busy the rest of the day with her routine duties, but when there was a lull, her mind kept coming back to the strange note and to Mr. Forsythe's leaving without a word. She read the note over and over again, trying to understand why she had received it and who would have known about what Elsie had told her.

No answers came to her, however, and by the time she had finished the light supper Nancy prepared for her, she had resolved that there was nothing to do but to go to the pier at the appointed time of ten o'clock to see what she could learn. It was out of the question to mention her plan to Nancy, however, since she would, without a doubt, protest. It was not unfeasible that Nancy would even keep an all night vigil to see that she did not leave the house.

She could not ask young Freddie, who had actually shown up, to saddle Lucy without raising suspicion. Furthermore, if she attempted to saddle her herself after Nancy had gone to bed, Nancy would surely hear her, since her room was on the stable side of the house. It was a walk of approximately a mile to the pier, and she did not relish the idea of making the walk alone in the dark. She would take Zack with her.

Nancy didn't make it easy for her, however. It had long been Alexandra's habit to invite Nancy into the parlor with her after supper for a chat, or at times to read to one another, either from the classics, which her father had taught Alexandra to love and Nancy to appreciate, or from Alexandra's favorite modern authors, Henry James or the Russian, Dostoyevsky, and even occasionally from one of Nancy's lurid romances. Recently, they had been reading an English translation of Dostoyevsky's *The Brothers Karamazov* and on this particular evening, Nancy had become so engrossed in the complicated interlocking love triangles of the characters, she read until it was quite late, and then she had to argue that Dostoyevsky's story was every bit as lurid as any of the romance novels she'd chosen. After that she insisted that there was work she'd left undone in the kitchen which couldn't possibly wait for morning. It was almost ten by the time she finally went to bed, and Alexandra still had the difficult task of getting a dog weighing eleven stone out of the house without making a noise.

Zack, with his habit of wanting to "talk" to her with his soft growls and almost human sounds, seemed to be asking, "Where are we going and what are you getting me into?"

It was enough to make Nancy poke her head out of her room and ask, "Is everything all right down there?"

"Of course. I'm just putting Zack out one last time." Alexandra hoped Nancy wouldn't notice that her voice was a bit unsteady. She hadn't sneaked out of the house since she was twelve. As it happened, Nancy was with her that time, and they'd both been nervous, and they'd both gotten caught.

When Nancy hadn't bothered to show any more concern after several minutes, Alexandra and Zack stepped out of the house into a moonless, star-stenciled night. The ground was familiar at first, lit here and there by a lamp shining through a cottage window, but as they neared the piers, the darkness became thick and oppressive as a heavy purple robe of fog billowed from the sea toward the land.

They both slowed their pace, and Alexandra instinctively caught Zack's leash up closer, wanting to feel the protection of his hulking body. She could hear the sea to her right, lashing at the shore and the wood pilings of the piers. Something, a large undeniable heaviness, loomed there as well, and Alexandra supposed it to be a fishing vessel.

She and Zack walked slowly, choosing their steps carefully. The note had said to come to the "old" pier. Alexandra was not intimately familiar with the docks, but she supposed the old pier to be the one that had fallen into disrepair. She had never clearly understood why it was in disuse and deteriorating, except that it had something to do with a superstition that had grown up in the area that ill fortune befell those who used the pier. A fitting place, she mused, to meet the ghosts of George Stirling and Lord Dunsford.

It seemed as if the whole parish was hallucinating, seeing ghosts and spirits at every turn. A ridiculous notion. Except now in this eerie darkness punctuated with the mournful sound of the sea, it seemed possible.

She felt Zack's body tense. He stopped, then moved slightly in front of her as if to protect her. She heard a low growl, deep in his throat. Her grip tightened on the leash, and she strained to hear or see whatever it was that had alerted Zack.

Zack growled again, low and menacing, and she felt him backing against her, pushing her back. Then suddenly she felt the leash ripped from her hand and sensed Zack bounding away from her, snarling and barking into the darkness. She started to call to him, but something stopped her—a presence, a heaviness surrounding her. Zack continued his wolfish bark, and then suddenly he screamed.

10

Darkness stalked Nicholas's coach as he and his driver made their way to London. The road from Newton to London was long, and even in the best of circumstances it was tedious. Travelers very quickly lost sight of the sea, and the scenery became pastoral, pleasant but unremarkable. As the darkness moved in, however, the route became menacing.

It would certainly be possible, and maybe even likely, that a coach driver could lose his way trying to follow a road that was not always clearly delineated even in daylight. And wasn't the *Times* always full of stories of members of the upper class being accosted by highwaymen along dark roads in the countryside?

It was foolish to travel at night, but Nicholas had gotten a late start, and he'd paid the driver double to drive all night so he could be in London by morning.

He'd also paid Freddie, Dr. Gladstone's stable boy, whom he'd met in the village, sixpence to deliver a note to Dr. Gladstone explaining what he'd done and instructing her not to go out alone until he returned, at which time he would remove to the quarters above the stable. Now, in retrospect, he wondered if he'd done the right thing by giving the note to the stable boy. He seemed a bit shiftless and unreliable, but Nicholas had thought at the time it was better to give it to a stable boy who was illiterate, than to one of the servants at Montmarsh and risk having them read it.

He had reasoned that if no one, save Dr. Gladstone, knew what he was doing in London, then there could be no messages forewarning certain parties of his arrival there. One could never be sure about such things, but it was best to be cautious, especially where murder was involved.

Under normal circumstances he would have been inclined to let the police handle the whole sordid affair. The fact that he had become so deeply involved in solving the murder might have, at first, been an excuse to see more of Dr. Gladstone. But the more he became involved, the more he began to share Dr. Galdstone's passion for uncovering the truth, and the more he became convinced that she was right about the kitchen wench. Elsie O'Riley was not Eddie's murderer.

After Nancy had told him this morning that Dr. Gladstone was still asleep when he called on her, he'd gone to the village where the talk everywhere was of the upcoming trial of Elsie O'Riley. There was also a great deal of praise for Squire Thomas Trowbridge, the justice of the peace who had convened his magistrate court so quickly, and equally as quickly had the prisoner bound over for trial. Although Justice Trowbridge had no legal training, Nicholas thought he seemed astute when he'd been compelled to give his testimony before him.

The assizes, made up of judges from the Queen's Bench in London, traveled to principal towns in each region to hold trials. They met in each county only once or twice a year, which meant, Nicholas hoped, there would be more time to find a way to prove Elsie's innocence. His hopes were dashed when Snow told him the assizes would convene in a fortnight. That had been the reason for the haste in holding the hearings before the justice. There might not be enough time. He would have to travel to London immediately to dig out the information he hoped to find.

How he wished he could represent Elsie properly in court.

But, as Snow had pointed out, he could not act as her barrister since he was to be a witness. Her hearing before the magistrate was her only opportunity to speak, and then she could only cross-examine witnesses, which she had not done, since she had no idea how to go about it.

She was not allowed to speak in her own defense at either the hearing or the trial. There were some rumblings that Parliament might change that law eventually, but unless it happened within a fortnight, which was impossible, it would do Elsie no good. There was a good chance she would hang for the murder of Edward Boswick, fifth earl of Dunsford.

After his brief sojourn in the village, Nicholas had gone back to Montmarsh, troubled by the fact that the English court system was so efficient. Then, feeling restless and with nothing to do, he had wandered about the house, empty now of guests and seeming very large and lonely. He began to feel hungry and decided to ask for a meal. But there were no servants to be found. He could hear their voices, however, and he finally found them in the kitchen.

" 'E was mad enough to kill Lord Dunsford right then, I'll tell ye that. And I'd wager all me buttons old Lord Winnie'd been planning to kill him ever since." It was the voice of a young man who spoke. Nicholas recognized him as Eddie's valet. Eddie had brought him with him from London for his stay in the country. Hearing the voice, Nicholas stepped just outside the door, so he wouldn't be seen as he listened.

"I don't believe ye at all." This was the high-pitched voice of one of the chambermaids. "Lord Winningham's no murderer. 'E's a kind man, 'e is. Treated me with such kindness as ye'd never believe each time he came out 'ere to Montmarsh. I was always the one to serve 'im, you know."

The valet's laugh had a superior ring to it. "Kind, ye say? Oh yes, 'e's kind enough if 'e thinks there's a chance 'e can get in yer knickers. Likes a bit o' pussy, 'e does. What man doesn't, even if 'e's ancient as old Winnie. But when Lord Duns caught 'im with that bloke from the theater district, I seen the murder in 'is eyes."

"But I still say, 'e's no—"

It was Mrs. Pickwick who interrupted her this time. "Yer just a child, Amelia. Ye don't yet know the ways o' the world. If word got around a man like Winnie likes doin' it with boys, it would ruin 'is name. It's easy to see how 'e could calculate murder was the easy way out." She turned to the valet. "But do ye really think he came here with it on his mind to kill the earl?"

"Sure it was on 'is mind." The valet was full of blustery self-confidence. "Heard 'im say it meself. 'I'll kill the bastard,' 'e says. 'E was just waiting for the right moment, 'e was. What's 'e got to lose? I ask you that. 'E knew Lord Duns could ruin 'im."

"Aye, and Earl Duns would do it, too," one of the older kitchen maids said. "He was a cruel one, that one was. Cared not a farthing for anyone but himself. He was bound to pay with his life for that cruelty, I say."

"He was a cruel one, all right, and it's the devil in him that makes him walk these halls after 'e's dead, then." Mrs. Pickwick's voice had dropped to a frightened hush.

"Ah, go on now. 'E ain't walkin' at all. Corpses don't walk." The valet was exhibiting his arrogance again.

"What about that strumpet, Mrs. Atewater?" Amelia said. "Didn't she say she saw the dead Lord Duns walkin' 'erself?"

"Ye don't believe 'er, do you?" The valet said. "She was raging vexed with old Duns for throwin' 'er over. Pure waxy, she was."

"Waxy enough to kill Lord Dunsford?" Amelia clearly was still trying to defend Lord Winningham.

"Ye think a woman could have killed Lord Duns?" The cocky valet was incensed. "Yer crazy, ye are. Lord Duns was no milksop. 'Twould take a man to kill 'im."

"Aye. More than the likes of Elsie," Mrs. Pickwick said.

"Pshaw!" The valet poured himself a glass of Lord Dunsford's best claret. " 'Tis only the nobs that wants to blame it on 'er. We all knows that. So they fixes it with the constable to get the girl so none o' them will 'ave to get too close to the gallows."

Mrs. Pickwick nodded her head, considering it. "Aye, the

constable's a strange one. Always thought so even when 'e was the schoolmaster. Always slipping off to London for God knows what, and . . ."

When the gossip turned to the constable, Nicholas left, quietly, for fear that if he stayed longer one of them would catch him eavesdropping. But their gossip about Lord Winningham as well as about Isabel Atewater had given him pause. True, it could be nothing more than gossip, but experience had taught him that too often the gossip of servants was grounded in unvarnished facts. He was convinced that it needed to be investigated. But there was little time to waste. If Elsie was bound over for trial in two weeks, he had to move quickly, and so he was now on a coach bound for London. His aim was to look into Lord Winningham's motive for murder.

The coach slowed to the speed of a man's gait, and Nicholas grew impatient. "Can't we move along a little faster?" he called to the driver.

The driver shouted back to Nicholas over his shoulder. "Them horses has chose to move through this blackness with caution, and I ain't inclined to dispute that decision."

Nicholas could see that the lantern the driver had placed at the front of the coach did little more than light up the rumps of the horses. And it was, indeed, a black and moonless night. Nicholas, though, had already thrown caution to the wind by his decision to make this night journey, and the slow pace at which they moved served only to frustrate him.

He was still grumbling to himself about the slow pace when the blast of a pistol ripped into the silence of the night. The horses shied and cried out with nervous snorts, then there was a voice shouting.

"Stop the coach, and you won't be hurt!"

The driver immediately pulled the frightened horses to a halt, but they danced nervously as the voice grew closer. "Passengers! All of you! Out!"

Nicholas, who had stiffened with fear at the first sounds of the commotion, now felt the fear dissipate as anger replaced it. How dare the hoodlums be so presumptuous! He'd like to teach them not to steal from innocent folks. Still, he knew there was danger, and he wished for the first time ever that he had taken Eddie's long-ago advice about carrying a pistol. He'd argued that it was barbaric and uncivilized. Eddie had laughed and taunted him, saying he'd find out what uncivilized was one of these days.

Now, it seemed they both had.

"Out, I say!" the voice, that of a young man, said again. With that, he jerked the coach door open and reached in to grab Nicholas's arm and pull him out. Another form, almost too shadowy to make out in the darkness, had climbed up to the driver's seat and struck the driver with something. The driver crumpled and hit the ground with a thud. The horses jumped, but the shadowy form reigned them in.

Just as the driver fell, the other highwayman pushed Nicholas against the side of the coach, and Nicholas felt the cold steel of a knife against his throat. The highwayman ripped his watch, along with its gold chain, from his vest. "Hand over your purse, and any fancy rings you might be wearin'!" he said.

Nicholas fished a purse out of his pocket and handed it over. "I've no rings or jewels." His voice was edged with the anger he still felt, and his mind spun as he tried to devise some way to overcome the young thug without risking his burying the blade in his flesh.

"You'll not be lyin' to me, sir, or I'll wack your fingers to get at the rings!" The man ran the edge of the blade along the fingers of Nicholas's right hand, and Nicholas felt a sharp pain and the warm ooze of blood. The man dropped the right hand, apparently satisfied that there were no rings on it. In the gap between seconds as the man dropped one hand and reached for the other, Nicholas lunged for his throat. The man stumbled back, and the knife fell, stabbing the ground a fraction of an inch from Nicholas's foot.

In the same moment Nicholas heard the report of the gun coming from the direction of the shadowy form on top of the coach, and he felt the slicing, ragged heat of a bullet at his head.

11

"Zack! Zack, where are you? Are you all right?" Terror
gripped Alexandra, rendering her almost unable to move.
The fog, growing thicker, weighed her down as well. She
forced herself to take a step forward in the darkness. And
then another, and another, moving toward that horrific
sound she'd heard coming from Zack.

There had only been one yelping scream, and then silence
except for the sound of the surf, oddly muffled in the fog.
She called out again. "Zack! Are you . . ."

Suddenly a hand clamped her mouth, and another arm,
encircling her body, pinned her arms to her side. A memory
of the night in the stable yard flashed in her mind, but this
was not the same person. The one who held her now was
smaller, perhaps only a boy, and he smelled of stale beer
and cheap tobacco.

"What is it yer doing here?" the boy asked. At the same
time she heard Zack growl, low in his throat, and then a
loud, ferocious bark. Next, pandemonium—Zack's bark, the
arm letting go, the sound of a scuffle, young voices shouting, "Kill the bastard! He's attacking!" And then another
whimper from Zack.

"Don't hurt him!" Alexandra screamed.

Zack growled, and she saw what she thought was the shadowy form of him lunge.

"Damnation! The bugger's tearing my leg off! Use the bloody knife for God's sake. Aaargh!"

Then suddenly the light of a lantern sputtered weakly through the fog and mist and a young voice yelled, "Let the woman go, you idjets! She's here to see me." And then the same voice directed at Alexandra. "Call the bloody beast off of the boys before he kills 'em!" The speaker held the lantern at arm's length in front of him so that the glaring light kept Alexandra from seeing his face clearly.

There was a moment's hesitation, and then, "Zack! Zack! Heel!" She had to call twice more before the dog could be convinced, and by this time, his victims were both groaning miserably. Finally Zack heeded her command and moved toward her. She put her hands on him, feeling in the darkness for a wound that might have made him cry out in pain. She felt a dampness around his mouth, but she couldn't be sure if it was blood or the profuse saliva that was characteristic of him. If it was blood, had it come from Zack or the boys? Then she felt the wet, matted hair on his head as well as evidence of a gash in his skin. He had been injured, but in the darkness, it was impossible to tell how badly.

The dog was tense and alert, pacing nervously and growling, low and menacing, even as the two injured young men tried to move away, scooting on their backsides.

The boy with the lantern shouted at them in anger. "You buggered clods! Didn't I tell you I had business here tonight?"

"We was just makin' sure it wasn't trouble she was here for, Quince," one of the young men on the ground whimpered. "How was we to know she'd 'ave the bloody bear dog with 'er? I think the beast 'as tore Artie's face off."

There was a sickening groan from the other boy. It sounded as if he was lying on the ground.

"Serves you right for bein' such fools," the boy with the lantern said. "Now off with you!"

"But, Quince—"

"Out of my sight, the two of you!" With that, he squelched the lantern's light.

"Wait!" Alexandra took a step toward the two boys as they stumbled away, but Zack blocked her with his huge body.

"Leave 'em be!" Quince's words were a harsh command.

"But they're hurt. Those wounds should be—"

"I said, leave 'em be." Alexandra could feel his hand like a stone weight on her arm, dragging her back. "I'll see to it later. For now we've got to talk." His voice was a harsh whisper, and she could sense, even smell, his fear.

Alexandra's heart was pounding out her own fear as well. Zack sensed it, growled, and took a menacing step toward Quince. Alexandra grabbed his leash and had to use both hands to restrain him.

"Can't we go some place more comfortable? Some place where I can see—"

"No! It's best we not be seen together, and it's best ye not tell anyone ye talked to me, ye hear?"

"Well, I—"

"If ye value yer life . . ."

"Good lord!"

"And if ye don't value yer own life, then think of the girl yer tryin' to save."

Alexandra's heart pounded even harder. Perhaps she should have heeded Mr. Forsythe's warning about coming here. "I . . . I'm afraid I don't understand—"

"What I'm doin', I'm doin' for Georgie. And ye best keep yer voice down, miss."

Alexandra's mouth was dry, and she was finding it difficult to speak at all, but she managed to whisper, "Of course, George Stirling was your friend." She paused, screwing up her courage, then added, "Do you know who killed him?"

There was a long moment of silence before Quince spoke. "Did the girl, the one they call Elsie, did she tell you she seen 'is ghost?"

"She said she'd heard him speak to her."

"And ye didn't believe 'er."

"I believe she thinks she heard him."

Quince's laugh was a hard, brittle sound. "Aye, but yer a clever one with words, ye are. But I tell ye for sure, I know who done the deed."

"Then you must tell—"

Zack suddenly became even more restless, and Alexandra felt him tense again. She sensed that his head had lifted, and he was sniffing the air, as if someone was approaching. Alexandra placed her hand on his head, being careful not to touch his wound. The touch was partly to soothe him and partly to read his body language as she whispered to Quince.

"If you know who killed George and the earl, you must tell the constable."

Quince drew back from her. "I won't talk to a copper, miss, and I ain't so willin' to talk to you if it wasn't for me doin' it for Georgie."

"Do you know who murdered Lord Dunsford?"

Quince leaned toward her and seemed about to say something when Zack let out another sharp bark. In almost the same instant, Quince moved quickly to grab Alexandra again, clasping his hand around her mouth and holding her arms against her sides in the same manner the other boy had done. Zack lunged at him, but he managed to back away.

"Somebody's coming." Quince's mouth was close to her ear, and his whisper was full of terror. "I ought to kill ye to keep ye quiet about this."

Alexandra tried to say something, but his hand on her mouth made it almost impossible to breathe and certainly impossible to speak. Zack barked, loud, harsh, and angry, and tried over and over again to lunge at Quince, but Quince's deft maneuvers kept Alexandra between him and the dog so that Zack could not attack without harming the one he was trying to protect.

A voice, muffled by the mist and fog, called out. "Who's there?"

Another whisper, hoarse and curdled with fear, came from Quince's lips, still close to her ear. "Hold the dog!"

She nodded, or tried to nod as much as his restraining

hand would allow and pulled Zack's leash shorter. Immediately Quince loosened his grip on her and fled. Almost instantly the darkness swallowed him, and the fog softened his footfalls.

Zack barked and strained at his leash, but Alexandra would not let go. She started to call out Quince's name, but the memory of his fear that someone might find out he had spoken to her kept her quiet. She resolved to try again to see him. She could come down to the piers again tomorrow in the light of day and ask for him. No, that would be unwise. He had not wanted anyone to know he had spoken to her, and he had threatened her with her own and Elsie's life if she revealed it. She would have to find another way.

"Zack," she said, still whispering. "Hush now. We must go home."

Zack obeyed her and stopped his barking, but he kept up a low, undulating growl that sounded almost like vowel sounds, as if he were trying to speak to her in her own language to warn her of danger.

"It's all right, Zack. We're going home now." She took a few steps forward, blind in the heavy darkness, allowing Zack to lead her. He had given up trying to talk to her and had resorted to his loud, threatening barks again. She followed the sound and bulk of him, and then screamed in fear when a human hand touched her face.

At the same time, Zack leapt, snarling, but Alexandra managed somehow, awkwardly, to get in his way, and it was she he knocked to the ground. Zack seemed confused. The voice she had heard earlier, muffled by the fog, said her name.

"Dr. Gladstone?"

Alexandra held her breath, puzzled for a moment. Then she said: "Mr. Atewater? Is that you? Zack! Stay!"

Two hands reached to bring her to her feet, gently. They both spoke at the same time. "Dr. Gladstone, what are you doing out this time of . . ."

"Mr. Atewater, I thought you were in . . ."

"I thought it was you I saw walking this direction, and I must confess, I followed you," Atewater said. He held her arm and led her away from the water toward the dim lights of the town.

In spite of her commands, Zack was still growling and lunging against the leash. Obviously the encounter on the pier had upset him. And there was still the possibility that he had been injured. She had Jeremy Atewater to deal with now, however.

"You followed me? I don't understand. . . ."

"Frankly, I found it odd that a woman would be out alone so late at night. Even with a dog as large as the one you have," Atewater said. "I thought perhaps I should keep an eye on you. It was so dark, though, I lost you. And then when I heard the dog barking, I followed the sound. To be honest, I was frightened you'd been attacked."

"Oh no, not at all. Zack was just barking at shadows. And . . . and I often walk Zack at night." Alexandra wasn't sure why she was lying. Why she felt the need to protect Quince. "But what are you doing here, Mr. Atewater? I thought you and Mrs. Atewater had returned to London. Zack, quiet, please."

Atewater, who was now leading her toward a street, walked briskly. The fog made light from cottage windows dance out of bounds. "You're quite right," he said. "We did plan to go to London, but at the last minute, I decided to stay. You see, Lord Dunsford and I were involved in a rather complicated business venture together, and I'm afraid his death precipitated rather a lot of work and decisions I'm forced to make. Mrs. Atewater went on without me. I took a room at the inn. More convenient than staying so far away at Montmarsh, you see."

"I see," Alexandra said, trying not to let her curiosity overcome good manners. She wanted to ask him exactly what sort of business kept him here and why he was out walking so late.

Atewater's grip tightened on her arm. "Forgive me for being presumptuous, Dr. Gladstone, but I must say, it's rather not a good idea for you to be in the habit of walking about so late. Especially in light of recent events."

"Perhaps you're right." Alexandra stumbled in the darkness as she tried to calm Zack. "Perhaps it's rather not a good idea for either of us."

"Point well taken. And I for one would have gone straight to my lodgings at the inn had I not seen you and felt compelled to—"

"Excuse me, Mr. Atewater, we're headed in the direction away from my house, and I'm afraid I really must return home. My housekeeper will be—"

"Of course! Forgive me, I'm afraid I don't know where you live." Atewater said.

"It's that way." She pointed toward her house. "And I must thank you for your concern for me tonight, and perhaps, if whatever kept you here isn't too consuming, I shall see you again." She was eager to get away to examine Zack. He was still acting odd, and she knew the wound was bleeding. Quince's ruffians had hurt him, and she wanted to see how serious his injury might be.

"Oh, but I can't allow you to walk home alone." Atewater took her arm again.

"But, Mr. Atewater—"

"Yes, yes, I know you're accustomed to walking alone, and you do have your dog to protect you, but I simply would never forgive myself if I allowed you to walk home and then learned some ill fortune had befallen you."

His firm grip and his long, measured stride confirmed that it would do no good to argue with him. She only hoped he would be quiet once they reached her door so that Nancy wouldn't awaken. She had too much to think about now to have to contend with Nancy.

Zack's behavior was even more erratic when they reached the house, and Alexandra was sure now that his low growls and occasional agitated barks would awaken Nancy, and she would have to be dealt with anyway.

When they reached the front door, and before she unlocked it, Alexandra reached down to touch Zack again, with the hope of calming him.

He yelped in pain, and Atewater drew back, alarmed.

"Sorry," Alexandra said, "I'm afraid Zack stumbled back there along the waterfront, and he must have hit his head on a rock." Alexandra was surprised at how easily the lie came to her lips. As she moved her hand gently along Zack's head, he cried out again as she touched the wound, the same sharp scream of pain she had heard in the darkness earlier. Perhaps they had stuck him only out of fear, but it made her angry nevertheless.

"My word! Do you need help with that animal?" In spite of his offer, Atewater's voice seemed reluctant.

"No, no, I'll be fine. I just want to get him inside and have a look at the wound." By now Alexandra had the door unlocked and was trying to lead Zack inside. But Zack kept stalling, looking over his shoulder as if he was expecting something unpleasant. Alexandra silently chided herself for getting him into a situation that had made him so over-wrought.

In the struggle to keep the dog going in the right direc-tion, she dropped her key, and the shawl she was wearing slipped to the floor. Atewater stepped inside to pick up both for her.

"Don't bother, please. You've done enough." Alexandra spoke in a whisper, still hoping Nancy would stay asleep.

"No bother," Atewater said. He stood, holding the key and the shawl, but Alexandra could not let go of the nervous Zack long enough to take them. They looked at each other in an awkward silence for a moment.

"Thank you so much for your help," Alexandra said fi-nally. "I'm afraid I'd best see to my dog now, and I know you must get back to the inn. Good night, sir." She led Zack off to the surgery, leaving Atewater to see himself out. Once inside, she talked to Zack in soothing tones while she ex-amined and cleaned the wound. It did, indeed, look as if he'd been struck with something. A rock, perhaps. While there was a cut that was bleeding and was, no doubt, tender, it didn't appear to be serious.

Zack's unusually nervous attitude had calmed somewhat by the time she led him out of the surgery, but he still insisted upon staying very close to her side. As they walked into the hallway, she was surprised to see that a lamp had been lit in the parlor. Alexandra took a deep breath and prepared herself to find Nancy waiting there to interrogate her.

She was startled when she saw that it was not Nancy who waited for her in the parlor but Atewater. He was standing next to the lamp table, the shawl and house key still in his hands.

"Forgive me." He appeared embarrassed. "I just . . . I just wanted to make sure you were all right."

"Thank you for your concern, Mr. Atewater, and yes, we're both—"

"What is going on down here?" It was Nancy, coming down the stairs in her nightdress and enunciating each word with annoyance. "All the racket makes . . ." She stopped three steps from the bottom of the stairway, looking first at Alexandra and then at Atewater. "Oh, I'm sorry. I didn't know you were entertaining. Shall I make tea?"

Atewater started to protest, but Alexandra stopped him after the second "no."

"You look as if you could use some tea, Mr. Atewater, and you gave me such a scare out there, I believe I would like some, too." Alexandra was feeling more relaxed now that she knew Zack's wounds were not serious. She turned to Nancy and gave a little nod, and Nancy replied with a look of exasperated curiosity before she turned away to the kitchen. Alexandra now realized that since she would have a great deal of explaining to do to Nancy anyway, she could keep Jeremy Atewater in her parlor a bit longer to find out why he was walking along the waterfront so late at night.

Alexandra, followed by Zack, crossed the room to take the key and shawl from her guest, along with his hat and cloak. After she put them away, she sat on one of the sofas. "Please," she said, indicating the one across the tea table from her.

Atewater sat and immediately seemed to relax. "You're very kind, Dr. Gladstone, and to tell you the truth, I could use a bit of relaxation."

Alexandra did her best to appear at ease herself. "Of course. Lord Dunsford's death has been quite stressful for everyone, hasn't it?"

"It has indeed." Atewater looked down at his hands, tense again. "To be perfectly honest, there's another reason for my wanting to stay." He looked up at her again.

Alexandra waited, trying to appear interested, but not too eager.

"It has to do with my wife."

"Your wife?"

"Yes, you see . . . Well, I'm not sure how well you know Isabel, but she is, shall we say, a rather spirited person."

"I see."

"And she . . . I don't want to be indelicate, Miss Gladstone, but I'm afraid she . . . shall we say, she . . . had an affair with Lord Dunsford."

Alexandra allowed herself only the slightest raise of an eyebrow.

"This is quite embarrassing."

"I'm so sorry, Mr. Atewater."

"Well, you see, the point is, Eddie—Lord Dunsford, that is—threw her over, and Isabel was quite upset. Not because she was in love with Eddie, mind you, but rather because her pride was hurt. She's not used to being turned down, you see."

Alexandra nodded, encouraging him to continue, Zack stirring restlessly at her feet.

"Of course we've had our rows over it, and of course my pride was wounded, and one would think now that poor Eddie is dead all the fuss would be over, but quite frankly . . ."

"Yes, Mr. Atewater?"

"I'm afraid that gives Mrs. Atewater a motive to kill the old boy, you see, and I don't want any of that to come out at the trial. So, while I am quite willing to testify as a witness, I want to protect her, because, of course, she didn't mention any of this to the justice. So now, at this point, it's unclear whether or not Mrs. Atewater will be called as a witness for the trial, and I'm hoping that my complete cooperation will render it unnecessary." His eyes went to a spot behind Alexandra, and when she turned around she saw Nancy standing in the entry with a tray.

"Tea, miss." Nancy walked toward the table between the two sofas.

"Thank you, Nancy. I'm sorry to have kept you up. You may go to your room, and I'll see to the tea things myself later." Alexandra didn't miss the frustrated look that flickered in Nancy's eyes as she turned away. Her curiosity was about to get the best of her, and there was no telling how long she'd been standing there with that tray, listening.

Alexandra poured the tea and handed a cup to Atewater. "You were saying, Mr. Atewater?"

"Oh, I'm afraid I've said too much." He accepted the cup and stirred in milk. "You see, I can't afford a scandal, and I hoped to come here to nip in the bud any problem that might arise concerning Isabel. That's why I was out walking tonight. I was trying to clear my head and trying to decide what to do."

"I suspect you'll just have to leave it in the hands of the prosecutor," Alexandra said.

"You're right, of course." Atewater put down his cup and put his head in his hands. "I don't know how it came to this. Lord Dunsford had his enemies, of course, but Isabel wasn't one of them."

"I must confess that I'm a little surprised at the idea of any suspicion falling on her." Alexandra was stirring her tea slowly. "Isn't it usually the cuckold husband who is suspect?"

Atewater raised his head to look at Alexandra. "Oh, of course I would be suspect, too, but, you see, there's no point in any of that coming out. I'm quite worried, though, since poor foolish Mrs. Atewater made the mistake of telling several of her friends in London she was going to kill Lord Dunsford for what he'd done to her."

"Oh?"

"She didn't mean it, of course. Just an expression, don't you know. She was just angry and hurt and embarrassed. Women do foolish things when they're upset."

Alexandra clamped her lips between her teeth.

"And truthfully," Atewater continued, "Mrs. Atewater

isn't smart enough to plan a murder or even be an accomplice."

"Indeed?"

"She is spirited, as I said. Perhaps a bit spoiled. And beautiful. But none too bright. Rather superficial at times, I'm afraid, so I shouldn't have been surprised that she was attracted to a man like Lord Dunsford. After all, she is attracted to flamboyance, and Lord Dunsford was that, all right, wasn't he? That red silk nightshirt he had on the night he died was just what we might have expected."

"Do you think the kitchen girl had an accomplice?" Alexandra still stirred her tea. She had forgotten to drink it. Zack was pacing the floor, drooling and growling low in his throat.

Atewater kept an eye on the dog as he answered Alexandra's question. "An accomplice? I suppose it's possible, isn't it? But who would it be? Another servant, perhaps? Lord Dunsford could be unpleasant at times, and it could be he'd set off one of them. Or maybe there was no accomplice at all. That girl could have done it by herself."

"You're convinced the kitchen girl is guilty, then." Alexandra tried not to sound too eager in her questioning.

"It appears that way, doesn't it? Oh, of course I know you believe the poor old boy was strangled to death and that Elsie couldn't have done it, but I'm not so sure. I certainly don't want to think Mrs. Atewater is guilty." Atewater pulled a watch from his vest and glanced at it. "Miss Gladstone, I must apologize for keeping you up so late."

"Please don't bother to apologize, Mr. Atewater."

"But I am sorry, and I really must get back to the inn. And forgive me, too, for burdening you with my troubles, although I must say, it has done me good to get this off my chest."

"I understand." Alexandra got his hat and cloak, and she and Zack saw him to the door. When he had gone, she hurried upstairs with Zack, hoping to make it safely to her room without encountering Nancy.

She found her waiting at the top of the landing, hands on her hips, glaring.

"It's late, Nancy, you should be in bed." Alexandra tried to sound as authoritative as her father always had, but it had never been easy for her with Nancy.

"And how am I supposed to sleep when you're up until the wee hours entertaining a gentleman?" Nancy still glared.

Alexandra tried a little dismissive laugh, still trying to find a way to get around her so she could go to her room. "You make it sound as if you think I'm a fallen woman."

Nancy crossed her arms in front of her. "I don't know what to think, now, do I? What with you sneaking out of the house like a schoolgirl, and . . . My God, what happened to Zack?"

"It's a long story, Nancy, and it's late. I'll tell you all about it later when—"

"You got yourself into trouble, did you not? I should think you'd have learned from our childhood that if you're going to sneak out, you must take me with you. Murderers everywhere, and one of them trying to kill you in your own stable, and still you go out alone! Why, people will be saying you've lost your mind. And I can't say I would disagree if it came down to—"

"Nancy, please. It's very late."

"I'm well aware of that, and it's for sure I won't be able to sleep at all tonight after all of this. Just what *were* you doing, and who was the gentleman you brought home to entertain?"

"Can't you please stop saying it that way? I wasn't *entertaining*."

"Then who was he? And what did he have to do with whatever it was happened to you and poor Zack? And where did you—"

"All right, Nancy. I see I won't have a minute's rest until I tell you everything. Come on into my room. You too, Zack."

Nancy sat cross-legged at the foot of the bed while Alexandra leaned against the headboard. Zack lay next to her, snoring softly, while she related all of the evening's events to Nancy.

"So young Quince never told you who killed the poor

earl, and you're lucky to escape with your life," Nancy said when the story was finished. "And besides that, there's more going on with the Atewaters than meets the eye."

"You've summed it up well," Alexandra said. "Now if you'll excuse me—"

"I know, I know, we both need our rest." Nancy was already on her way to the door, but she turned around just as she reached it. "But don't go thinking you'll get out on your own again. I'll have my eye on you, I will." With that, she was gone.

Zack refused to move to his customary place on the floor and slept the entire night with his spine curled against her. Apparently he, as well, was going to make certain she didn't leave.

Alexandra was awakened from her all-too-brief sleep the next morning by Nancy knocking loudly on her door.

"Wake up, Miss Alex! Wake up! There are already patients at the door needing to see you, and soon, miss. Two boys with nasty wounds."

Alexandra dressed hurriedly, and by the time she was downstairs, Nancy had shown the patients to the surgery. In spite of the fact that she did not know their faces, Alexandra knew who they were as soon as she saw them and the nature of their wounds. They were the two boys who had tangled with Zack at the pier. She went to work immediately, treating and dressing their injuries, which should have been tended last evening.

"This is a dog bite." She was cleaning the face of the younger of the two boys, and she was remembering one of them crying out, *I think the beast has tore Artie's face off.* She glanced at the two boys as she spoke, hoping to gauge their reaction. They said nothing, but their eyes darted toward each other. Artie's face was far from torn off, but there was a nasty gash there that was inflamed and obviously painful, judging by the boy's pale face and the marks tears had made streaming down his dirty cheeks. Now he was shivering, indicating that chills had set in.

"Nancy," she called. "Bring me a mixture of—"

"Here it is, miss." Nancy spoke to her from the doorway

where she was carrying a bowl and pestle. "A mixture of elm and lobelia leaves with a sprinkling of bloodroot to keep down the proud flesh."

Alexandra nodded, feeling grateful for Nancy's efficiency. Obviously, she had made the same diagnosis and prepared the mixture in anticipation of Alexandra's orders. She also immediately went to a cabinet and pulled out supplies for stitching up the wound.

"I hope the animal wasn't rabid," Alexandra said, still watching for the reaction of the boys.

The expression in their eyes grew even more alarmed, still, they said nothing for several seconds. Finally the older one, who had only a few puncture wounds on his hands, spoke. "You're the one, ain't you? The one at the pier last night with the damnable beast."

Alexandra didn't answer, but she looked up from her work, and the boy's eyes caught hers.

"Quince said you're the one," the boy continued. "He told us to come here. That was before . . ."

The boy seemed unwilling to say more, but the younger boy, Artie, urged him. "Go on, tell her."

There was a long silence and Alexandra had to encourage them to continue. "Quince told you to come here before . . ."

"Quince is dead," the older boy said. "Murdered."

12

***

It took Nicholas a moment to realize that the cry he heard following the gunshot had come from him. He became aware of a warm trickle of blood down his face and into his eyes and of a burning sensation high on his forehead, and he realized the bullet had only grazed his head. Yet, he was bleeding profusely. He heard the two men who had accosted him run away into the darkness. His confusion lingered as he tried to decide whether to pursue them or see to his own wound.

In the next instant he heard someone groaning and remembered the coach driver. Wiping the blood away from his eyes, he moved in the direction of the sound.

"Is that you, Driver? Are you all right?" He groped his way in the darkness until he stumbled upon the driver, still lying in a crumpled heap on the ground.

The man groaned again. "Oooh, me bloody head feels like it's been crushed." He groped for Nicholas's hand. "Where's the coach? And the 'orses?"

As if in answer, one of horses neighed from a short distance away where the team had run with the coach. Apparently the darkness kept them from traveling too far.

"Oooh! Me bloody head!" the driver said again as Nicholas helped him get to his feet. "How about you, sir? Are ye all right?"

"Yes, quite. Just a little scrape." Nicholas dabbed his forehead with his handkerchief.

"Did the buggers rob ye blind? Where'd they go? I hope ye shot 'em dead." The driver kicked at the ground as if he was looking for the bodies.

"They only got a few pounds, and no, they're not dead. They simply ran away." Nicholas felt relieved that the bleeding from his forehead had subsided.

"Well, that's the young for ye." The driver spoke over his shoulder as he hobbled toward the coach and horses. "None of 'em's got any backbone. None of 'em wants to do the job right. Not even the bloody thieves."

London was just beginning to awaken when the coach with its two wounded pulled up to Nicholas's residence in Kensington. He offered to have Morton, his manservant, take the driver to his own personal physician to see about his head wound, but the driver refused. In the end, Nicholas gave him five pounds and extracted a promise that he would see a physician on his own. The driver took the money and left Nicholas with the distinct impression that he had no intention of keeping his promise.

For his own part, Nicholas was equally unwilling to take the time to see a doctor, but he allowed Morton to clean the wound, which did indeed turn out to be superficial. While Morton was seeing to the wound, Nicholas was compelled to answer a barrage of questions about his well-being and about what exactly had occurred and whether or not the thieves were recognizable.

It was out of character for Morton to be either curious or talkative, but given the circumstances and their long-term relationship, Nicholas was willing to forgive the impropriety.

"I'm afraid I do have some bad news, however." Nicholas spoke as he removed the soiled linen shirt he wore. "Lord Dunsford is dead."

Morton accepted the shirt. "Yes, sir. The news has

reached London. I understand there was a big funeral. Almost all of Parliament was there, as well as the queen herself. I was surprised you didn't return for the funeral, sir."

"I'm afraid I've gotten involved in some of the legal aspects of Lord Dunsford's death. Found it difficult to leave."

"Yes, sir. Shall I draw your bath, sir?"

Morton, who now seemed assured Nicholas had not been seriously harmed, was his old efficient and proper self again. There were no probing questions about why Nicholas had returned or whether or not he might be going back to Newton-Upon-Sea. Nicholas would confide in Morton eventually, but for now, he wanted to concentrate on finding Lord Winningham, as well as finding out as much about his alleged motive as possible.

Once he was bathed and dressed and had convinced Morton to replace the bandage on his forehead with a smaller, less conspicuous one, he left for Winningham's London house. He was in need of sleep, but the bath and a light meal had revived him.

He had thought for some time about what he might say to Lord Winningham. It was obvious he couldn't very well ask him outright about the incident the servants had been discussing and whether or not he'd killed Eddie to keep him quiet. All he could hope for was to talk to him, to try to get him to talk as well. He also wanted to check on the valet's story and see if there was a way to prove or disprove it. That would require his paying a call on Isabel. He'd learned in his limited contact with her that she seemed to know all the worst gossip about everyone.

When his carriage stopped in front of the Winninghams' residence, he told the driver to wait, then walked to the front door to knock. There was an unusually long wait before a servant finally came to the door.

"Nicholas Forsythe," he said, handing the butler his card. "I'd like to see Lord Winningham, please."

"Lord Winningham is not present." The butler started to close the door, but Nicholas stopped him by putting his hand on the door frame.

"Perhaps I could wait, then."

"I'm afraid that's not possible, sir. Lord Winningham is not expected back for several days." He started to close the door again, and again Nicholas stopped him.

"Gone is he? But he's hardly had time to return from Montmarsh. Why would he be gone again?"

"I'm sure I don't know, sir. Now if you'll excuse me . . ."

"What's wrong, Garret? Who's there?" Lady Margaret, the countess of Winningham, emerged from the parlor, craning her wrinkled and sagging neck to see what was happening. "Is that you, Nicholas? Why, of course it is. Show him in, Garret."

Garret stood aside and without allowing his eyes to focus on Nicholas, took his hat and cloak.

The countess walked toward him with her hands outstretched. "Oh, Nicholas, I'm so glad you're here." She caught her breath. "My dear, what has happened to your head?"

"Just a scratch, my lady. A silly accident."

She allowed him to kiss one of her hands. "Garret, see that we have tea in the morning room."

Nicholas followed his hostess into a room with walls papered with delicate pastel flowers and hung with blue velvet drapes. Several sentimental paintings of pastoral scenes vied with the patterned wallpaper. A rose-colored settee and chairs were clustered around a tea table, and a collection of miniature paintings and photogravures as well as crystal and porcelain figurines added to the clutter.

Lady Winningham looked equally overly decorated in her ruffled lace collar and cuffs and her old-fashioned lace cap.

"Nicholas, my dear boy, it is so kind of you to call." Lady Winningham settled herself into one of the lurid settees. "You have no idea how upset I've been over the events at Montmarsh and with no one to console me now that Winnie's gone off." She fanned herself with a lace handkerchief. "It was terribly distressing, you know, and you'd think that Winnie would be more understanding. But he's nowhere near as sensitive as you are, dear boy," she said as she leaned slightly toward him.

"Lord Winningham was compelled to travel again?" Nicholas had to force himself not to shrink back from her.

Lady Winningham gave her handkerchief a little fling, as if she were brushing the idea away, and the heavy sweet scent of gardenias wafted around her. "Winnie's always running off. To Norfolk mostly. Although he hates it there, in spite of the fact that the estate is quite grand and lovely. Too remote, he says. Too many country bumpkins, he says. Our son is living there now, with his wife, who in spite of her impeccable lineage, has no taste at all when it comes to decor."

"Indeed," Nicholas said with a furtive glance around the room. A maid brought in a tray of tea and sandwiches, and Lady Winningham began to pour.

"Our son will inherit, of course, and he's quite happy there and does an excellent job of overseeing the estate. Winnie always says so himself, so I don't understand why he's always running up there to see about it. Winnie can be terribly obtuse at times. And our daughter-in-law, who will one day be Countess Winningham after I'm gone, simply does not have the élan one needs for the title, although, as I said, her lineage is impeccable. But one learns to recognize that it takes more than bloodlines, doesn't one? My own bloodlines, I admit, are not so impeccable, but one is, nevertheless, born with a certain affinity, don't you agree? Winnie recognizes this, too, of course, and he has little patience for the country-lass image our daughter-in-law projects. No more than he has patience for the remoteness of Oxbow, our estate in Norfolk. So why is he always in such a state to go there? It's rather mysterious. In fact, he seemed quite anxious to be home the whole time we were at Montmarsh. I think that brassy Mrs. Atewater got on his nerves. Do you think it is right that I told the justice I saw her coming out of poor Eddie's room? I rather wish I hadn't, for it means I shall have to testify again." She placed a hand delicately on her chest and tried to look weakened. "But one has to do one's duty to the queen, doesn't one?"

When Lady Winningham finally stopped her chatter long enough to take a breath, Nicholas put down his teacup and threw another morsel of bait to her. "Of course you did the right thing by telling the justice everything, my lady. And as for Lord Winningham, perhaps he simply doesn't want to worry you with his affairs." Nicholas's pun was unintentional. He quite literally suspected, judging by his reputation, Lord Winningham was indeed having an affair and using his travels to Norfolk as a cover. But there had never been any evidence or gossip either, for that matter, that Lord Winnie dallied with any other than the opposite sex. Perhaps his indiscretion the valet mentioned, if it happened at all, was just an experiment, but one that could cost him his reputation. Was Lord Winningham sufficiently worried about that to commit murder?

The countess sank back into her chair and assumed a suffering expression. "Not wanting me to worry certainly has never been his concern before. The hours he keeps! Why, many are the mornings when he's been out all . . ." She stopped herself, as if she had said too much and fanned herself with her handkerchief again, causing the overwhelmingly sweet scent to waft toward Nicholas. "I don't know, dear boy. I never concern myself with the affairs of our estates. And anyway, Winnie can be terribly inconsiderate. He never tells me anything."

Nicholas made himself reach for her hand. "Now, now, Lady Winningham, you mustn't get yourself worked up, I know the events at Montmarsh were stressful for you."

She put her other hand over his, and Nicholas thought he could see a forced tear in her eye. "You are such a comfort, dear. I've needed someone to confide in. Especially since Winnie's been acting so strangely lately."

"Strangely?" Nicholas allowed his fingers to close slightly tighter around her hand.

"Why, yes." She gave him a wan, affected smile. "I thought he actually seemed to be avoiding Lord Dunsford for a while, and then I was surprised when he accepted his invitation to join him at Montmarsh, although one could hardly afford to refuse such an important social event, could one? Still, Winnie seemed rather edgy the entire time we were there. Wanted to come home early. But then after the . . . the unspeakable event, he actually seemed to relax a bit. That is until we left for home, and he became edgy again and said he would have to leave soon for Norfolk. It seemed foolish to make such a long trip when he'll have to make yet another trip to Montmarsh in less than a fortnight. We will both be compelled to testify, you know. I should think I've done my duty by testifying at the preliminary hearing and shouldn't have to return for the trial. One does hope the Queen's Bench recognizes there are certain limits as to what a lady wishes to do."

"Of course," Nicholas said, although he wasn't at all sure of what Lady Winningham had said. He was still thinking about Lord Winningham. It was indeed odd that he'd gone off to Norfolk with the trial date so near.

"I should have thought Winnie would be as upset about being called as a witness as I am." Lady Winningham patted her bosom with her handkerchief. "Oddly enough, though, he said something about it all being his good fortune."

Nicholas leaned forward. "In what context, Countess?"

Lady Winningham slipped her hand from his and leaned back in her chair again, a weary gesture. "Oh, I'm not sure. I was weeping over poor Eddie's death, and Winnie said something to me about how in the midst of tragedy, one can find good fortune, but then, as I said, he became edgy again and said he had to make sure his fortune wasn't lost by the diligence of others and that one had to be careful what he said in court. Which I'm sure you know, my dear boy."

Nicholas frowned. "Just what was the good fortune he was speaking of?"

"I'm sure I don't know. Could it be he thought he was fortunate to have the opportunity to help solve poor Eddie's murder by appearing as a witness at the trial?" Lady Winningham shook her head. "Not like Winnie at all, you know. He hates that sort of thing. I rather think it had something to do with an investment, although what, I can't imagine. It's just that Eddie was always pulling his friends into investments with him. I'm surprised he didn't do the same to you." Lady Winningham fanned her bosom again.

"Oh, he tried," Nicholas said, "but after so many refusals on my part, I'm afraid he came to think of me as a needlessly conservative stick-in-the-mud."

The countess sat up and leaned toward him again. "No, no, dear boy, you are most certainly not a stick-in-the-mud." She gave his left cheek an affectionate little pinch.

"You are very kind, my lady." Nicholas managed to escape her grasp and get to his feet. "And now, I think I am causing you to tire, and I must take my leave." He lifted her hand and kissed it again.

"You are such a dear boy." She fell back in her chair and tried once more to look weakened. "But please do come again."

"Of course," Nicholas said on his way out of the room, although he hoped he would never be compelled to keep that promise.

By the time Nicholas left Lady Winningham, he was beginning to feel the effects of a sleepless night, and he was compelled to drop his investigation long enough to sleep. It was late morning before he awoke, and he set out immediately to try to find Isabel.

It was two days before he found her. At least by then he no longer needed to wear his head bandage and was spared the necessity of telling her his accident story.

He met up with her at last when he had his driver take the coach to her house one more time. She was just walking down the front steps to her waiting carriage. She was elegantly attired in a walking-out dress of orchid-and-violet striped taffeta and a flower-bedecked summer bonnet tied under her chin with a violet silk ribbon. A dainty parasol was tucked under one arm, and she was pulling on her white kid gloves as she came down the steps. Just as Nicholas stepped down from his carriage, she glanced up.

"Nicky! What a pleasant surprise!" In spite of her bright voice, Nicholas could see the strain on her face.

He made a pseudo-bow. "I'm afraid I've come at an inopportune time."

"If you've come to see Jerry, I'm afraid he's not here, and I don't expect him back for several days." Nicholas was surprised to note that there was no flirtatious lilt to her voice.

"It is you, madam, I hoped to call upon."

She raised an eyebrow, and a wicked smile played at the corners of her undeniably sensuous mouth. "Then I hope you'll be so kind as to join me in my carriage. I was just going to pay a visit to my dressmaker, but perhaps if you'll join me, we'll have a bit of refreshment first. I know the most delightful little place."

Nicholas touched his hat and bowed his head slightly again. "How kind of you, madam. I should be honored." He turned to tell his driver to wait for him there, then helped Isabel into her carriage, feeling grateful that at least he wouldn't be obliged to spend another hour sipping tea in the stifling confines of a lady's parlor. He settled in the seat next to Isabel, and she gave him a beaming smile. She had positioned herself to be seen as they rode down the street, and she was, Nicholas noted, definitely worth looking at. The colors of her gown made her eyes look violet, and the luxurious dark hair that peeked from under her bonnet made a striking contrast to her creamy pale skin.

"And now, Nicky, to what do I owe the honor of your call?" She gave him a radiant smile that did not quite hide the hint of distress in her eyes.

"I wanted to inquire after your health. Obviously the recent events at Montmarsh were difficult for you."

She turned to look at him and placed a hand on his arm. "Oh, Nicholas!" She was trembling. "It really was dreadful, wasn't it?"

He patted her hand and said nothing. She leaned toward him even further, and he felt her warm breath on his face.

"I really did see him, you know," she whispered. "Eddie, I mean. After he was . . . murdered."

"Isabel, my dear . . ."

"He came walking out of the stables. He was wearing his tweeds with bits of hay stuck on them everywhere." She was shaking, and her face had turned a ghastly white. She turned away from Nicholas and leaned her head against the backrest of the carriage seat. "Jeremy's no help. He thinks

I've gone daft, and now he's not here, and I've no one to turn to."

"Are you sure it was Eddie you saw? Could it have been one of the other guests whom you, in your grief, mistook for Eddie?" Nicholas kept his voice as low and soothing as possible.

Isabel sat upright again and looked him squarely in the eye. "It was Eddie, all right. No one else would look so fit in those clothes. And I know that body as well as I know my own."

She turned away, with her back to him, and Nicholas thought at first that she had turned away out of embarrassment for an untoward confession. But when he saw she was shaking with sobs, he knew he was wrong. She was consumed with genuine grief.

Nicholas spoke softly. "Isabel, my dear, why do you think the dead Eddie would appear to you?"

"Why to punish me, of course." She turned toward him again and spoke without hesitation, dabbing at her eyes with a handkerchief. "He could be so cruel."

"Punish you?"

Isabel sighed heavily. "He didn't like that I was trying to hurt him by . . ." She ducked her head. "By flirting with you."

"Ah." Nicholas nodded his head.

"Eddie was cruel, but he couldn't stand others being cruel to him." She sniffed and touched her handkerchief to her nose. "The truth is, I can't stand cruelty either. I only hoped it would stop if I . . . Well, it didn't stop, did it? He's still found a way to be cruel."

"Isabel, what are you trying to say?"

"Oh, let's do stop talking about it." She glanced at the street. "Look, here we are at that delightful little place I told you about."

The carriage driver had stopped in front of a quaint restaurant. Fashionably dressed men and women sat at sidewalk tables, engaged in animated talk and carefree laughter. Women hid their laughter behind lacy fans, except for what showed in their eyes, and men looked pleased with themselves for whatever reason.

"It's really *the* place to be seen." Isabel was making an all-too-obvious effort to appear happy as Nicholas helped her from the carriage. "Let's do sit inside, though, Nicky, dear. I'm afraid that, under the circumstances, I won't look my best in sunlight." She dabbed at her eyes again.

They were shown to a table inside, where the ambiance was decidedly more that of dim light and discreet secrecy. At Isabel's suggestion, they ordered a bottle of very expensive but very elegant French wine.

When Isabel finished two glasses of wine and had started on her third, Nicholas made several attempts to steer the conversation back to exactly what it was Isabel thought would stop Lord Dunsford's cruelty, but always without success. She even managed to brush off his direct question of her being in Eddie's room the night he was killed.

"Oh Nicky, Lady Winningham is such a gossip. You certainly don't believe her, do you? But let's not talk about her. What, pray tell, are you doing back in London so soon? You seemed to be quite taken by that Gladstone woman." Isabel gave him a coquettish look over her glass. "I should have thought you'd find an excuse to stay there with her. And haven't you been called as a witness for the prosecution along with the rest of us?"

"It's true," Nicholas said, deciding to return to his original mission. "I shall be a witness, as, I suppose, shall you, but since we have a few days, I decided to come see Lord Winningham, but he's in Norfolk."

"Winnie?" Isabel drained her glass and giggled. "He's not in Norfolk. He's gone back to Newton. He's to be a witness as well."

"But so soon?"

"Soon?" Isabel said a bit too loudly, so that Nicholas glanced around to see who might overhear. "Of course it was too soon. And Jerry's there too soon, also."

"Jeremy's already in Newton?"

"Yes." Isabel slurred the word so it sounded like "yesh." She leaned closer. "If you ask me, they're both there to make sure nothing goes wrong and that horrible girl will hang, and that will be the end of it."

"How will they do that?" Nicholas asked.

Isabel's laugh was cynical. "Money, my dear. They can buy people, you know. Prospective jurors, judges."

"But why?" Nicholas asked, although he feared he knew the answer.

"Why?" She was weaving slightly. "Well, Jerry kept saying something about having to make sure I hadn't caused a scandal. He's afraid my little affair with Eddie will come out at the trial and it will embarrass him." She giggled. "Or make it appear as if he has a motive to kill poor Eddie for ravaging me. So he's back there doing all he can to see that it doesn't come out. But I assure you," she said, waving her glass, "Jerry couldn't care less about who I sleep with. He only cares about how it affects his reputation. Could you pour another glass for me, Nicky, dear?"

Nicholas obliged her with another glass. "But why would Lord Winningham feel the need to go back so soon?"

"Winnie?" She giggled again. "He's got his own worries." She leaned forward weaving slightly. "If you ask me, he had more reason than anyone to kill the poor bastard." She took another sip of wine and licked her lips. "Winnie's not exactly a saint, you know, and Eddie caught him with his pants down, and some other poor bastard's down, too, it seems." She giggled and sputtered, spewing wine all over Nicholas.

When Nicholas had mopped his front off with a napkin and Isabel had helped herself to another glass of wine, she was then inclined to gossip about other people, no matter how hard Nicholas tried to steer the conversation. When she had finished the bottle of wine, Nicholas led her, with both of his hands firmly on her arm, out to her carriage and instructed the driver to take them home.

Once he had seen Isabel safely inside, he instructed his own driver, who had waited for him, to take him home where he immediately made preparations to return to Newton. Isabel had substantiated Lord Winningham's motive, as well as confirmed that perhaps others, including herself and

Jeremy Atewater, had their own motives. But there was still
work to be done. He wanted to know if there was more in
Eddie's past that could more definitely point to someone's
motive to kill him. He would try to use his status as barrister
and kinsman, how ever distant, to talk to banks, his club,
his soliciter.

Isabel found herself indelicately ridding herself of the contents
of her stomach soon after Nicholas left. She was obliged to
take a long nap and awoke late in the day with a headache.
It was more than the liquor that made her head ache, though.
She knew what Nicholas Forsythe was trying to learn something from her. She only hoped Jeremy would be successful
at buying whomever he had to buy.

13

Alexandra felt sickened at the words she had just heard. "Quince is dead?" Her voice trembled as she spoke.

The two boys didn't answer, but they exchanged glances, wide-eyed and frightened.

She glanced at one first and then the other. "How was he killed?" She found that her voice was still weak.

" 'E was tied up first, so's he couldn't struggle, by my reckoning. Then 'e was choked to death. Had a rope around 'is neck, 'e did," the older of the two said. Both had dirty brown hair, but the older one had a thin face and a long, lanky body. He appeared to be about sixteen, close to Elsie's age. The younger one's face still had the plump round-ness of a child, and he couldn't have been more than eight or nine.

Alexandra felt a moment of shock at the boy's words. "A rope around his neck . . ."

"Same as the earl hisself." The boy's voice was little more than a whisper. He expressed the same thought Alexandra was thinking.

"How did you know how Earl Dunsford died?" she asked. Both boys looked frightened, as if they were afraid they'd

said too much. The younger one, Artie, shook his head as
if to deny it, and the older one shrugged as he answered,
"A person hears things, don't he? On the streets, I mean.
Some are sayin' that girl done it. Strangled Earl Dunsford,
then cut 'im with a knife."

"But she couldn't have killed Quince," Alexandra said.

The boy shook his head slowly. "Not while she's in
chokey."

"Then who killed him?" Alexandra leaned toward the
boy, her voice urgent.

Both boys looked frightened, and the older one looked
around as if he might be afraid someone was listening.
"I . . . don't know," he said. He looked as if he might bolt
from the room, so Alexandra spoke again, quickly.

"Why did Quince tell you to come here?"

Artie, who was eyeing the needle and catgut Nancy was
preparing, answered this time. "He said you could 'elp us.
Said you was a doctor, didn't he, Rob?" It was the first time
Alexandra had heard the older boy's name. "Told us to
come here last night, but we was afraid."

"Afraid?"

Rob, who was holding the wrist of his damaged right
hand with his left, nudged the younger boy, as if to tell him
he was saying too much, but Artie, the younger, kept talking. "It's got so dangerous. Quince says we never should
have got greedy and hooked up with them London . . ." He
stopped speaking when Rob gave him a second, particularly
sharp nudge in the ribs with his elbow.

"The boy don't know what 'e's saying. 'E's just a baby
seein' the bogeyman everywhere. 'Course we wasn't afraid.
We just thought we wasn't hurt bad at first."

Alexandra could see the fear in Rob's eyes, in spite of
his denial. Artie was crying, but trying hard not to show it.
Both were terribly afraid of something. But what? And
why?

"It wasn't just that you was a doctor. Quince said you
seemed like a person we could trust," Artie blurted. It
sounded like a plea for help. "Said maybe if things got bad,

we should . . ." Once again he was silenced by a sharp jab in the ribs.

Alexandra studied both of their faces in silence for a moment. Finally she spoke. "Do you think that whoever killed Quince will come after the two of you as well?"

Neither of them spoke, but she saw the answer in their frightened eyes.

"Who?" she asked. "If you want me to help you, you've got to tell me who you're afraid of."

Neither boy spoke. Although Artie looked as if he wanted to, his friend's hard grip on his forearm was a warning against it.

"Is it someone in London?"

"We're afraid of no one." Alexandra saw Rob's grip on his companion tighten as he spoke.

She stood up suddenly. "You're lying!" she said sharply, deciding to take another tact. "You know who killed Quince, and I think you know who killed Earl Dunsford as well. You can both go to prison if you know who the murderer is and you don't tell. Or if you don't go to prison, you both know you could be killed, too."

"But we don't know his name!" Artie was crying so hard he could hardly speak.

Rob grabbed both of his shoulders and shook him hard. "Stop yer blubbering, ye bloody—"

Alexandra grasped Rob's hands firmly and pulled them from the crying boy. "Leave him alone. He has a right to be frightened, and if you had your wits about you, you'd be frightened as well." She sat down beside the crying child while Nancy stood by silently, observing everything with her sharp eyes and keen mind. "You said you don't know his name, but do you know what he looks like? Anything about him?" Alexandra asked.

Artie sobbed, finding it difficult to speak, but before he could say anything, the older boy blurted, "What 'e means is, we know it's some bloke from London. 'E came to Quince with an offer. Said 'e wanted us to be 'is partner. Said 'e would be the head and we would be the hands."

It was clear that the more they revealed, the more frightened both boys became. Rob had dropped his voice to a whisper, and he couldn't stop darting his eyes about, looking out the window, at the door, and all around the room as if he expected someone to be listening.

"He was going to be the head, and you were going to be the hands? To do what?" Alexandra tried to keep her voice low and calm, but both boys dropped their eyes and refused to look at her, Artie still sniffling. She pressed further. "To steal something? Jewels perhaps?" She remembered how, during dinner at Montmarsh, there had been a chance remark about a ring of young thieves in the area stealing jewelry and money. The constable had mentioned it as well. Elsie's beau, George Stirling, they'd all said, was part of it.

"Ye 'ave yer fine life here in yer warm house, miss. Ye can't know what it's like to 'ave a lank belly and the cold o' winter on ye." Rob spoke up suddenly, sounding troubled and defensive. "All I ever took was a loaf o' bread and maybe once or twice a shank o' meat. All right, and maybe once or twice a few coins for a glass of ale. But no rich gent was going to miss them coins, now was 'e? And Artie here," he nodded to indicate the younger boy, " 'e was just gettin' into it, and Quince had took 'im under 'is wing. Quince was like that, 'e was."

The boy stopped suddenly. Alexandra was afraid to speak, afraid if she urged him to say more, he would run away.

"Quince never meant no harm," the boy said finally, looking down at his hands again. " 'E come to us with what the London bloke had said. Said the bloke would tell us when it was ripe to pick the jewels, said 'e would tell us where. It was mostly ladies, it was, and Quince said we wouldn't be takin' anything they really needed. And we wasn't to hurt a one of 'em, Quince said. We was to get a cut of the loot, see."

Alexandra nodded, holding her breath, hoping he would continue.

"I know what yer wantin', miss," the boy said. "Yer wantin' the name o' the London bloke, but Quince never told us. We only seen 'im once, and the light weren't too good."

Artie, wide-eyed, moved his head slowly from side to side to show he didn't know either. "It started goin' bad, though, when Georgie got it, only he—"

This time it was Artie who stopped his friend from saying more with a hand laid firmly on his arm.

"When Georgie got it," Rob continued, giving young Artie a reassuring look, "Quince said 'e'd had enough and 'e was sorry 'e got us into it. But it was too late, wasn't it? Now Quince is dead and we is next."

"Is that why Quince told you to come to me?" Alexandra asked. "Because he knew you were in danger?"

" 'E said we could trust you, miss. And if we can't, well then, we is dead any way you look at it."

Alexandra stood and paced a few steps, then turned back to the boys. "Did anyone see you come here?"

"We got our ways," the older boy said.

"Am I to assume that means no one saw you?"

Both boys looked at each other, then back at Alexandra and nodded their agreement.

Alexandra paced a few more steps. "Obviously you can't leave here." She glanced at Nancy, who gave her a troubled look but said nothing. Alexandra went to the basin to wash her hands again, then picked up the needle. "This is going to hurt."

Nancy sat down beside Artie and took his hands. "Tell me about yourself, boy. How did you come to be in Newton?"

Alexandra punctured the boys flesh with her needle, and he howled loudly, not at all distracted by Nancy's tactics. Rob's face grew pale and he turned away. By the time she had finished, Artie was limp and leaning against Nancy. Alexandra prepared a poultice with the mixture of herbs Nancy had brought in, then bandaged the side of Artie's face and jaw. Next, she turned her attention to the Rob's hand and cleaned it thoroughly. She could see the wound was less serious than Artie's, and the bleeding had long since been stemmed. With Nancy's help, she brought the edges of the wound together and secured them with adhesive plaster and wrapped a light bandage around his hand.

She stood then, and moved toward the door, motioning for Nancy to follow. "Wait here," she said to the boys, ignoring the alarmed look that spread across their faces.

"That one is no more than a baby!" Nancy whispered when they were in the hallway. What are we going to do about them?"

"I want you to prepare Father's room for them."

"Prepare your father's room for them? Miss Alex, I don't have to tell you who those two ruffians are, do I?"

"I am fully aware of who they are." She was also fully aware that, in spite of her words, the tone of Nancy's voice made her warning sound less than convincing.

Nancy made another weak attempt at protesting. "One of 'em's just a baby, but still . . ."

"Just prepare the room, Nancy, and take them up now, before patients begin to arrive. Needless to say, no one is to know they are here, and they are not to come out of the room. We will take their meals to them."

Nancy pointed a finger at Alexandra and opened her mouth to protest, but she swallowed her words and said simply, "Yes, Miss Alex," before she left to prepare the room.

Neither boy protested when she told them they would be staying in her house, but they both seemed edgy when Nancy came to fetch them. She was still trying to be angry. "If your father was alive . . ." she said as she entered the surgery, but she never finished her sentence. Instead, she looked at Artie's round, wounded face, and Alexandra could see her anger dissolve. "Come along, boys." She took each by the arm and led them out. "A nice hot meal will do you good, and maybe even a bath, then we'll see how you like . . ."

Alexandra made her morning rounds, eager, for once, to hear the local gossip, hoping it would lend some insight into the murders. The talk was not of murder, however, but of the impending trial for Elsie O'Riley and of Priscilla Blackburn's funeral. The Blackburn funeral would, of course, be considerably less grand than that of the Earl. No members of Parliament nor any representative of the queen would attend. It was to be held that afternoon. No funeral was mentioned for the young man called Quince. In fact, his death had caused hardly a stir.

"One o' them ne'er-do-wells down at the pier kilt, was he?" Nell Stillwell, the butcher's wife, said. "Serves 'im right, I says. They've broke into our shop more than once to relieve us of our finest cuts." Her eye was worsening, and Alexandra had begun to fear it would require surgical removal. She remembered Nell's words: *If some things would but die, 'twould end our troubles, wouldn't it?*

When she visited Mrs. Pickwick at Montmarsh, she was disturbed to see that her mental state had worsened again.

"A body ought not to be up walking around when he's dead. It seems a downright sin." Her voice was strained as she busied herself packing things into a valise. "I seen him again. The late earl hisself." Her eyes were wide with fright as she turned to Alexandra.

"Mrs. Pickwick, you must not fret over this." Alexandra spoke as soothingly as possible. "You've been under a great deal of strain. The mind can play tricks on a person in that state."

"I'll be leaving soon," Mrs. Pickwick said, ignoring Alexandra's attempt at comforting her. "I've sent for my brother in Colchester to come fetch me. I won't be staying around where unnatural things are happening."

"Mrs. Pickwick—"

The cook shook her head. "Now don't go telling me it's because of the strain of Lord Dunsford's death. It's got nothing to do with strain, I tell you." She placed a folded winter jacket into the valise. "Why that poor stable boy, Jamie, seen him, too. Near scared him out of his wits, it did. Now he's run off."

"He's seen Lord Dunsford? Are you sure? Did he tell you that?" Alexandra was pushing her, thinking if she could force her to think rationally and logically she would come out of her frightened state of mind.

"Sure he told me," Mrs. Pickwick said. "Come running

in, he did, bawling and scared out of his wits, claiming he saw Lord Dunsford running down the driveway."

"When?" Alexandra asked, still pressing her.

Mrs. Pickwick shook her head. "I don't know. Time means nothing to me in my state." She closed her eyes. "Yesterday, I think it was. Yes, the same night Mr. Forsythe left."

"He left at night?" Alexandra's interest was piqued.

"Late in the day, it was. Said he would travel all night. And don't go asking me why he left, for I don't know. Them nobs has always got urgent business in London, you know."

"Did he say anything to you when he left?"

"Now why would he be talkin' to the likes of me?" Mrs. Pickwick's voice had gained strength with her growing emotion.

Alexandra picked up her medical bag, preparing to leave. "I thought perhaps he might have left a message for me."

Mrs. Pickwick continued her packing. "He left with nary a word to anybody except the stable boy to help him with his trunks. And now the guests is all gone, which is what we'd all be if we had any wits about us. I'll be leaving as soon as my duty to the queen's court as witness is over, and it's without a position to go to, I tell you. It's danger of starvation I'm facing, but you don't see that keeping me back, do you?" She folded one of her large aprons into a precise and neat square. "I'll be here for the trial and to see that poor Blackburn woman buried in holy ground before I go, and that's it. I must say, you won't see Priscilla Blackburn up and walking around after she's dead. Not a decent woman like her. May God bless her soul. No, she knows what's proper, she does, and you can thank God for that."

Alexandra went home, after she'd tried unsuccessfully to find Jamie.

The next day, as she and Nancy prepared to attend Priscilla's funeral, Alexandra wondered if she should tell Constable Snow what she'd learned about the jewel thief ring. But wouldn't it betray those two boys who trusted her? Or did her duty to obey the law take precedence over their

trust? To her surprise, she found herself wishing Mr. Forsythe was there to talk with and to help her work her way
through the muddle.

She still had not decided what to do as she and Nancy
made their way on foot from their home to the church in
the village.

"I hope, for your sake, that those two boys don't rob you
blind while we're gone," Nancy said as they walked.

"How can they rob me blind when they're locked in Father's room like prisoners?"

"Ha! That shows how gullible you are, missy. Those two
have no doubt escaped from prisons mightier than yours.
What's it to them to pick the lock of a cottage?" Nancy's
tone of voice and the fact that she'd called her "missy"
reminded Alexandra of when they were younger. Nancy
was forever trying to educate her in the ways of the world.
It was, she always said, her payment for the senior Dr. Gladstone's allowing her to share Alexandra's classroom with
her.

"Well, suppose they do get out; they won't go far with
Zack there to keep them in line."

Nancy shook her head. "Zack's a clever animal, all right,
but do you really think the poor beast understands that he's
supposed to keep those two rascals in the house when what
he's been trained to do is keep them out?"

"Zack understands." Alexandra's attention was immediately distracted by the sight of a man she'd just seen from
a distance coming out of the Blue Ram.

"Are you all right, Miss Alex?" Nancy had obviously
seen her face and was concerned.

"Quite all right," Alexandra said. "It's just that . . ."

"Yes, miss?"

"That man." She was still looking toward the tavern
where the gentleman she was certain was Lord Winningham
still stood, speaking to someone. "He looks familiar."

Nancy followed her gaze. "What man?"

"That one there. See, he's just going into the Blue Ram
again."

"How can you tell? It's so far away, and besides, there are three men going into the tavern."

"He's the one dressed like a gentleman. I think it's Lord Winningham."

Nancy shrugged. "Never heard of him. Is he another one of Lord Dunsford's friends?"

"Yes," Alexandra said, "and I find it rather odd that both Winningham and Jeremy Atewater would be in Newton this long before they have to be here as witnesses."

Nancy's eyes brightened. "You think they know something about the murderer?"

"There's certainly no logical reason to think that," Alexandra said, in spite of the fact that it was the very thing she was thinking.

By the time they reached the church, a large crowd had gathered. There were townsfolk, fishermen, and many of the other tenement farmers from Montmarsh. There was, of course, no representative from the earl's family, since the heir had yet to move into Montmarsh.

The wet nurse Alexandra had hired sat with Seth and his older son and held the surviving twin in her arms. Alexandra sat next to Nancy. Watching Seth, who could not stop crying, and his two-year-old son, who looked bewildered, Alexandra's mood darkened. In spite of the fact that death at childbirth was all too common, she couldn't help feeling that it was partly because of her own lack of knowledge that Priscilla was dead.

She knew she had to get past the self-recrimination, however; otherwise, she would never be able to serve her other patients. Nancy, who sensed her mood, reached to cover her hand with her own.

After the church service and the graveside ceremony, and after Alexandra had offered her condolences to Seth, she turned away to begin the walk home with Nancy. That was when she found herself face-to-face with Constable Snow.

"There's been another murder," he said. "A young man. I think you may know something about it."

14

"Dr. Gladstone! Are you quite all right?" Constable Snow
frowned as he looked at her face.

"I am never quite all right when I have lost a patient."
Alexandra's mouth had suddenly gone dry. She knew the
real reason for any change in her countenance he had ob-
served had to do with what the constable had just said, as
well as the fact that she'd lost a patient. But she hoped to
divert his attention until she could collect her thoughts.

"Of course," he said. "I'm sorry. I should have known.
Forgive me for being so abrupt."

Alexandra mustered as much poise as possible. "You
were speaking of a murder?"

He shook his head. "I'm sorry. Perhaps tomorrow would
be a more opportune time."

Alexandra felt Nancy tug at her arm, a signal that they
should leave. In spite of that, Alexandra blurted, "I'm afraid
you've aroused my curiosity, Constable." She was aware of
Nancy's glare. She didn't need Nancy's glare to tell her she
had spoken in spite of her own better judgment.

Snow seemed to consider it for a moment. "You know
of whom I speak, of course," he said finally.

"I'm not sure I do, nor am I sure why you think I know anything about a murder." There was another urgent tug on her arm.

"Excuse me, miss. You told me to make sure you got back to the surgery on time to see a few more patients." Nancy spoke boldly, in spite of the fact that they both knew Alexandra had asked for no such thing.

Snow ignored Nancy's disguised plea. "Dr. Gladstone, it's unlike you not to be forthright. You cannot help but know that I'm referring to the young man known as Quince."

"And why do you assume I know this?" Alexandra heard a desperate sigh from Nancy.

"Two young men of his acquaintance came to your house shortly after he died. They must have told you."

Alexandra bristled. "Are my house and surgery under surveillance? Indeed, is it customary for one's home and business to be watched by government officials when one is a law-abiding citizen?"

"There are no government officials watching your home or your surgery, Miss Alexandra. We were watching the young men." Snow had taken on a scolding tone, sounding very much as he might have when he was a teacher and she a student. He had even used the name he had used for her when she was his student.

"The young men?" Alexandra was struggling to keep her composure, convinced now that she should have taken Nancy's hint and used the earlier opportunity to walk away. It was too late now, though, and she was even more aware of Nancy's edginess as she stood beside her. She knew, too, once they returned home, she would have Nancy's scolding to face for allowing her curiosity to get in the way of good judgment.

"Yes, the young men," Snow said. "You know of whom I speak. The two who came to your house early yesterday morning. Rather too early, I would think. Especially since you returned so late last night after your meeting with the victim."

Alexandra heard Nancy's breathing change to a rapid,

shallow pattern, and she, herself, stiffened. "You were watching me as well, then." She managed to sound calm and detached in spite of the fact that her anger as well as her anxiety were growing.

"I was trying to watch young Quince, Dr. Gladstone, but it was quite dark, as I'm sure you know, and I was unable to see clearly. I was not even certain, until you just confirmed it, that you had, in fact, met with Quince."

"I have confirmed nothing, Constable." Alexandra was afraid she would not be able to stay calm much longer.

"Neither have you denied meeting with Quince." Snow met her gaze with a steely glare of his own.

"That fact does not constitute an affirmation." She stared back at him.

Nancy tugged at her arm and leaned toward her to speak in an urgent whisper, her hand covering the side of her mouth so Constable Snow would not hear. "You best not say any more, not until you talk to the likes of Mr. Forsythe."

Alexandra was certain she was right. If she were prudent, she would say no more without the advice of a solicitor, if not a barrister such as Mr. Forsythe. Knowing that, she still could not stop herself from asking the question that nagged relentlessly at her.

"Tell me, Constable, why are you so interested in this person you call Quince, as well as the two young men you say you saw come to my home? Does it have to do with the other two recent murders?"

"It has to do with police business, Dr. Gladstone." Snow's glare had turned to steel again.

"Am I in some danger as a result of having seen those two young men as patients?"

"I don't know." His answer was curt, as if he was afraid he might say too much.

"And why do you think I might know something about the other young man's death?" she asked. "The one you call Quince."

Snow gave her an accusing look. "I spoke with another young ruffian at the pier, and he told me Quince had told the two injured boys to see you. He also told me the two boys were bitten by a large dog and that the dog belongs to you."

So it was true he had not actually seen her. He had taken the word of the unnamed boy at the pier, and he was only conjecturing that the boys might have said something to her about Quince's murder. He was fishing, and knowing that gave her a bit of leeway.

"Two young men did indeed come to my front door yesterday morning as I'm certain you know because your spying—excuse me—your *surveillance* confirmed that fact." She watched his face for some reaction to her veiled criticism, but he remained stoic. She continued. "I'm not certain why the gentleman you called Quince would tell them to come to me, since I don't know him." She was careful not to say she had never met him, but was a half-truth any less grievous than an outright lie?

Nancy, growing more nervous by the minute, spouted her own half-truths. "We best be going now, Dr. Gladstone. Remember, one of your patients has urgent need of you today."

Snow once again ignored Nancy and spoke directly to Alexandra. "Perhaps it is your reputation as a physician that got them to you, then." His tone was innocuous, but his eyes were probing.

She gave him a noncommittal nod and a half smile.

"Nevertheless, I must caution you about walking along the waterfront late at night," Snow said. "Even a respected physician with a large dog is not invulnerable."

"Thank you for your concern, Constable, and I will remember your warning. Good day, sir." Alexandra started to walk away, but Snow stopped her with a sharp reprimand.

"You have not told me what you know about the murder of Quince!"

Alexandra turned around slowly, once again sensing Nancy's tension growing. "I beg your pardon?"

Snow took a step toward her and spoke in a hushed, urgent voice. "What did those two tell you?"

She chose her words carefully. "We spoke mostly of their

injuries. Lacerations and puncture wounds. Perhaps they were caused by an animal, but since I did not actually witness an attack, I'm afraid I can't be sure."

"The two boys were never seen leaving your house yesterday morning. Are they still there?" Snow's expression was stern, and, it seemed to Alexandra, his tone was almost threatening.

Alexandra managed a dismissive little laugh. "I maintain a simple surgery, Constable Snow. I don't run a hospital. Or a hotel."

"But you do know where they are."

Alexandra sighed. "I can only hope they are someplace where their wounds will be cared for. Do they have parents, Constable Snow?"

He was silent for a moment, glaring at her. "They live along the waterfront with other ruffians. They live by theft."

Alexandra tried not to let her own gaze falter. "I see," she said.

There was another silence, another glare, then Snow said, "I will be in contact, Dr. Gladstone."

"It will be my pleasure," Alexandra said as he moved away.

Nancy breathed a heavy sigh and waited until he had put several feet between them before she spoke. "You escaped that one by the skin of your teeth, now didn't you?"

"I'm not sure we've escaped anything yet," Alexandra said, watching Snow's back as he walked away.

"But you were a clever one, you were. The way you handled him, I'm not sure I could have done better myself. I've taught you well, if I do say so."

"I just lied to a policeman."

" 'Twasn't a pure lie. You just failed to elaborate, which is a lady's right, I say."

"Something made me want to protect those boys," Alexandra said. "I have a feeling they know something that's dangerous for them to know."

"Why, sure they do," Nancy said. "And it's plain that the constable thinks they know something, too."

Alexandra shook her head, perplexed. "I'm not sure his

knowing where they are would bring them harm. I just felt I couldn't betray them now."

Nancy gave her a knowing look. "And it could be dangerous for you, now couldn't it? Didn't I tell you that from the first?"

Alexandra nodded. "That you did." Then with a resigned sigh she said, "Let's go home, Nancy. I've got to stop acting on instinct and think this through."

"That's one thing you haven't been doing much of lately. Thinking, that is. If I may say so." Nancy spoke as they made their way through the churchyard toward the road. Alexandra ignored her impertinence, but she remembered again her father continually warning her, since she and Nancy were playmates, that she was not cultivating the proper relationship with a servant.

Alexandra was not stern, but she could, however, be defensive. "You're saying I haven't been using my head, Nancy?"

"Well, you aren't thinking straight when you bring strange men in off the street in the middle of the night, now are you?" said Nancy, showing her impertinence again.

"Jerry Atewater is hardly a stranger. He's a respectable London banker, whom I met at Montmarsh. As I told you, I happened to see him while I was walking Zack." Alexandra knew she sounded a bit too defensive.

"If I may say so, what's a respectable London banker doing in Newton? And in particular, what's he doing walking along the waterfront in the middle of the night?"

"He said he was here to—"

"And another thing," Nancy interrupted, "if I may say so, it's just a bit odd that—"

Alexandra snapped at Nancy. "Oh, for heaven's sake stop saying 'if I may say so.' You know as well as I that, with or without permission, you always say anything that comes into your head."

She was aware of Nancy's sideways glance at her and of her sudden silence, which, Alexandra was certain, was meant to signal that she had been unreasonably harsh. She'd spoken that way out of frustration and confusion. It had just

occurred to her that Constable Snow had not mentioned seeing Jeremy Atewater at the pier. It would have been difficult
for him to have missed him. Was there some sort of con-
spiracy between the two of them to spy on her? And if so,
why?

"Speaking of Mr. Atewater," Nancy said, obviously unable to maintain her silence for too long, "it seems a bit
odd, does it not, that the constable didn't mention seeing
him at the pier?"

It was not the first time Nancy had seemingly read her
mind. Alexandra's only response was an almost undetect-
able nod of her head.

Nancy continued. "And I wonder just what that Mr. Atewater was really doing out there. He wasn't walking there
just to enjoy the evening; you can be sure of that. There are
certainly other places around Newton more pleasant than
the smelly old pier if a person's in the mood for a nice
walk. And are you sure you've told me everything that happened out there? How can I help you if you don't tell me
everything?"

Alexandra stopped and turned to her before they reached
the churchyard gate. "Help me what?"

"Why, get to the bottom of all of this." Nancy sounded
indignant. "You know you always did need my help. Wasn't
I the one who showed you how to bait a hook and catch a
fish when the rector's son bet you two pence you couldn't
do it? Wasn't I the one who convinced your father, God
rest his soul, that it wasn't really gambling you'd engaged
in, as that sore loser and calumnious knave of a rector's son
told him, but rather that he had simply paid you to teach
him how? Wasn't I also the one who helped you when—"

"We are not talking about childhood misadventures now,"
Alexandra interrupted. "This is far more serious than that.
Three people have been murdered, and you have no business probing into any of that." There was a moment of
silence while they glared at each other. "And besides," Alexandra said, "your help is expensive. As I remember, you
took half of my winnings for rescuing me from that business
with the rector's son."

Nancy tried, unsuccessfully, to suppress a smile. "And as I remember you were grateful enough to pay me a few pence more than I asked for."

"Nevertheless—"

"And have you thought of this," Nancy said, not giving Alexandra a chance to protest more, "just why were Mr. Atewater and the constable *both* out at that pier? Were they both after you? Or were they after something else? Maybe something they were afraid you'd find before they could. Was it you they meant to kill instead of that young man, Quince? If you ask me, you need my help now even more than—"

Alexandra interrupted her as she opened the churchyard gate and stepped into the street. "Come now, Nancy, your imagination is running away with you!" She feared her voice betrayed her lack of conviction. She had given no thought to the fact that what happened to Quince was meant to have happened to her, but Nancy's speculation was not entirely unreasonable, she had to admit.

15

Alexandra saw no more of Jeremy Atewater for the next several days. Talk around the village was that he had gone back to London. Lord Winningham must have returned as well, since she saw no more of him either.

The only time she saw Constable Snow was when she tried to visit Elsie again. Snow told her he could not allow it, since there was no medical reason to see her. Alexandra hoped that meant she was no longer hallucinating.

Even Mrs. Pickwick was marginally better, at least to the extent that she no longer spoke of seeing Lord Dunsford's ghost. She was clearly edgy, however, as well as eager to make her escape from Montmarsh.

If Constable Snow was still looking for Rob and Artie, he did not come to Alexandra's home to search for them. Alexandra knew she could be breaking the law by harboring them, but she could not convince herself that they would be of any value to Snow, since they most certainly would not tell him anything. In the meantime, she would allow them to stay in the interest of their safety.

The two of them had been given the run of the house, except during surgery hours when someone might see them or when guests were expected. Nancy had given them tasks around the house, which they seemed happy to perform in exchange for her stews and meat pies, and especially her chocolate biscuits.

On the surface, it appeared that Newton-Upon-Sea and, to some extent, Montmarsh, had returned to normal. There was, of course, talk of Elsie's trial as the date grew near, but even that seemed nothing out of the ordinary.

It was the Sunday before the trial was scheduled when Alexandra and Nancy returned home from the church that Alexandra was reminded things were far from normal.

The moment she unlocked the door and stepped inside, she sensed that something was wrong. She glanced at Nancy, who appeared tense and ill at ease as if she, too, thought something was wrong.

Zack, in the meantime, had roused himself from his resting place near the hearth and was barking with excitement. That in itself was odd. He usually greeted Alexandra or Nancy with a subdued, gruff bark, along with a nudge with his nose.

"Zack's trying to tell us something," Nancy said as she removed her hat and placed it on the rack.

"I think you're right." Alexandra knelt down to rub Zack's neck and look into his eyes. He cocked his head and barked again.

"I'll just take a minute to see about the boys before I make your tea, miss," Nancy said, as if she had somehow understood the message in Zack's bark. She was practically running up the stairs.

Alexandra followed her with equal exigency, and Zack followed right behind, still barking, until they reached the door to the room that had been her father's, but now had become the boys' room. Both Alexandra and Nancy hesitated and looked at each other, sharing some inexpressible fear before Nancy knocked lightly on the door.

"Rob? Artie?" Nancy waited, breathless, her knuckles still poised a few inches from the door. She leaned closer. "Hello? I was wondering, would you like me to bring you up a bit of luncheon? Tea perhaps? And there are some scones in the larder that are still fresh." Again there was no response.

Alexandra stepped in front of Nancy and grasped the doorknob. It was not locked, and she had specifically told Artie to keep it locked. She opened the door and stepped inside. She felt a sudden hollowness in her stomach. No one was there. Zack was quiet, as if there was no need to bark now. No need to tell them the boys were gone.

"Dear God!" Nancy cried and ran into the hallway calling their names. "Artie! Rob! You best not be up to mischief, or I'll see to it myself that you get a proper thrashing! Rob, where are you?"

"It's no use, Nancy. They're gone." Alexandra handed her a flyleaf torn from one of her father's medical texts. She had just found the page on the floor. Rob had used it to pen a note in the same crude handwriting she had seen before. She watched as Nancy silently read the words.

We seen the kiler. We have to run or we wil be muddred. Run or you will be muddred to.

Nancy glanced at her, still holding the flyleaf. "Do you suppose the murderer came here looking for them? Or was it you?"

Alexandra shook her head. "I don't know. But they recognized him. Or her."

"But they said they didn't know the killer's identity."

"They said they didn't know the name. That doesn't mean they wouldn't recognize a face."

Nancy's face paled. "He could be after you, as well, you know. Or she, as you say."

Alexandra found she could not speak.

"But why?" Nancy asked. "Why would anyone kill any of those three boys?"

Alexandra paced the hall a few steps, rolling the flyleaf she had taken back from Nancy into a tight cylinder. "Because each of them had something the killer wanted? Or because each of them knew something that could be damaging to the killer?"

"And all that talk of ghosts," Nancy said. "Things that

won't stay dead. It's as if the whole county has been possessed by a demon."

Alexandra stopped her pacing and turned to face Nancy. "There's more than one corpse that walks among the living!"

Nancy gave her an alarmed look. "What did you say?"

Alexandra turned back toward the stairs, calling back to Nancy. "I'll need a few things in a satchel small enough to tie to my saddle. Get them ready for me, please. Enough for one night's stay." She hurried down the stairs. Nancy ran to the landing and called down to her.

"Where are you going?"

"Montmarsh," Alexandra said over her shoulder. "And I may not be home until morning. I'm going to find that ghost."

"What!" Nancy scrambled after her. "You'll do no such thing! Not when there's a murderer loose. And he's after you, too! Or she's after you! Didn't that boy say as much in the note he left? It's because you know too much, too, isn't it? And what do you mean a ghost?" Nancy's voice had risen several decibels by the time she caught up with Alexandra at the bottom of the stairs.

"I'll be as safe at Montmarsh as I am here." Alexandra hurried toward the back door, headed for the stable and for Lucy. Nancy was right behind her, still protesting frantically.

"Of course you'll be safer here. You'll have Zack to warn you."

Alexandra tried to ignore her, mostly because she knew Nancy was right. She gave instructions to Freddie, whom, she was surprised to see, had shown up for work. She turned back to Nancy. "I'll leave Zack here for your protection."

"And who will protect you?" Nancy demanded.

"I will be all right, Nancy," Alexandra said. "Remember? You taught me everything you know."

Montmarsh loomed before her, shrouded in a sticky summer haze. It seemed darker somehow, and even Lucy sensed it.

She slowed her pace, and then stopped completely, throwing her head about. Alexandra, sitting sidesaddle, nudged her with her left heel.

"Go on, Lucy." She kept her voice low and calm, but she had to nudge the mare again and to speak to her before she resumed a reluctant advance toward the imposing country house.

Alexandra dismounted and was about to secure Lucy's reigns to a post when she saw Mr. Forsythe riding a large bay gelding along the path that led from the back of the house. He must have returned to testify at the trial. She recognized the gelding he was riding as one that belonged to the earl's estate.

He saw her at almost the same moment and waved and called to her. "Dr. Gladstone!" He urged the horse to a quicker trot and stopped in front of her. "How wonderful to see you. I was just on my way to your house." He dismounted and walked toward her.

"How nice to see you again." She knew her reply sounded stiff and formal.

A troubled frown moved across his face like a cloud. "Is something wrong?"

"Of course not."

"I thought of posting you a letter describing all I have learned, but I knew I would most likely return before the letter arrived."

"All you have learned?"

He gave her another puzzled look. "You got my message, of course."

"Your message?"

"I sent a note to you by your stable boy telling you that I had to leave rather suddenly, and that I would have much to discuss with you when I returned."

She found herself inexplicably relieved that his sudden departure had not been out of rudeness after all. "I'm afraid I received no such message."

"Ah," he said with an amused expression in his eyes, "then that explains your discontent."

"Discontent?"

"Well I did rather expect a warmer welcome."

"I must apologize if I was rude, Mr. Forsythe."

His response was an all-too-confident smile as he secured Lucy's reigns and took Alexandra's arm to lead her toward the house. "To satisfy your curiosity," he said, "I will tell you that I made a rather quick journey to London to—"

"I have no curiosity," she lied, "and there is no need to make me privy to your business in London."

"Ah, but there is a need, my dear Dr. Gladstone." His tone was not at all defensive. "You see, the reason for my journey was because of our mutual concern for Elsie O'Riley."

"Indeed?" Alexandra saw that he had now grown quite serious.

"I overheard some of the servants talking and realized the possible motives on the part of at least some of Eddie's guests were even stronger than I thought, and with the trial occurring so soon, I had to get to London to try to learn as much as possible."

Alexandra wanted to ask what, precisely, he had learned as well as who, precisely, were the guests with strong motives, but he went on talking.

"Unfortunately, I had learned everything of importance by the second day, and I'm afraid my week spent going through Eddie's files was not as productive as I had hoped. There should be some interesting testimony, however, judging by the guests who have returned as witnesses. We'll all be staying at Montmarsh during the trial. Even Isabel, who did her best to keep from having to testify, is here."

"Is there hope for Elsie?"

Mr. Forsythe shook his head. "In spite of the fact that several people obviously could have had a motive to kill poor Eddie, there's no concrete proof they would even attempt such a thing.

Alexandra would have pushed him for more of an explanation of the supposed motives, except that they had, by now, entered the great hall of Montmarsh and were met by the butler. He took Alexandra's hat and riding crop in a resigned manner and announced that, in the absence of the heir apparent, only a light supper would be served in the dining room tonight.

"Since it was always the custom of the late Lord Dunsford to make his guests comfortable, I shall accommodate you," he said, sounding as if, in truth, he was loath to do so. "Excuse me, Mr. Forsythe," he added. "It was my understanding that you would be taking your evening meal elsewhere."

"I'm afraid I've changed my mind." There was a hint of irritability in Mr. Forsythe's voice.

"Indeed," the butler said. He turned to Alexandra. "And will the lady be spending the night?"

Mr. Forsythe, still sounding irritated, attempted to answer for her. "Of course not, she—"

"Yes," said Alexandra in the same moment. "I must see after Mrs. Pickwick." She had conceived the excuse during her ride to Montmarsh. She was determined to stay the night to look for the so-called ghost.

Mr. Forsythe looked at her in surprise while the butler, unperturbed, merely nodded. "I'll have one of the maids ready a room for you." He bowed again as he left.

"And please have someone see to my horse," she said.

"You're going to spend the night?" There was a hint of eagerness in Mr. Forsythe's voice now, along with surprise.

"Yes." Alexandra was busy removing her gloves. "It has become clear to me that someone needs to talk to that corpse that walks about Montmarsh." She glanced at Mr. Forsythe and smiled benignly, hoping to ward off any protest.

He looked at her askance. "Dr. Gladstone, as I said before, you're a sensible, educated woman. Surely you don't believe—"

"Don't believe there's a corpse walking about? A number of people have seen it, Mr. Forsythe."

He still looked puzzled. "But that doesn't mean—"

"I should think at the very least it should be looked into. I intend to do that, and since the corpse apparently only appears at night, I'm going to spend the night here."

"Well, of course!" he said. "We'll both stay up and investigate it together. Perhaps Elsie can call him, or it, as a witness for the defense."

"There's no need to be patronizing, Mr. Forsythe."

"I am by no means patronizing. I am quite serious."

"Are you?"

"Certainly! When one has eyewitness accounts from a feather-brained socialite, a hysterical cook, a man in his cups, and an ignorant, frightened serving girl, of course one must be *quite* serious about investigating."

Alexandra looked at him, saying nothing for a long, chilling moment. "I see your point, Mr. Forsythe, but you must admit it is a rather odd coincidence that all of these people, even though you imply they are incompetent, have seen the same thing."

There was another second before he spoke and his expression softened. "Of course, you're right. Please forgive me, Dr. Gladstone, I—"

"Apology accepted," she said, cutting him off. She walked up the stairs, hoping to find her room. After one of the maids pointed it out to her, she unpacked the small satchel containing her nightclothes and a few toiletries Nancy had packed for her. As she shook out her nightdress, she considered whether or not she should go downstairs to join the other guests for a buffet supper. Would she be able to glean any more information from them? Or would her presence somehow intimidate them and keep them from revealing anything?

Eventually she decided to make her way down to the dining room. Jeremy Atewater and Lord Winningham were the only two in the room.

"Well, of course I have an academic interest in the trial." Lord Winningham punctuated his speech with occasional grumbling harumphs. "You see, I read law for a year before I went into the military."

Atewater was about to reply when he saw Alexandra. He was unable to hide his surprise. "Dr. Gladstone? I say! What brings you here?"

Alexandra's only reply was a nod and the slightest of smiles. She watched as Atewater moved toward her, a quick, liquid movement, like a drop of water running down glass. Lord Winningham, in the meantime, stepped to the buffet to help himself to a slice of roast beef, which was floating in a rather questionable-looking gravy. As he moved closer to her, she caught the scent of whisky on his breath and heard him mumble, "Good God, even the locals are turning out for the bloody circus."

Alexandra ignored his last remark and tried to look pleasant as Atewater approached and took her hand to kiss. He was about to speak when Isabel's voice, thin as a fingernail on slate board, overrode his. "Hello, Jerry, dear. I hope I'm not interrupting anything."

Atewater once again appeared off guard. "Isabel! What are you—"

"You didn't expect me to show my face in public, did you? But I came to stand by my loyal husband while he made sure I was not touched by scandal." Her voice was like raw silk, a curious mixture of coarse and smooth, and her eyes were gleaming. Perhaps with anger. Perhaps, simply, from too much wine. She came to stand beside Atewater and linked her arm through his in a possessive gesture while her eyes fixed on Alexandra. A smile flickered at her mouth. When she spoke, she did not move her eyes from Alexandra. "Hello, Winnie. You've come for the bloodletting, I see."

Lord Winningham, who had by now seated himself at the table and was attacking the roast beef, looked up, surprised. "Bloodletting? What bloodletting?" The knife and fork he gripped in each hand stood like sentries on each side of his overflowing plate.

"Why, that trial. There are sure to be plenty of wounds." Isabel slipped her arm from her husband's and sat down across from Lord Winningham. "Have you spoken with the judge and the jurors yet? I'm sure Jerry has."

"Isabel!" Atewater's tone was scolding.

"Well, one does have to protect one's interest, you know." Isabel's voice was sugary with feigned innocence. "Don't you agree, Winnie?"

"I have no idea what you're talking about, madam." Lord

Winningham's words rolled in his throat like thunder.

Isabel laughed and reached across the table to pat Lord Winningham's bald head. She then leaned over to inspect the buffet and at the same time made a waving gesture toward Atewater and Alexandra. "Don't let me interrupt you two. Just go on with what you were doing." She gave the boiled potatoes a suspicious poke with the serving fork.

Atewater's face was red with restrained anger, while Lord Winningham appeared tense. He still had not gotten back to the business of eating. Atewater poured himself a glass of wine and sipped it, brooding, while he leaned against the wall.

Alexandra watched all three of them for a few seconds before she moved to the buffet and picked up a plate. She had just placed a slice of bread from the still-warm loaf on her plate when Isabel spoke to her.

"You're an awfully quiet little mouse, Miss Gladstone. Did you come back to spy on all of us?"

"Of course not," Alexandra said, spreading butter on the bread.

"Then why are you here?"

Alexandra laid the knife aside and locked her eyes on Isabel's, not speaking for several seconds. Finally she said evenly, "I have a patient in the household, Madam Atewater. Mrs. Pickwick, the cook, suffers from a nervous condition. She imagines that she sees the corpse of Lord Dunsford walking around."

Isabel kept her defiant gaze locked on Alexandra for a few seconds longer before her mouth trembled slightly and she looked away. She laid a single potato on her plate and sat down, but she seemed unable to eat.

Alexandra took her plate of bread and butter to the table and sat at the opposite end, thinking she would have done better to have asked the maid to bring her supper up. A heavy atmosphere of tension hung in the room like a dirty fog.

Presently, Mr. Forsythe appeared in the arched doorway. He gave her a polite smile, then she saw a flash of wariness in his eyes when he surveyed the other guests. He went to the buffet to make his choices, then sat down across from Alexandra. He glanced at her as he cut his beef and seemed to be asking, "What's going on?" with his eyes. She responded with the slightest of shrugs. The only sound in the room was the occasional clink of silver against a plate and the servant's footsteps as he walked around the table refreshing the guests' wine. Scowling, Atewater still leaned against the wall. Lord Winningham was making an effort to eat, and Isabel merely pushed the potato around her plate with her fork.

"Oh, for heaven's sake!" Isabel said finally. She dropped her fork, stood, and threw her napkin on the table. Mr. Forsythe stood up in deference to her sex, and Lord Winningham made a halfhearted attempt to do the same. She walked around the table to Mr. Forsythe, leaned toward him to whisper something in his ear, and left the room without even glancing at her husband, who still slouched against the wall.

This time it was Alexandra who gave Mr. Forsythe a what's-going-on look. His answer, as he seated himself again, was a troubled frown and the slightest rise of an eyebrow, which Alexandra found impossible to decipher. In the meantime, Atewater slammed his wine glass on the sideboard and followed his wife out of the room.

"What is everyone so bloody on edge about?" Lord Winningham's language indicated he had either forgotten or did not care there was a lady present.

Alexandra ignored the language and spoke calmly to Lord Winningham. "I'm afraid it's the upcoming trial that has everyone on edge, my lord. And you as well, it seems."

Lord Winningham rolled some incomprehensible words around in his throat again and gave her a troubled glance. He didn't bother to stand when she stood and made her way out of the room. Mr. Forsythe followed her into the hallway.

"Cheerful lot, aren't they?" he said when he caught up with her.

"Yes." Alexandra kept walking.

"And you, too, I see. Your mood's about as dark as the others'."

"I'm sorry," she said. "I'm thinking of the ghost."

"Oh, of course."

There was something in the tone of his voice that made her turn around. "You still think I'm foolish to believe those people actually saw a ghost."

"Not at all."

She could see he was lying. "I should think that a learned man such as yourself, a man who has studied logic and jurisprudence, could see the logic in my thinking."

"Mmmm," he said.

"Mind you I did not say that I am convinced a corpse does actually walk the grounds of Montmarsh. I am all too aware of what happens to a body after death, but I am convinced that three women as well as Lord Winningham have seen *something*, and it is my feeling that it all has something to do with the murder of Lord Dunsford as well as the murders of young George and young Quince."

"Quince?" Mr. Forsythe was alarmed.

"Murdered on the beach. It's gone too far. The first death was going too far."

"I couldn't agree more, but—"

"I bid you good night." When she was in her room, she dropped to the bed and leaned back on the headboard for a moment, trying to collect her thoughts.

She was still contemplating just how to begin her search for the ghost when her eyes were drawn to the window. The disembodied head of Edward Boswick, fifth earl of Dunsford, floated by outside.

16

❧❧❧

*Alexandra tried to scream, but there was no sound. Fear con-*stricted her throat and her heart flailed in her chest. Yet, her curiosity bade her get out of bed and go to the window. In spite of her resolve, terror roared in her ears as she moved, slowly, cautiously, toward the window. She reached out and touched the sheer curtain, pulling it back gingerly with the tips of her fingers, as if to touch it more firmly would some-how put her in contact with the unholy thing she had seen.

There was nothing outside the window now except the void of night wrapped in a film of fog. Pushing the window open with less timidity, she leaned forward into the darkness and turned her head right and left. And there, to the left, walking along a ledge and illuminated by light from what she knew to be Mr. Forsythe's window, she saw the form of a man who had undoubtedly supported the supposedly disembodied head. She recognized the unruly tuft of hair and the wide-set eyes she had seen only seconds before. He turned away from her with a frightened jerk and tottered on the ledge to regain his balance. It had been some trick of light and shadow coupled with the fog that had made the head seem disembodied as the man peered into her window.

She called to him as he moved with uncertainty along the ledge, his back, clad in the fashionable tweeds of a gentleman, pressed hard against the stone wall of the house.

"Who goes there?"

There was no answer, and he disappeared into the ether of night. Had he jumped? Of course, he had to have. There was no other plausible answer. If he had jumped from such a height, he would undoubtedly have either injured or killed himself. She closed the window and turned back into the room and lit a candle. With haste, she drew on a dressing gown over her nightdress and picked up her bag, along with the candle, and hurried out the door to the great staircase.

Her bedchamber and the window from which she had seen the figure were at the back of the house, and she didn't know whether to leave by the front entrance and skirt around the house and all its various wings and gardens, which would certainly be a considerable distance, or to try to find her way to a back exit.

Ultimately she decided on the latter, hoping to bump into a servant who could give her directions, but there were no servants to be found. Eventually, though, she found the kitchen and at last the back stairs. As she hurried down them, she spied a shadowy figure moving along, close to the massive walls of the house. Not wanting to alarm him, she didn't call out, but hurried across the garden, padding along soundlessly with her feet encased in soft slippers. The figure turned around just as she approached him and caught her quite by surprise. She raised the candle even with his face.

"Mr. Forsythe!"

He clasped her forearm for a moment and spoke in an excited whisper. "There's someone out here. I saw him walking along the ledge, and by God, it looked for all the world like Eddie. He was wearing those old tweeds that were his favorites."

The architecture of the house caught Alexandra's eye, and it took a moment for her to respond. She could just make out in the shadows that, from where the man appeared to have jumped, he could have, with sufficient agility, landed on a wing of the house, protruding at a right angle from the main house and at a lower elevation. And from there, she surmised, it was possible that he could have found his way to the ground without too much risk.

"I saw the figure, too," she said finally, "but I think he—"

Before Alexandra could finish her thought, they both heard a cough and saw the tweedy figure again, limping toward the stables. Both took pursuit. Alexandra, nursing the candle flame, moved cautiously and fell behind while Mr. Forsythe, who was more familiar with the landscape, raced ahead of her. She heard a thud, a groan, and then sounds of a struggle, more coughing, and, finally, Mr. Forsythe's voice.

"Who are you? Damn you, tell me who you are and why you're wearing the earl's clothes."

There was another thud, more struggling and groaning, and then a frightened voice. "Ach! What is it yer wantin' with me? I done nothin'. I swears it!" It was not the voice of the earl, and certainly not the voice of a ghost.

As Alexandra's eyes grew more accustomed to the darkness, she could distinguish the two forms. Mr. Forsythe seemed to be the larger of the two, and he was pulling the intruder to his feet.

"Now, you scoundrel, let's have a look at your face!" Mr. Forsythe had one of the man's arms twisted behind his back, and he forced his head back by grabbing the shaggy hair at the nape of his neck. Alexandra raised the candle and looked into the frightened eyes of someone who was scarcely old enough to be called a man and whose face had sprouted only the beginnings of a beard. The beard vied for space on his visage with the spots and pustules of adolescence. But his bone structure, high forehead, and wide eyes resembled the earl. Those similar features in the dim haze outside her window had led her to think it could have been the earl.

He coughed again.

"Who are you?" Mr. Forsythe said, giving him a shake. "Tell me or I'll have you thrown in prison, but not before I break your arm first." He gave the young man's arm another twist.

Alexandra had never seen that brutal side of Mr. Forsythe, but the young man apparently took him seriously. "Enough! Enough!" he said between groans. "My name is George. George Stirling, it is."

"George Stirling?" There was both surprise and suspicion in Alexandra's voice.

"You're lying!" Mr. Forsythe said at the same time, twisting his arm to what Alexandra feared would be the breaking point, but she heard no crack. His bones were young and strong.

Nevertheless, the young man groaned pitifully in pain. "No, I ain't lyin'. I swears. I'm George Stirling, and I ain't dead like you thought."

Mr. Forsythe relaxed his grip somewhat. "Why were you playing dead? And why were you sneaking around on that ledge like a thief? Because that's what you are, I wager."

George shook his shaggy head. "I ain't a thief no more. And I was looking in windows to see who was 'ere. I got business with one of 'em, I does. And as for playing at being a dead man, it was so as not to be one. There's them what want's me dead, there is."

Alexandra leaned closer. "Who wants you dead?"

"With all due respect, miss, I ain't fer tellin' ye. How do I know ye ain't one of 'em."

Mr. Forsythe gave him another shove. "Neither of us has any reason to see you dead, and if you are who you say you are, you'd better tell us everything you know if you want to save Elsie."

With that warning, George became agitated. "Elsie's all right, ain't she? Ye ain't harmed her, have ye?"

"She's all right now," Mr. Forsythe said, "but she'll hang soon unless we can help her. Start by telling us everything you know about Lord Dunsford's death."

"And why would I be tellin' you anything? I knows not who you are. The lady, I've seen around the village. They say she's a doctor like her daddy before her. But you, you're one o' them London dandies what befriends the likes of the earl, may his soul burn in hell! I don't trust the likes o' you." George spat the words out furiously.

"George," Alexandra said before Mr. Forsythe could issue any more of his threats. "Mr. Forsythe is a barrister who is trying to help Elsie, just as I am. And he speaks the truth when he says we need your help."

George was silent, weighing what she had said. In the flickering candlelight, Alexandra could see fear mingled with confusion, and she noticed that his cough had subsided. Finally he broke his silence.

He looked at Mr. Forsythe. "Yer going to speak for her in court? See that she's not hanged?"

"I cannot act as her attorney, since I've been called as a witness, but I shall do all I can to see that she doesn't hang," Mr. Forsythe said.

George eyed him suspiciously. "And how do I know you speak the truth?"

Alexandra spoke quickly. "I will vouch for him. He speaks the truth."

George's suspicious gaze turned to her, but it softened slightly. "Elsie trusted you. . . ." He turned back to Mr. Forsythe. "Unhand me, and I'll tell ye all I knows."

Mr. Forsythe tightened his grip again. "Do you take me for a fool? How do I know I can trust you not to flee as you did before?"

"And how does I know I can trust ye to keep your word to help Elsie? And for that matter, not to try to stick me with the bloody earl's murder?"

It was Mr. Forsythe's turn for a moment of silence. "Very well," he said at length. "I'll give you my word as a gentleman, and I'll take yours as fairly given. But mind you, if you try to escape, I'll have no mercy the next time I have you in hand." With that he dropped his grip on George. They stood there for a moment, looking at each other with suspicion until Alexandra spoke.

"All right, then. Now that you're both acting like civilized people, let's retire to the kitchen and you can give us your information, George."

George gave her a frightened look. "No, miss, I'll not walk into that house in plain sight."

"And why not?" Mr. Forsythe sounded as if he was beginning to lose patience.

"For fear I'll be kilt, that's why." George seemed to be trying to shrink into the darkness.

Mr. Forsythe took a step toward him. "You gave me your word—"

"Aye, and my word is good, but I'll not be going into that house unless it be into the cellars."

"The cellars?" Mr. Forsythe was sounding perturbed again.

"That's where I stays now, unless I has business with Quince, or I has to talk some sense into Elsie, or other business to save me own neck."

"If you're afraid of something here, why stay?" Mr. Forsythe asked.

The expression on George's face seemed to suggest he hadn't considered that before. "Well . . . I been safe so far, ain't I? What with all the dandies gone." He looked down at his hands. "Anyway, I knows no other place, does I? Or how to get there if I did know. And with Elsie close to help me . . ."

"Elsie thinks you're a ghost, you know." This from Alexandra.

"Pshaw!" George said. "She knows now I'm flesh and blood, same as you. She was just trying to protect me, she was, although it's true she thought me dead at first."

"Damn! What are you talking about, man?" Mr. Forsythe looked as if he might be ready to grab George again.

George took a step forward and gestured for the two of them to follow. "Come along to the cellars, and I'll tell ye all I can, if 'twill help my Elsie."

He led them across the back garden to an outside entrance to the cellar, and then down the steps into the dank environs of the underground room. By the time they were all three inside, Alexandra's candle had grown short of wick and begun to sputter. She feared they would soon be shrouded in darkness, and the prospect left her edgy. In spite of the fact that she was more willing than Mr. Forsythe to give George the benefit of the doubt, she was not so foolish that she didn't consider that he could have been lying about his innocence as well as what he might do in a darkened dungeon, if he had a mind to.

She needn't have worried, at least for the moment, however. As soon as George saw the candle sputter, he reached up to a dusty shelf and retrieved a fresh candle, which he lit with the dying flame from the one Alexandra held. He then gestured toward a rickety chair for Alexandra, then perched himself on top of a barrel of salted pork. Mr. Forsythe found his own seat on the lid of a large trunk.

"All right, boy, now tell us what you know of the death of the earl of Dunsford." Mr. Forsythe was using his intimidating barrister's voice.

"I knows not who done it." He sounded as if he'd dealt with barristers and the courts before and was reluctant to say too much.

Mr. Forsythe stared at him in silence, a stern expression on his face. Alexandra was tempted to speak up and ask George simply to begin at the beginning and tell them how it came to be that everyone thought him dead. She thought better of it, however. After all, this was Mr. Forsythe's game, just as medicine was hers, and he was not likely to appreciate her interference any more than she would appreciate his trying to tell her how to remove a diseased limb.

Eventually Mr. Forsythe cleared his throat and shifted around a bit on the trunk. "Very well, George, perhaps then you can explain to us in more detail the circumstances of your supposed death and why Elsie perpetrated that scene in Lord Dunsford's dining room accusing him of killing you, if, as you say, she knew you were alive all along."

Alexandra smiled ever so slightly. Perhaps Mr. Forsythe was better at this than she thought. She turned to George and saw him shaking his head.

"Oh no, ye got it wrong now, sir. At that time Elsie thought I was kilt, and she thought it was the earl what done it."

Mr. Forsythe leaned forward. "But it wasn't the earl?"

"Oh no, sir. 'Twas somebody else what kilt me."

"And who might that be?"

Alexandra saw George's shoulders stiffen and his eyes dart nervously. "I . . . I never got a good look at 'im, sir." His agitation had brought the cough back, probably a symptom of consumption. It was most likely in the early stages, since he showed no signs of emaciation. It must have been the cough Mrs. Pickwick had mistaken as Earl Dunsford's habitual cough.

Mr. Forsythe was silent, and Alexandra suspected he was thinking the same thing she thought. The boy was lying because he was still afraid for his life. And, it appeared, not willing to take the risk even to save Elsie.

"Very well," Mr. Forsythe said at length, "why did Elsie think the earl had killed you?"

"Quince told 'er, but don't be askin' me why he thought that. I ain't fer knowin'."

Again, Alexandra felt he was lying. Perhaps Mr. Forsythe did as well, but he moved on to another question. "Exactly how did this unknown person attempt to kill you?"

"Strangled me. Left me for dead, 'e did." He pulled down his collar to reveal a dirty rag encircling his neck, apparently hiding a wound. "Strangled me same as 'e done the earl, but 'e never came back to finish me off with the knife as 'e did the bloody earl."

Mr. Forsythe nodded and leaned back against the wall as he glanced at Alexandra and then back to George. "And just how did you know the earl was both strangled and cut with a knife?"

"Why ain't that what the doctor lady said? That 'e was both strangled and stabbed?"

"Indeed it is," Mr. Forsythe said. "But, pray tell me how you knew she said this."

George seemed to consider for a moment whether or not he wanted to answer the question. Finally, he said, "There was some what was talking about it in the kitchen."

"The servants, you mean?" Mr. Forsythe said.

George nodded.

"And did they know you were listening?"

"Oh no, sir. I thought it best that none knew I was around. Especially since the murderin' bastard was in the . . ."

Mr. Forsythe exchanged another quick glance with Alexandra, then leaned toward George again with even more intensity. "Go on, George. You were about to say the murdering bastard was in what?"

George shook his head and dropped his eyes. "I don't know, sir. I was just scairt, that's all."

"If you don't tell me everything, how do you expect me to help you or Elsie?" Mr. Forsythe again spoke in his intimidating barrister's voice.

George raised his eyes to Mr. Forsythe again. "Expects you to 'elp me?" His tone was once again defiant. "I expects nothing from the likes of you, sir."

Once more the boy's eyes darted nervously, as if he was looking for a quick way to escape. Alexandra suspected then that the rapport Mr. Forsythe had developed with George was gone. She suspected, too, that Mr. Forsythe realized it as well, as he appeared to make a conscious effort to speak in a softer timbre. "But you said you wanted to help Elsie, George. You must tell me everything you know about—"

George was seized by a fit of coughing, and it was several seconds before he could speak. "I knows nothing," he said, choking. He stood and, still coughing, made a quick move toward the door.

"Wait!" At the urgent sound of Alexandra's voice, the boy hesitated and turned around. "Before you go, you must let me have a look at your neck." She moved toward him with what she hoped was authority, yet without enough aggression to frighten him even more.

George's hand went to his throat, and he seemed confused, as if undecided whether to flee or to allow her to examine what was obviously a painful wound.

"This will only take a minute." Alexandra now spoke in a low, soothing voice, and she reached her hand toward the dirty rag around his neck and untied it. The wound was several days old and not healing properly. It had become infected as well. "You must first let me clean it," she said, leading him to the chair. With a gentle push, she forced him to sit again and spoke over her shoulder to Mr. Forsythe. "Bring me a basin and some hot water from the kettle on the stove upstairs, as well as another basin of cold water. Then look around until you find some clean linen. A napkin or a dishcloth will do as long as it's clean. I shall need two of them."

She heard, rather than saw, Mr. Forsythe moving toward the exit to do her bidding while she looked at the angry red-and-blue mark on George's neck. She was holding his head back, gently, with her left hand. There was still some bruising and broken blood vessels on his neck, and in one place the skin had been broken. That was where the infection had set in.

She called out to Mr. Forsythe, who was on his way up the stairs. "Bring a bit of soap along with the water, please, if it's about." Her eyes were still on George, and she had the feeling that if she turned around, he would escape.

"How long have you had the cough?" she asked.

He shrugged. "A goodly while, I reckon."

"Any pain in your chest?"

"Not much. Just a bit of pleurisy now and then."

"And blood flecks when you cough? Shortness of breath?"

His eyes widened, and he shook his head and turned away from her. Alexandra suspected that he did, indeed, have the symptoms she had named, but denial eased his fears.

Within a few minutes more, Mr. Forsythe returned with a basin of water in each hand and the cloths across his arm. He placed everything on the trunk on which he'd been sitting. He seemed agitated. "George," he said, "perhaps you could just tell me—"

"Not now!" There was a quiet, but sharp tone to Alexandra's voice. She tested the water in one of the basins with a finger, then, seeing it was not so hot as to be scalding, picked up one of the cloths and fished the soap out of the water to bathe the wound while Mr. Forsythe stepped aside. "You must keep this clean," she said, speaking to George as she worked. "It will help rid the area of infection." She saw George's eyes widen in what she interpreted to be fear. "The infection is not severe," she said, still keeping her voice low and soothing, "but it can become severe if proper

care is not taken." She wiped away a spot of pus and spoke
to Mr. Forsythe again, still without looking at him. "Find
me a bit of yeast, please. It will likely be upstairs in the
larder."

"A bit of . . . ?"

"Yeast," she repeated, and this time turned to look at him.
She saw the puzzled look on his face. Although he must
surely have heard of the substance, it was clear he had no
idea what it looked like. It was possible that a man of his
station might not even know what a larder was. "It's of a
soft texture, yet solid. Gray in color, and it will have a rather
exaggerated odor of fresh bread." She pointed above them.
"It will most likely be on a shelf in that small room up
there, just off the kitchen, the larder, where the other food-
stuff is kept."

Mr. Forsythe moved toward the exit again, and Alexandra
turned her attention back to George. "I shall mix a concoc-
tion of the yeast with some of the sweet oil I have in my
bag, and you must drink a tablespoon of the mixture several
times a day. You should also have a poultice of elm and
lobelia about your neck. If you will be so kind as to come
by my surgery early on the morrow, I will prepare it for
you. I will also give you a tonic for your cough." She was
now dipping the cloth in cold water and holding it to his
neck. George winced every time she touched the wound.

"There was a great deal of pressure applied to your neck,
was there not?"

George nodded in response to her question.

"Enough, I would venture, that you found it impossible
to breathe and you lost consciousness."

Again George nodded, and she sensed that he was relaxing at least to a small degree.

"Well, then I can certainly understand why, if Elsie saw
you that way, she thought you dead."

"Aye, they all did. Even Quince, and he's not an easy
one to fool, I'll tell you that. As for Elsie, they tell me the
poor girl was near out of her mind with grief for me. Loves
me, that one does."

Alexandra saw Mr. Forsythe stick his head back into the

cellar, as if to hear better. "You're very fortunate to have someone like Elsie love you." She moved one hand behind her back and surreptitiously waved Mr. Forsythe away, then handed George the cloth dampened in cool water. "If you'll just hold that to your throat when you need it for comfort. But mind you, don't keep it there if it begins to irritate."

"Thank ye, my lady."

"Dr. Gladstone will do. I have no title."

"Aye, Dr. Gladstone."

"Have you eaten, George?" She was suspicious that his diet, in general, was lacking, which was often the case with consumption. The malnourished condition seemed to encourage tubercles of the lungs.

"It's been some time, now that you mention it," George said.

"I'm surprised you found anything to eat at all." She removed the cool cloth and inspected the wound again.

"It weren't so hard a task to find a few scraps after the house was asleep," George said. "If Elsie hadn't got thrown in chokey, she could 'ave 'elped me."

Alexandra gave him a surprised look. "Elsie?"

"Aye, I had to tell her the truth, didn't I? Couldn't 'ave her goin' on with her grievin', could I? I told 'er that night after she threatened all them nobs with a knife." He laughed. "Lor', but I wish I coulda seen 'er. 'Twas the next mornin' before dawn she run away because the bloody killer put the knife next to 'er bed to make it look like she done it. Tried to bury it, she did, but that bastard Jamie saw 'er and grassed on 'er."

Alexandra said nothing as she replaced the cloth and went about placing her supplies back into her bag. Her silence seemed to bother George.

"Now don't go blaming 'er for lying to you when she told you she seen me ghost. 'Twas me what told 'er to lie. It was best none knew I wasn't kilt. She was scairt at first, after you talked to her, then she said she was wrong to mistrust you. 'Set up that meeting wif Quince and the lady doctor,' she says to me. 'They's both got brains, though I never liked 'im' she says. Quince was a smart 'un all right.

Could read and write, 'e could. Wrote that note to ye hisself. Even taught some o' them young boys the readin' and writin'. Never got around to learnin' meself, though."

Alexandra continued to arrange the supplies in her bag, hoping George would keep talking now that he was more relaxed.

"I could do with a bit of cream, you know. I ain't et so regular today, since . . ." George's voice trailed off as if he was afraid he would say too much, but all the while he was glancing toward the pails of milk which had been set in the cellar to cool.

"I'm afraid the cream's not risen yet," Alexandra said, glancing at the milk. "Fresh milk will have to do." She found a dipper next to the pails, scooped it full of milk, and handed it to George. "You put a great deal of trust in your Elsie, don't you?" she said.

George swallowed and nodded. "Aye, she's a good 'un, that one is, and I was sorry to give 'er such a fright when she seen me after me resurrection. But I knew not what else to do but come 'ere for 'er 'elp. It was she what found me these duds when me own was soiled with me own vomit from the strangling. Little did I know, though, that I was jumping from the kettle to the fire by comin' 'ere. But how was I to know, since I knows not the ways of the dandies?" He looked down at his hands. "If Elsie was 'ere, she'd 'elp me. But now that she's in chokey I knows not what to do." His voice broke and he wiped his hand across his eyes in a quick movement.

Alexandra did her best to keep her voice even. "You are very frightened, of course, because it's dangerous here for you."

George nodded, but said nothing more. He kept his eyes focused straight ahead.

"As dangerous as it was for the earl. The person who killed him is here." Alexandra's voice was almost a whisper.

George nodded again, still looking away.

"And you want to help Elsie."

George's eyes darted to her face, and he stared at her, frightened. "I . . . I want to 'elp 'er, sure, but . . ."

"Then tell me who—"

Before she could say more, George stood and bolted up the stairs and outside. Alexandra tried to follow him, but he was too quick for her. By the time she reached the exit, he had disappeared into the darkness. She turned her head, searching in all directions, but all she saw was Mr. Forsythe emerging from the kitchen. He had a small jar in his hand, which he offered to her. "I hope this is yeast."

Alexandra took the jar absently. "I frightened him away," she said.

"You . . ." Mr. Forsythe turned his head in all directions, peering into the darkness.

"I'm sorry." She turned back to the cellar to fetch her bag.

"Did you learn any more?" he asked, hurrying after her.

"Only that he believes his would-be killer also killed the earl. And he confirmed the killer is here, but he didn't know that when he came here for Elsie to help him. It seems he only recently found out, and now he doesn't know what to do. He's afraid to leave for fear he'll be followed and afraid to stay for fear he'll be found. He wants to help Elsie, but he fears that, too. It seems, though, his instinct for survival is stronger than his love for the girl."

"If the poor cowardly bastard's too frightened to leave, then we'll find him."

"I'm not so sure," Alexandra said. "He's not terribly bright about figuring out what to do, but he could be on his way away from here now, under the cover of darkness, unless . . ."

"Unless what?"

"Unless he decides to kill the murderer first."

Alarm marked Mr. Forsythe's face. "But isn't he too cowardly to attempt anything like that?"

"I'm not sure. Under the right circumstances, I think he would kill to save his own life. I think he's afraid the murderer will track him down."

"My God, if that's true, then we've got to stop him." He paced back and forth in the small open area of the cellar. "We do know it is someone here in this house he's after."

"And it's one of the guests, I'd say."

Mr. Forsythe stopped his pacing and looked at her. "How can you be sure?"

"I'm not absolutely sure, of course, but remember, I said he didn't know the killer was here at first. What was it he said? He didn't know he was jumping from the kettle to the fire by coming here? Since the servants are here all the time, and he knew that, it must mean it wasn't one of them who attacked him. He would have been too afraid to come here if he knew that beforehand."

Mr. Forsythe pondered it. "You may be right," he said, "but we still don't know why he was attacked in the first place."

"Perhaps I know someone who does know why," Alexandra said.

"Who?" Mr. Forsythe asked.

"Quince's boys. Alexandra picked up her bag. "And I must talk to them as soon as possible."

Mr. Forsythe stood, as if to stop her. "Not tonight, Dr. Gladstone. It's dangerous, and anyway, you don't know where to look. If those boys think they're in danger, they won't go back to their usual place at the docks, knowing the killer would know how to find them there."

Alexandra sat down, feeling defeated. Mr. Forsythe reached to touch her hand.

"You're tired, my dear. You must rest. I suggest you retire to your bedchamber."

She shook her head. "I should not be able to rest for worrying about that poor girl. And for worrying about George killing someone."

"I'll search for him, of course, but you must go back to your room. Our best hope is that he's too cowardly to follow through and that even if he weren't, he doesn't have wits enough to get in by picking a lock. And as for Elsie, we'll do the best we can for her tomorrow. We'll just have to do it from the witness stand."

Alexandra raised her eyes to look at him. She had no doubt that he would do his best, and she had no doubt that his best was exceedingly competent, but she also knew that circumstances weighed heavily against Elsie O'Riley simply by virtue of the fact that the man she was accused of killing was an aristocrat, and she a mere scullery maid. She saw in Mr. Forsythe's eyes that he was thinking the same thing. Elsie O'Riley would surely hang.

17

In spite of Mr. Forsythe's insisting that she not do it, Alexandra joined him in searching the stables, the grounds, and as much of the house as possible for George. Although Mr. Forsythe agreed with Alexandra that he still was most likely somewhere on Montmarsh property, he conceded, along with her, that George had eluded them, and they would be better off trying to gain a few hours of sleep and continue the search in the morning.

Before Alexandra retired to her assigned bedchamber, however, she tried to look in on Mrs. Pickwick again. However, she found that she was unable. Mrs. Pickwick had locked her room, just as she had been instructed.

Taking some comfort in that, Alexandra returned to her own room and locked the door, but she slept very little. There was a killer sleeping somewhere under the same roof. Would he or she kill again? Would George kill first? Had all the guests and servants locked their doors as they had been warned to do? Would George not have wits enough to find a way past the locked doors, as Mr. Forsythe had suggested?

She was up very early the next morning, out of bed and

dressed even before the servants were about. Once again she looked around for George, but found him nowhere. When she went to search the stables, she saw that, in fact, she was not the only one awake. Jamie, the stable boy, was up. In fact, he looked as if he had not been asleep.

"Are you not feeling well, Jamie?" Alexandra asked.

"Today's the day, ain't it?" he said. "The day for Elsie's trial. He looked as if he might cry. "She'll hang, won't she?"

Alexandra reached to touch his arm. "There's a very good chance of that, yes."

"I never meant to grass to that copper about Elsie. I had to tell him I saw her bury that knife, didn't I? But I never meant—"

"You told the truth, Jamie. No one can blame you for that."

A tear escaped. "But now she's going to hang."

"If she hangs, Jamie, it's not your fault. You must remember that."

He nodded, sniffed back his tears and ducked his head. Presently, he spoke. "Shall I saddle your mare, Doctor?"

"Not yet, thank you." Alexandra knew she could not leave until she assured herself that everyone in the household was accounted for. She lingered over breakfast in the dining room until Lord Winningham showed up. He seemed distracted and nervous, but at least he had not been murdered in his sleep. Mr. Forsythe was next. She could see in his eyes the same concern she felt, and they were both relieved when the Atewaters came down together. Apparently they had been quarreling. Isabel was pouting and distant, while her husband save for a warm greeting to Alexandra, was cool to everyone.

Alexandra left soon after breakfast. When she arrived home, she found Nancy waiting for her in the parlor. A pot of tea, steaming, sat on a table next to her. Before she could say good morning, she was met with an onslaught from Nancy.

"I hardly slept at all last night, but what else could a body expect with you out of the house and a murderer running about." Her lack of rest was evident in the mud-colored circles under her eyes.

"Well, I'm perfectly safe," Alexandra said, hanging up her own coat. By this time Zack had rushed to her side, nudging her with his nose while he danced with the joy of seeing her again. She stooped to hug him and to rub his back.

Nancy, meanwhile, was looking at her as if she wasn't certain she could believe her. She picked up the teapot to pour two cups. "And how was Mrs. Pickwick?" With her suspicious tone.

"Very well," she said, in spite of the fact that she had no idea of her present condition. So kind of you to ask." Alexandra moved to the tea table, Zack sticking close to her side.

Nancy dropped two lumps of sugar and a drop of cream in Alexandra's cup and four lumps, along with a generous splash of cream, in her own. "And why wouldn't she be well?" She stirred her tea with quick, forceful strokes, as if it were the tea she was peeved with and not Alexandra. "She's strong as an ox, and, I dare say, in no need of a doctor watching over her the whole night long." She tapped her spoon on the cup with enough force to cause Alexandra to wince.

"Of course, Nancy. You're right." Alexandra sat down and reached for her own cup, which she stirred slowly. Zack lay down at her feet.

Nancy glanced up at her with a surprised look on her face. "Did I hear you say I'm right?"

"Certainly. You know as well as I that was just an excuse. I really only went for a romantic liaison with Mr. Forsythe, who is back at Montmarsh for the trial."

Another surprised look from Nancy before she set her cup and saucer on the table with a little too much vigor. Then, in spite of her attempts to stay angry, she laughed. "Oh, that it *would* be the reason!"

Alexandra smiled and took a sip of her tea, savoring both its sweetness and its warmth.

"But," said Nancy, trying hard to regain her scolding demeanor, "enough of your teasing, miss. It wasn't a lover you were after, I'm thinking, but a killer. And it's not be-fitting. If your father were alive—"

"But he isn't alive, Nancy, and I'm now, as you have so often reminded me, a woman of a certain age. Of an age, I should say, in which I am capable of making my own de-cisions and taking my own risks. And furthermore, I suspect the real reason you're angry is because you couldn't go searching for this murderer yourself."

Nancy stood and, in a huff, gathered up the tea dishes. "I've got better sense, I have. And besides, I have no in-terest in such gory matters." With that, she walked to the kitchen.

Alexandra sighed and shook her head at Nancy's haughty manner, but she couldn't scold her. She could only smile, knowing Nancy's reaction was only because she had spoken the truth. She couldn't resist, however, one last jab. She called out to Nancy's back.

"You didn't ask whether or not I found the murderer."

Nancy stopped, but did not turn around.

"Unfortunately I didn't, but I did see the ghost."

The dishes Nancy had in her hands rattled dangerously as she spun around. "You saw . . ."

"Yes, I saw the ghost. One of the supposed murder vic-tims. A living corpse, if you will."

"There you go with your teasing again!" She was doing her best to look stern, but her face had gone white.

"Of course, you're right," Alexandra said, standing to take the cups and saucers from her. "It's not a matter to be flippant about." She spoke with her back to Nancy as she started for the kitchen.

Nancy hurried after her. "Then you must tell me—"

"The so-called ghost was young George Stirling, who is no corpse at all, but a living body." Alexandra put the cups and saucers in the basin Nancy kept for washing dishes, then sat down at the large wooden table in the center of the room. Nancy sat down across from her.

"You're speaking of the young George who was killed by some of his fellow ruffians down at the waterfront?"

Alexandra nodded. "The same. Only, he wasn't killed, although he most certainly was left for dead. And I don't believe the attempt at murdering him was done by any of his fellow ruffians."

"Then who?"

"I don't know, except that young George seemed to think it was the same person who killed the earl, and therefore it had to be someone at Montmarsh, either a guest or a servant."

"Elsie O'Riley?"

"No, not Elsie. George was her lover; she wouldn't attempt to kill him. And the earl died of strangulation and was stabbed as an afterthought to make it look as if Elsie was guilty. George's would-be killer also tried to strangle him and botched the attempt. Elsie is not strong enough to have strangled either of them. And probably not strong enough to have driven the knife that deeply into the earl's chest."

"But Artie and Rob know who the killer is, and they're afraid of him," Nancy said.

"Remember, it could be a woman."

Nancy gave her a skeptical look. "A woman strong enough to strangle a man?"

"It's possible. But she would have to be bigger than Elsie."

A pensive expression replaced Nancy's skeptical look. "Someone big and strapping and used to hard work, such as, say, Mrs. Pickwick?"

"Or someone trim but fit, such as Madam Atewater."

Nancy's eyes widened. "Madam Atewater? The gentleman you were entertaining has a wife?"

"Nancy, how many times must I tell you . . . Oh, never mind." She stood, feeling restless. "I've got to concentrate on finding the killer before George does and before Elsie O'Riley is hanged for something she didn't do."

"How are you going to do that? If I may be so bold to ask."

"I could start by finding George again, or by finding Artie and Rob. They know who the killer is."

"But they've sense enough to hide from her—or him—and you're not likely to find them."

Alexandra sighed. "Perhaps you're right. Perhaps it's best to leave it to the constable and the courts, while I attend to my own business of seeing to the infirm. I'd best be off to make my rounds." She walked away, headed for the surgery to fill her bag with supplies.

Nancy called out to her back. "If you think you're going to trick me into thinking you're going to drop the matter, then you take me for more of a fool than I am."

Alexandra tried to ignore her. Within a few moments, she was out the door, mounted on Lucy, and, with Zack trotting beside her, on her way to her rounds.

It took less time than usual, since almost no one was at home. They had left early for the tavern, which was traditionally set up as a courtroom when the assizes met.

The light schedule gave her time to take Lucy and Zack home before she walked down to the piers in search of Artie and Rob. She had to endure the glaring looks and rude remarks of several unsavory-looking men, but she continued to ask of the boys' whereabouts. No one admitted even to knowing the boys, and she was about to abandon her search when she saw Old Beaty standing in the shadow of a rotting ship's hull.

She was certain he had seen her as well, but when she walked toward him, he turned and walked away. She called his name, but he pretended not to hear her. His strange behavior piqued her curiosity, and she followed him a short distance until he disappeared around the corner of an abandoned warehouse. She followed again, but as she rounded the corner, he was nowhere to be found. She was about to give up when she heard his voice.

"Aye, Dr. Gladstone, 'tis me, John Beaty." He stepped out from behind a jumble of fallen bricks and other debris from the abandoned building. It was then she realized he had obviously walked away from her in order to make sure no one else was near. "You're searching for someone, I takes it." His voice was little more than a whisper.

"Indeed I am, for two boys, Artie and Rob, they're called. Do you know them, by chance?"

"I knows them not, my lady, but you best call off yer search for 'em, whoever they be." Old Beaty, still whispering, kept looking around, as if he feared someone was listening.

"You do know something. Otherwise, why would you be warning me to—"

"Me rheumatism is much worse today, Dr. Gladstone, and I was just on me way to yer surgery for a bit more of yer wonderful tonic. Perhaps ye could help me along." He hobbled toward her, exaggerating his limp.

"Why, of course, Mr. Beaty." She took his arm and led him toward her house. For the price of a glass of whisky, she could have the benefit of whatever it was the old fox knew.

When they reached the house, Nancy did not greet them at the door. When Alexandra called to her, there was no answer, and a quick glance into the garden told her she was not there. She had, no doubt, walked the short distance to the market district to purchase something.

Alexandra led Old Beaty into her surgery and helped him sit in one of the chairs, then she reached for the medicinal whisky she kept on the top shelf of her cabinet and poured some in a glass for him.

"Now," she said, handing it to him. "Tell me what you know of Artie and Rob?"

Old Beaty took a swallow of the whisky, let out a long sigh, and wiped his mouth with his sleeve. "I told ye the truth. I knows them not." He took another long swallow of the amber liquid, draining the glass, and extending it to her. "A wee bit more, perhaps."

"Mr. Beaty, I'm afraid I—"

"I knows them not, but I knows they are among the young band of thieves headed by that boy, Quince, may God rest his soul." He raised an eyebrow as if to ask if that tidbit and the promise of more was not worth another glass of whisky.

Alexandra reached for the bottle again. Old Beaty extended his hand for the glass to be filled, but Alexandra held back. He glanced at her.

"Perhaps there is more you can tell me," she said.

He hesitated a moment, then shook his head. "Aye, yer a cruel woman, ye are." He sighed again. "All right, I tell ye the truth. I knows not the boys, and I knows not any of their names, but they is more than petty thieves, I'll tell ye that. Word is among me old mates there at the docks they works for one of the nobs that has connections here through the late earl, may God rest his soul. The nob sets it up for 'em by telling 'em who has the jewels and such and where it is, or sometimes when one of the rich dandies or his lady will be on the coach to or from London. The boys does the stealin' and gives the nob a cut of the profit." Old Beaty looked longingly at the whisky.

"Who is this so-called nob you're talking about?"

Old Beaty kept his eyes on the whisky, but Alexandra still didn't offer it to him. Finally he glanced at Alexandra and shook his head. "I knows not, but the talk is, the earl was in on it, too, and something went bad that got him killed."

Alexandra handed him the glass, which he once again grabbed eagerly and drank deeply. Old Beaty seemed certain the killer was one of the guests, nobs, as he called them, which was what George had led her to believe. But did that mean she could trust that Old Beaty really was telling the truth and telling her everything he knew? She wasn't sure.

She glanced at him as he took another swallow of the whisky. "What did you mean when you told me once that if I found the corpse I'd find the killer?"

Old Beaty held the empty whisky glass in both his hands and rolled it between his palms, looking down at his knees. "I'd heared all that talk about the jewel thief ring, and I'd heared one o' the boys was kilt, but I never believed it. I thought 'e was maybe injured and fearful, so 'e was hiding."

"Why didn't you believe he was dead?"

Old Beaty raised his head to look at her. "Why, if 'e'd been dead, Quince would have buried 'im. Quince may have been a thief, but 'e was a good Christian boy, 'e was. 'E'd

see his boys got buried proper. No, Quince sends 'im off
to hide, if you ask me. Wanted 'im to leave the town, I'd
wager, but the way it looks, the poor bloke was lovesick
for yer Elsie, so 'e stayed around to be with 'er."

Alexandra was silent a moment, trying to sort it out in
her mind. When she spoke, it was in a careful, thoughtful
tone of voice. "So both Quince and George knew something
they weren't supposed to know, and whatever it was got
Quince killed and almost the same for George."

Old Beaty nodded. " 'Tis the way I sees it."

There was no more from Old Beaty. He only continued
to shake his head and roll the glass between his palms.

Alexandra stood and placed the whisky back on the top
shelf in the cupboard. She was feeling a bit guilty about
using it to ply answers from Old Beaty. It appeared he was
becoming addicted to it, and if she fostered the addiction
she was breaking her oath to do no harm. She would have
to deal with her guilt another time, though. For now, she
had a murderer to find.

She turned to her guest. "Thank you, Mr. Beaty. You've
been most helpful."

He looked a bit crestfallen when he saw there was to be
no more whisky, but he managed a gracious response. "Glad
to be of 'elp, Doctor." He hobbled toward the door. "Ye'll
be coming 'round with more of ye wonderful tonic, won't
ye?"

Alexandra gave him a gentle pat on the shoulder. "Of
course I will, but I'm thinking of a small change in the
prescription."

He gave her a worried look and bade her good-bye. When
he was gone, Alexandra paced the floor for a time, still
trying to sort all the facts in her mind. She tried to relive
the events of the night Lord Dunsford was killed and of the
next morning when she examined the body. While there was
reason to suspect several of the guests, nothing came to her
except the fact that she had to try once again to find George.

She had to saddle Lucy herself for the four-mile ride to
Montmarsh, since Freddie, as usual, had wandered off.
When she reached the estate, no one answered her knock.

Obviously all the guests and several of the servants had been called as witnesses, and the rest, with no master around to stop them, were attending the trial. The front door was locked, but she did manage to find a door at the back that had been carelessly left open.

The door gave access to the servants' quarters, which, like the rest of the house, appeared empty. She searched each of the rooms, though, and then let herself into the kitchen, which was as silent as a tomb. If the guests expected to be served a luncheon on this day, they would be disappointed. If the heir to Montmarsh didn't show up soon, the house would be in chaos.

She searched the attic and down in the cellar, but all in vain. She went back into the house to search more rooms, calling out George's name, but her voice echoed eerily down empty halls.

The house was enormous, and she knew she could never search every room in the short time she had before her duty as a witness bade her leave. And even if every room was searched, George could easily be in one wing of the house while she was in another.

At least, she had to try the rooms on the wing where the guests had stayed the night of the murder. The door to the first room was left slightly ajar, and when she slowly pushed it open, the hinges squealed, sending shivers through her body. Cautiously, she stepped inside. The room had obviously been Lord Winningham's. She recognized the coat that was now flung carelessly on a chair as the one he had worn the night before.

"George," she called softly. "George. Are you here?"

She was answered only with silence. She made a quick search of the room and then left, leaving the door partially opened, as she had found it. Her search of all of the other rooms proved to be equally futile, and she had only one more on the wing to search, the room in which the earl had died.

That chamber, like the others, was uninhabited, and the bed in which the earl had died had been cleaned and neatly made, so that it now looked as benign as any other room.

In spite of that, she could not help but see, in her mind's
eye, the gory sight of his sheets and his natty silk nightshirt
turned dark in one spot with his blood.

She turned away to leave, but turned back again with the
unexplainable feeling that she was missing something. But
what? She had no time to ponder it, because she had to get
to the trial in time to testify.

She rode Lucy to the Blue Ram, now set up as a courtroom. In spite of the fact that the windows were open, the
room was hot, and, as she had suspected, it was packed with
observers, whose perspiring bodies contributed to both the
rank odor and the sensation that the air was liquid. Among
the observers sitting on one of the benches was Nancy,
damp curls plastered against her glowing face where they
had escaped her bonnet. She also saw the Atewaters and
Lord Winningham along with Mrs. Pickwick and Mr. Forsythe, all of whom would testify, if they hadn't already.

Elsie sat alone at a table near the front looking pale and
frightened and very young. Alexandra took a seat on one
of the tavern chairs next to Nancy.

Nancy leaned close and whispered, "I'm surprised it took
you so long since all your patients are here at the trial."

Alexandra responded with a benign smile and then whispered. "I thought you told me you have no interest in such
gory matters."

Nancy stiffened and refused to look at her. She kept her
eyes on the prosecuting attorney, who had just sworn in Mr.
Forsythe.

The prosecutor's robe billowed over his portly frame,
giving him the look of an enormous bewigged ball rolling
toward the witness box. When he spoke—"State your name,
please"—his voice had a deep, hollow sound, thunder coming through a tunnel.

"Nicholas Andrew William Forsythe." Alexandra could
see the worried expression on Mr. Forsythe's face even
from so far away. That must mean things were not going
well for Elsie.

"Were you a guest at the country house of Lord Edward
Boswick, fifth earl of Dunsford, on the night of August

sixth?" The prosecutor raised his eyes to look at the ceiling as he spoke.

"Yes," Mr. Forsythe said.

"Who were the other guests present?" The prosecutor was still looking at the ceiling with a bored expression on his face.

A sound, something like a growl, escaped the throat of the judge. "Mr. Crudgington, I think by now the court knows who was at the dinner. You've asked the same question of every single witness so far."

The prosecutor dropped his eyes and his head to look at the justice. "Excuse me, my lord, I was merely trying to establish that all of the witnesses were indeed present at the dinner."

The judge picked up a handkerchief and patted his glistening face with it. "I think you've established that, Mr. Crudgington. Just get on with the business at hand."

The prosecutor seemed to puff himself up even more to hide his chagrin. "Very well. Mr. Forsythe, describe the events of the evening of Lord Dunsford's death."

The judge mopped the back of his neck under his periwig and leaned toward the witness box. "Did you observe the defendant enter the dining hall, Mr. Forsythe?"

"I did, my lord."

"Then begin with that."

Mr. Forsythe obliged by describing how Elsie came rushing into the dining hall brandishing a knife and threatening Lord Dunsford for killing her Georgie.

The prosecutor glanced at the jury, which, Alexandra noticed, was comprised mostly of local merchants. Among them was Dave Stillwell, the butcher, who, Alexandra remembered, was already convinced of Elsie's guilt long before the trial, by virtue of her being Irish.

"Do you see the young woman who made those threats in the courtroom?" the prosecutor asked.

"I do."

"Will you point to her, please."

Mr. Forsythe hesitated a moment, and Alexandra saw his jaw tense before he pointed to Elsie.

A look of satisfaction spread across the broad expanse of the prosecutor's face. "When was the last time you saw Lord Dunsford alive?"

"It was quite late," Mr. Forsythe said. "The two of us lingered in the library after all the other guests had gone to bed. Then, after we'd finished our brandy, we said good night at the top of the stairs, and Lord Dunsford went one way to his bedchamber, and I the other."

"And when did you realize he was dead?" the prosecutor asked.

"Not until the next morning. I left the house rather early for a ride in the morning air, and when I came back, I discovered his body in his room."

Mr. Forsythe was asked next to describe what he saw.

"It was a grisly scene. The earl's head thrown back and twisted slightly to the side, mouth agape, eyes bulging, a bit of blood making a dark stain on Lord Dunsford's night-shirt . . ."

"A bit of blood?" the judge asked.

"It was difficult to tell how much at first, my lord, since Lord Dunsford was wearing a red silk nightshirt. But there was a slightly darker stain on it, and Dr. Gladstone said—"

"Dr. Gladstone will have her own opportunity to testify, Mr. Forsythe," the judge said. "Please, just describe what you saw."

Mr. Forsythe continued to described the scene just as Alexandra remembered it.

"I must confess I did not notice the mark on Lord Dunsford's neck until Dr. Gladstone pointed it out," Mr. Forsythe said.

"You were not asked to describe things you did not notice." It was the prosecutor who spoke this time, and who was literally looking down his nose at Mr. Forsythe. "And you needn't speculate on anything Dr. Gladstone saw, as the judge has instructed you, and as, being a barrister, I'm sure you already knew."

Once again the judge leaned toward Mr. Forsythe in the witness box. "You were apparently the only one of the guests to see the body before the constable and the doctor arrived."

"Yes, my lord, I believe that is what they claim."

"Proceed," the prosecutor said.

"None of the other guests had emerged from their bed-chambers when I returned from my ride," Mr. Forsythe said, "and when I started upstairs to my room to change out of my riding clothes, I saw Eddie's door ajar, so I stopped and peered inside, hoping to have a word with him."

The judge frowned. "Whose bedchamber?"

"Lord Dunsford's, my lord. Edward Boswick, fifth earl of Dunsford."

"Let the record show that Eddie and Edward Boswick, fifth earl of Dunsford, are one and the same." The judge gave Mr. Forsythe a stern look. "We must keep the record straight."

"Of course, my lord."

"Proceed," the judge said with a nod of his head to Mr. Forsythe.

"When I saw the body, and it was clear to me that he had been murdered, I left his room, secured a key from the housekeeper to lock the room, and instructed the staff that no one was to enter, and then I sent one of the servants for the constable. By this time, the others were arising, and I told them the awful news. They all appeared shocked, as one might expect."

"You say you gave instructions that no one was to enter?" the prosecutor once again had his face lifted upward as if waiting for God to shower blessings on him.

"Yes, of course. I thought it best to make certain the crime scene was not corrupted," Mr. Forsythe answered.

"As one would expect of a barrister," the judge said.

Prosecutor Crudgington nodded slightly, and then, with his back to Mr. Forsythe, said, "No more questions."

Mr. Forsythe made no move to leave the witness box. Instead, he spoke to Crudgington's back. "Excuse me, sir, but I believe it may be of some interest to you to know that George Stirling is not dead."

Crudgington turned around as quickly as a man of his

girth could turn. "It is for me to decide what is of interest
to me. You may step down, Mr. Forsythe."

"George Stirling?" The judge wore a puzzled frown.

"The person the defendant referred to as Georgie, my
lord," Mr. Forsythe said. "And I believe Elsie knew he was
alive by the time Earl Dunsford was killed, so she had no
motive to kill him."

Crudgington's face turned red with rage. "Mr. Forsythe,
you should know that kind of ridiculous speculation is of
no value to—"

The judge interrupted, while at the same time holding up
his hand to silence Crudgington. "Why, Mr. Forsythe, do
you believe this man George Stirling to be alive?"

"Because, my lord, I have spoken with him myself."

"Mr. Forsythe," Crudgington said, all but shouting,
"whether or not you imagine yourself to have spoken with
this person has no bearing on this case."

The judge turned a gaze, hot with anger, on the prosecutor. "Mr. Crudgington, sit down. And you will refrain
from interrupting me." While Crudgington moved away, the
judge turned back to Mr. Forsythe. "I assume your conversation with this George Stirling does have some bearing on
the case. Otherwise, you would not have mentioned it. Now,
pray tell, what did he say that you think is of importance."

"He said, first of all, my lord, that he was severely strangled and then left for dead by the same person who killed
Lord Dunsford."

There was an excited murmur in the courtroom, and the
judge pounded his gavel for silence. "Go on, Mr. Forsythe.
Did Mr. Stirling know this person?"

"He did, indeed, sir."

"And he revealed his name to you?"

"I'm afraid not, but—"

Crudgington threw up his hands. "Of course not! You are
wasting my time and the court's time, Mr. Forsythe. Now
if you will kindly step—"

"But he led me to believe the killer was at Montmarsh,"
Mr. Forsythe said. "And I believe he plans to kill him for
putting the blame on Elsie."

An even louder excited murmur issued from the crowd and brought the judge's gavel down several times. When the room was finally quiet, the judge spoke again. "Mr. Forsythe, you say he *led* you to believe. You, of all people, should know that kind of speculation is not admissible. Did he or did he not say the killer is at Montmarsh?"

Mr. Forsythe wore a troubled look. "My lord, I am only trying to point out that there is reason to doubt the guilt of—"

"Mr. Forsythe," the judge interrupted again, "unless you can produce this George Stirling, it will be very difficult for me to give much consideration to what you allege he has told you. Can you find him and bring him here to testify?"

"I'm afraid not." Mr. Forsythe appeared quite nervous now, a fact that seemed to cheer Mr. Crudgington.

"And why not?" The judge sounded unquestionably annoyed.

"He has disappeared," Mr. Forsythe answered. "And all my attempts to find him have been in vain."

The judge was silent for a moment, apparently contemplating all that Mr. Forsythe had said. Finally he spoke. "Constable Snow, you will make every attempt to locate one George Stirling. Mr. Forsythe, you will cooperate with the constable and tell him everything you know about where and when you last saw Mr. Stirling." He turned then to the prosecutor. "Mr. Crudgington, who is your next witness?"

"Dr. Alexandra Gladstone, sir."

The judge hit the desk with his gavel again. "There will be a brief recess before Dr. Gladstone is called."

The murmur of voices resumed after the judge left the courtroom, and Nancy turned to Alexandra to speak to her. "You must be careful, miss. Don't say anything to get that poor girl hanged."

Alexandra hardly heard her. She was still reliving the scene of Lord Dunsford dead on his bed. She was only vaguely aware of Mr. Forsythe at the front of the courtroom, surrounded by people, and of his glances at her as if he wished to speak to her.

Nancy touched her arm. "Miss Alex, are you all right?"

Alexandra stood up suddenly. "I must leave, Nancy." She tried to push her way through the crowd, but Nancy caught her hand.

"But, miss. You have to testify in five minutes. You must wait."

"No!" Alexandra pulled her hand away from Nancy's. "I know who the murderer is, and I'm afraid George is about to be the next victim."

18

❧

Alexandra found it difficult to get through the crowd. Her role as "next witness" made her something of a celebrity. Everyone wanted to talk to her.

"That dirty little scullery maid killed the earl, didn't she?"

"What can you say to prove 'er innocent?"

"Is that Forsythe dandy lying, miss, or is 'e crazy?"

"Who killed the poor bloke? Was it Stirling?"

"I'm sorry," Alexandra said, pushing her way through. "I've been admonished not to talk about the case. Please excuse me. I must get through." As she tried to make her way past the crowd, she looked for the person she knew to be the murderer, but to no avail. She knew the killer must be looking for George now that Mr. Forsythe had testified he'd seen him at Montmarsh. She knew she had to find George first if she was to save his life.

By the time she finally reached the door, the five-minute recess had ended, and she heard the bailiff asking for quiet. Everyone turned away from her, leaving her in the hallway as they returned to their seats.

The court would be called to order soon, and she would be called to testify, but she could not stop. As soon as she

was on the street she saw that it was empty of both pedes-
trians and carriages. She hoped that meant she had gotten
out ahead of the killer and could get to George first.

She reasoned that because of Mr. Forsythe's testimony,
the killer would go to Montmarsh to look for George, and,
in spite of the fact that her repeated searches for him had
yielded nothing, she still thought George was most likely at
Montmarsh. He had said he thought that would be the safest
place for him once the killer was out of the way. He was
not right, of course, but George's intelligence was lacking.
Also, he was obviously afraid of trying it on his own in
some unknown place.

She found Lucy where she had left her outside the tavern
and rode as fast as she dared without risking tiring her too
much all the way to Montmarsh.

When she arrived, she saw a carriage waiting in front
without a driver. That must mean the killer had left the
tavern ahead of her. She rode to the back of the house and
slid off of Lucy and left her to graze untied and unfettered.
She hurried to the back door, hoping it was still open. She
hoped, too, that the patch of wild grass just outside of Montmarsh's manicured lawns would keep Lucy from straying
too far.

Her heart was pounding and her breathing still coming in
gasps as she reached the door. It was, indeed, still open,
and she took a cautious step inside and then another and
another, trying not to make a sound, not knowing whether
to call out to George or to call out the murderer's name as
a way to alert George that he was in danger.

She stopped suddenly and caught in her breath as someone moved out of the shadows and stood in front of her.

"Dr. Gladstone?" Isabel laughed. "I never expected it to
be you."

"Shhh!" Alexandra placed a finger to her lips. "What are
you doing here?" She spoke in an urgent whisper.

"I followed Jerry." Isabel spoke none too quietly. "I've
long suspected he had a mistress. But you of all people? I
knew if I followed him and caught the two of you, he could

no longer threaten to divorce me for my own little indiscretions, and—"

She was interrupted by a scream, throbbing with terror. It seemed to be coming from beneath them. From the cellar! It was followed by the sound of a struggle and the muffled sound of groaning. Alexandra turned away from Isabel and ran out the door and toward the cellar. She had just reached the bottom step when she saw Jeremy Atewater emerge from the shadows, his left arm covered with blood and blood oozing from between the fingers of his right hand where he held his wounded arm. He stopped when he saw her.

"So it's you," he said, echoing his wife's words.

"Where's George?" She knew the answer almost as soon as she'd said the words. As her eyes grew accustomed to the darkness, she saw him sprawled, lifeless, in a pool of blood on the cellar floor. His own knife was clutched in his hand with the blade lying across his sliced and bleeding neck.

"You knew, didn't you?" Atewater continued to move toward her as he spoke, and she instinctively backed up the stairs, then turned and ran. She saw Isabel standing at the top of the cellar stairs, wide-eyed and frightened.

"Jerry! What does this mean? How could you . . ." Isabel never finished her sentence; instead she screamed and tried to run away, but she stumbled on the train of her skirt and fell directly in front of Alexandra. There was no time to avoid her, and Alexandra tripped on Isabel's prone body, falling to the ground.

Alexandra scrambled to stand, but she felt Atewater's blood-dampened hand grab her arm and pull her to her feet. In the same instant she glanced down and saw that Isabel was unconscious. She'd hit her head on the short stone wall that lined the path to the stables.

Atewater twisted her arm behind her, forcing her back against him. She could feel the blood from his wounded left arm soaking into her dress. "I should have killed you myself when that idiot I hired because I thought you were on to me bungled the job that night at your stables." He tightened his grip. "But I found that I'd rather come to like you, and I kept hoping maybe you didn't know the truth after all." He placed his mouth close to her ear and whispered, "Ah, what fools you ladies turn us into, just with your winning ways. Now I shall have to do what I should have done long ago."

"If you've severed an artery in your arm, you'll die first," Alexandra said.

Atewater laughed. "It will do you no good to try to frighten me, Doctor. The wound is superficial. George is no better with a knife than the idiot from the waterfront I hired to kill you."

In the next second he had something around her throat, pulling it tight, sending daggers of pain to her head and shoulders as it pressed into the wound she'd sustained a few days before. He let go of the arm he had twisted behind her back and used both hands to tighten the cord.

Instinctively, she grasped at the cord, trying to loosen it, then knowing, as it pulled even tighter, that she should attack him in some way to get him to drop the cord. His eyes, or his injured arm. But she could not think how to do it as the world around her grew darker and darker and her breath, trapped in her throat, could not get to her lungs. Her lungs were on fire, and the old wound at her throat sent a roaring tide of pain throughout her body. When her eyes started to ache, she knew they were beginning to bulge, just as Lord Dunsford's had. Then she heard her own ghastly choking sounds.

Suddenly there was another sound, deep, loud, closer, filling her first with terror and then with relief just as some enormous form sent her and Atewater staggering backward, crashing to the ground.

"After him, Zack. Don't let him go!" It was Nancy's voice calling to the dog. Atewater, in the meantime, was screaming in terror as Zack clamped his enormous jaws onto his wounded arm.

Alexandra, still dazed, called out to Zack to stop just as two more forms moved past her and, when Zack backed away, pulled Atewater to his feet. It took a moment for her to realize that it was Mr. Forsythe and Constable Snow.

Much later, when she was propped up in her bed with half a dozen pillows and Zack curled into an enormous ball on the floor beside her, she saw Mr. Forsythe again. He, along with Lord Winningham, Isabel Atewater, and Constable Snow, was standing at the foot of her bed. Nancy was hovering over her with a steaming cup of tea. She realized she must have blacked out, just as George had when he had been left for dead.

Remembering George, she sat up suddenly. "Someone has to see to George; I think he may be—" Her voice was hoarse.

"Now, now, miss, you mustn't fret. Here, drink this." Nancy thrust the teacup toward her.

"But—"

"It's been taken care of, Dr. Gladstone," Constable Snow said.

Alexandra was still agitated. "It was Atewater. He killed Lord Dunsford, but I don't know why he—"

"Please don't trouble yourself." Snow's voice was low, almost soothing. "We got a full confession from Mr. Atewater."

"But how did you all get here. . . ." Alexandra felt disoriented and had to fight a feeling of anxiety.

"You can thank Nancy for that," Mr. Forsythe said. "When you failed to appear as a witness, it was she who told us where she thought you'd gone and why. We all got to Montmarsh as quickly as we could. Nancy insisted on stopping here first to pick up Zack. Rather fortunate that she did, I should say."

"And George, you must tell me whether he—"

"George is dead." Mr. Forsythe's voice was quiet. She had suspected it all along, of course, but she needed confirmation, and she was grateful that Mr. Forsythe knew how wrong it would be to keep it from her. "Atewater didn't fail the second time," he said. "But young George put up a good fight. He wounded Atewater."

"Atewater was the one who was using those boys. Getting them to steal for him." Alexandra looked at Mr. Forsythe again for confirmation of what she had just said, but it was Isabel who responded.

"The bastard! He never told me how desperate he was. He had to turn to stealing because the bank was failing. Now we're both disgraced!"

Lord Winningham patted her arm and murmured, "Now, now."

"And George was a part of his ring of thieves," Alexandra said.

Mr. Forsythe shook his head. "Not exactly. George had taken part in some of the petty thievery with Quince and the boys, but he was never in on the big heists. Atewater didn't think he was smart enough."

"But why would Atewater kill Lord Dunsford and George? Was the earl involved somehow with the robberies?"

"No, Eddie wasn't a part of that nasty business," Mr. Forsythe said. You could say it was Eddie's nasty personality and George's ego that got them killed, each in his turn. You see, when George got left out of the big jobs, he thought he could get even with Atewater by telling Lord Dunsford what was going on. He thought the earl would go to the police. But Eddie, true to form, didn't bother with the police. Instead he set out to blackmail Atewater."

"Oh, and of course Jeremy wouldn't stand for that," Isabel said.

"You're quite right," Mr. Forsythe said. "He went after George first out of revenge and thought he had killed him. Eddie thought so as well, and it frightened him. You may have noticed how nervous he was at his dinner party when he'd only just heard of George's supposed death. He knew Atewater would be after him, as well."

"Then why was he so foolish as to leave his door unlocked to allow Atewater to get into his room that night?" Alexandra asked.

There was a moment of embarrassed silence. Mr. Forsythe cleared his throat. "Eddie did lock his room, of course." Another awkward silence.

"Oh, for heaven's sake," Isabel said. "You may as well know the truth. Everyone else does. Jeremy used my key to get into Eddie's room. Yes, I had a key."

"I say, quite enough of this," Lord Winningham said, patting Isabel's arm.

"Did Atewater tell you all of this?" Alexandra asked.

"He did," Constable Snow said. "I find it interesting how men will confess everything when they're in a tight spot. Survival instinct, I suppose." He studied Alexandra's face for a moment, a finger placed to his pursed lips. "I suspect you had already figured out much of this. But I can't quite see why you put yourself in contempt of court by fleeing to Montmarsh to confront Mr. Atewater when you were supposed to be in the witness-box."

"I'm afraid I shall disappoint you, Constable, when I confess that I didn't know all of the details. I only knew that Jeremy Atewater was the killer, and that I wanted to keep him from harming George."

"I'm not at all disappointed, Dr. Gladstone. Merely curious as to how you knew about Mr. Atewater."

"We all are," Isabel said. "Even I didn't know it was Jeremy. How did you possibly know?"

Alexandra put her teacup aside. "It was Lord Dunsford's red silk nightshirt."

"What?" Isabel said, as everyone else murmured their surprise.

"It was while I was listening to Mr. Forsythe describe the murder scene to the prosecutor that I began to visualize the scene and the earl in his red silk nightshirt. Then I remembered that Atewater had mentioned the nightshirt once, commenting on how foolish the earl was to wear it. But no one had been in that room to see what he was wearing except Mr. Forsythe and me and the constable. Even when the earl's body was removed from the house, he was covered with a sheet."

Alexandra glanced at Isabel. "I think you may have seen

the earl in his nightshirt, Mrs. Atewater, because I know you were lurking outside his room, but I suspect it was only out of curiosity. And, in spite of the fact that you are a relatively strong, athletic woman, I did finally come to believe that you were not, in fact, strong enough to overcome a man the size of Lord Dunsford."

Alexandra, growing even more hoarse, leaned back into her pillows, which made Nancy exclaim, "You're tired now, miss. I'm afraid it's time your guests leave."

"You're certainly right, I'm sure," Snow said. "It will be a day or two before I need that statement." He gave Alexandra a courtly bow and turned to leave.

"Wait!" Her voice was weak as well as hoarse. "What about Elsie?"

Snow turned back to her. "Charges have been dismissed, and she has returned to the care of Mrs. Pickwick at Montmarsh, who, I might add, has decided to stay on until the new heir arrives. When you've had time to recover, Elsie will want to express her gratitude."

Alexandra nodded.

Snow cleared his throat and shuffled about in an uncharacteristically embarrassed manner. "I'm afraid there is one other thing, Dr. Gladstone."

"Yes?"

"You have been held in contempt of court for not being present to perform your duty as witness before the Queen's Bench."

"But if the charges against Elsie have been dropped—"

"That is of no consequence, I'm afraid," Snow said. "I'm sorry, Dr. Gladstone." She watched as Snow once again turned away to exit the room. Lord Winningham, in turn, took Isabel's arm. "May I offer you a ride, madam? I'm certain this has all been far too stressful for a person of such delicate constitution. My carriage is waiting outside."

There was a flicker of surprise in Isabel's eyes, replaced quickly by a coy expression. "How kind of you, Lord Winningham." She slipped her arm through his. "It is seldom that a lady meets a man who is so sensitive and understanding."

"Nancy, will you see everyone to the door, please," Alexandra said.

Nancy hesitated, then nodded and reluctantly left the room with Mr. Forsythe following behind.

"Mr. Forsythe." When Alexandra called to him, he turned around to face her. "I must know about the two boys who came here seeking my help. Artie and Rob. I think they may have been part of the jewel thief ring, but I didn't want to mention it in the presence of Constable Snow."

"Artie and Rob?" Mr. Forsythe frowned, considering the names. "I believe those are the names of your new stable boys."

"My what?"

"I'm afraid Nancy took it upon herself to fire your old one and hire new ones."

"Nancy's a bit cheeky, I'm afraid."

"Mmmm," Mr. Forsythe said.

Alexandra frowned, troubled. "But when the investigation is complete, the boys may be implicated. I'm not certain, of course. I'm only saying they may be."

"Then they shall be in need of a good barrister."

A slight smile touched her lips. "Of course."

Mr. Forsythe nodded again. "Good-bye, Dr. Gladstone. Nancy is right, you need your rest."

"Mr. Forsythe!" Alexandra said again, and once again he turned around to face her. "I must tell you thank you for your interest in this case and for your most capable help. I admire your intelligence."

"And I admire your intelligence as well, Dr. Gladstone." And then, as if it were an afterthought, he added, "Perhaps we shall be working together again."

"A lovely thought, but I can't imagine under what circumstances."

Mr. Forsythe raised an eyebrow. "Remember, Dr. Gladstone. Your new stable boys aren't the only miscreants here. You're facing a contempt of court charge. You'll be in need of a barrister as well." A slightly wicked smile crossed his lips before he turned to leave.

And now
an exclusive preview of

Savage Run

the new Joe Pickett novel
by acclaimed mystery writer
C. J. Box

1

On the third day of their honeymoon, infamous environmental activist Stewie Woods and his new bride Annabel Bellotti were spiking trees in the Bighorn National Forest when a cow exploded and blew them up. Until then, their marriage had been happy.

They met by chance. Stewie Woods had been busy pouring bag after bag of sugar and sand into the gasoline tanks of a fleet of pickups that belonged to a natural gas exploration crew in a newly graded parking lot. The crew had left for the afternoon for the bars and hotel rooms of nearby Henry's Fork. One of the crew had returned unexpectedly and caught Stewie as he was ripping off the top of a bag of sugar with his teeth. The crew member pulled a 9mm semiautomatic from beneath the dashboard and fired several wild pistol shots in Stewie's direction. Stewie had dropped the bag and run away, crashing through the timber like a bull elk.

Stewie had outrun and out-juked the man with the pistol and he met Annabel when he literally tripped over her as she sunbathed nude in the grass in an orange pool of late afternoon sun, unaware of his approach because she was listening to Melissa Etheridge on her Walkman's head-phones. She looked good, he thought: strawberry blonde hair with a two-day Rocky Mountain fire-engine tan (two hours in the sun at 8,000 feet created a sunburn like a whole day at the beach), small ripe breasts, and a trimmed vector of pubic hair.

He had gathered her up and pulled her along through the timber, where they hid together in a dry spring wash until the man with the pistol gave up and went home. She had giggled while he held her—*this was real adventure*, she'd said—and he had used the opportunity to run his hands tentatively over her naked shoulders and hips and had found out, happily, that she did not object. They made their way back to where she had been sunbathing, and while she dressed, they introduced themselves.

She told him she liked the idea of meeting a famous en-vironmental outlaw in the woods while she was naked, and he appreciated that. She said she had seen his picture before, maybe in *Outside Magazine*?, and admired his looks—tall and raw-boned, with round rimless glasses, a short-cropped full beard, and his famous red bandana on his head.

Her story was that she had been camping alone in a dome tent, taking a few days off from her freewheeling cross-continent trip that had begun with her divorce from an anal retentive investment banker named Nathan in her home town of Pawtucket, Rhode Island. She was bound, eventu-ally, for Seattle.

"I'm falling in love with your mind," he lied.

"Already?" she asked.

He encouraged her to travel with him, and they took her vehicle since the lone crew member had disabled Stewie's Subaru with three bullets into the engine block. Stewie was astonished by his good fortune. Every time he looked over at her and she smiled back, he was poleaxed with exuber-ance.

Keeping to dirt roads, they crossed into Montana. The next afternoon, in the backseat of her SUV during a thunderstorm that rocked the car and blew shroudlike sheets of rain through the mountain passes, he asked her to marry him. Given the circumstances and the super-charged atmosphere, she accepted. When the rain stopped, they drove to Ennis, Montana, and asked around about who could marry them, fast. Stewie did not want to take the chance of letting her get away. She kept saying she couldn't believe she was doing this. He couldn't believe she was doing this either, and he loved her even more for it.

At the Sportsman Inn in Ennis, Montana, which was bustling with fly fishermen bound for the trout-rich waters of the Madison River, the desk clerk gave them a name and they looked up Judge Ace Cooper (Ret.) in the telephone book.

Judge Cooper was a tired and rotund man who wore a stained white cowboy shirt and an elk horn bolo tie with his shirt collar open. He performed the ceremony in a room adjacent to his living room that was bare except for a single filing cabinet, a desk and three chairs, and two framed photographs—one of the judge and President George H. W. Bush, who had once been up there fishing, and the other of the judge on a horse before the Cooper family lost their ranch in the 1980s.

The wedding ceremony had taken eleven minutes, which was just about average for Judge Cooper, although he had once performed it in eight minutes for two Indians.

"Do you, Allan Stewart Woods, take thee Annabeth to be your lawful wedded wife?" Judge Cooper had asked, reading from the marriage application form.

"Anna*bel*," Annabel had corrected in her biting Rhode Island accent.

"I do," Stewie had said. He was beside himself with pure joy.

Stewie twisted the ring off his finger and placed it on hers. It was unique; handmade gold mounted with sterling silver monkey wrenches. It was also three sizes too large. The judge studied the ring.

"Monkey wrenches?" the judge had asked.

"It's symbolic," Stewie had said.

"I'm aware of the symbolism," the judge said darkly, before finishing the passage.

Annabel and Stewie had beamed at each other. Annabel said that this was, like, the *wildest* vacation ever. They were Mr. and Mrs. Outlaw Couple. He was now *her* famous outlaw, although as yet untamed. She said her father would be scandalized, and her mother would have to wear dark glasses at Newport. Only her Aunt Tildie, the one with the wild streak who had corresponded with, but never met, a Texas serial killer until he died of lethal injection, would understand.

Stewie had to borrow a hundred dollars from her to pay the judge, and she signed over a traveler's check.

After the couple had left in the SUV with Rhode Island plates, Judge Ace Cooper had gone to his lone filing cabinet and found the file. He pulled a single piece of paper out and read it as he dialed the telephone. While he waited for the right man to come to the telephone, he stared at the framed photo on the wall of himself on the horse at his former ranch. The ranch, north of Yellowstone Park, had been subdivided by a Bozeman real estate company into over thirty 50-acre "ranchettes." Famous Hollywood celebrities, including the one who's early-career photos he had recently seen in *Penthouse,* now lived there. Movies had been filmed there. There was even a crackhouse, but it was rumored that the owner wintered in LA. The only cattle that existed were purely for visual effect, like landscaping that moved and crapped and looked good when the sun threatened to drop below the mountains.

The man he was waiting for came to the telephone.

"It was Stewie Woods, all right," he said. "The man himself. I recognized him right off, and his ID proved it." There was a pause as the man on the other end of the telephone asked Cooper something. "Yeah, I heard him say that to her just before they left. They're headed for the Bighorns in Wyoming. Somewhere near Saddlestring."

*   *   *

Annabel told Stewie that their honeymoon was quite unlike what she had ever imagined a honeymoon to be, and she contrasted it with her first one with Nathan. Nathan was about sailing boats, champagne, and Barbados. Stewie was about spiking trees in stifling heat in a national forest in Wyoming. He had even asked her to carry his pack.

Neither of them had noticed the late-model black Ford pickup that had trailed them up the mountain road and continued on when Stewie pulled over to park.

Deep into the forest, Stewie now removed his shirt and tied the sleeves around his waist. A heavy bag of nails hung from his belt and tinkled while he strode through the undergrowth. There was a sheen of sweat on his bare chest as he straddled a three-foot thick Douglas fir and drove in spikes. He was obviously well practiced, and he got into a rhythm where he could bury the 6-inch spikes into the soft wood with three heavy blows from his sledgehammer; one tap to set the spike and two blows to bury it beyond the nail head in the bark.

He moved from tree to tree, but didn't spike all of them. He attacked each tree in the same method. The first of the spikes went in at eye level. A quarter-turn around the trunk, he pounded in another a foot lower than the first. He continued pounding in spikes until he had placed them in a spiral on the trunk nearly to the grass.

"Won't it hurt the trees?" Annabel asked as she unloaded his pack and leaned it against a tree.

"Of course not," he said, moving across the pine needle floor to another target. "I wouldn't be doing this if it hurt the trees. You've got a lot to learn about me, Annabel."

"Why do you put so many in?" she asked.

"Good question," he said, burying a spike in three blows. "It used to be we could put in four right at knee level, at the compass points, where the trees are usually cut. But the lumber companies got wise to that and told their loggers to go higher or lower. So now we fill up a four-foot radius."

"And what will happen if they try to cut it down?"

Stewie smiled, resting for a moment. "When a chainsaw blade hits a steel spike, the blade can snap and whip back.

Busts the saw-teeth. That can take an eye or a nose right off."

"That's horrible," she said, wincing, wondering what she was getting into.

"I've never been responsible for any injuries," Stewie said quickly, looking hard at her. "The purpose isn't to hurt anyone. The purpose is to save trees. After we're done here, I'll call the local ranger station and tell them what we've done. I won't say exactly where we spiked the trees or how many trees we spiked. It should be enough to keep them out of here for decades, and that's the point."

"Have you ever been caught?" she asked.

"Once," Stewie said, and his face clouded. "A forest ranger caught me by Jackson Hole. He marched me into downtown Jackson on foot during tourist season at gunpoint. Half of the tourists in town cheered and the other half started chanting, 'Hang him high! Hang him high!' I was sent to the Wyoming State Penitentiary in Rawlins for seven months."

"Now that you mention it, I think I read about that," she mused.

"You probably did. The wire services picked it up. I was interviewed on *Nightline* and *60 Minutes*. *Outside Magazine* put me on the cover. My boyhood friend Hayden Powell wrote the cover story for them, and he coined the word 'eco-terrorist.' " This memory made him feel bold. "There were reporters from all over the country at that trial," Stewie said. "Even the *New York Times*. It was the first time most people had ever heard of One Globe, or knew I was the founder of it. Memberships started pouring in from all over the world."

One Globe. The ecological action group that used the logo of crossed monkey wrenches, in deference to late author Edward Abbey's *The Monkey Wrench Gang*. One Globe had once dropped a shroud over Mt. Rushmore for the president's speech, she recalled. It had been on the nightly news.

"Stewie," she said happily, "you are the real thing." He

could feel her eyes on him as he drove in the spiral of spikes and moved to the next tree.

"When you are done with that tree I want you," she said, her voice husky. "Right here and right now, my sweet, sweaty . . . *husband.*"

He turned and smiled. His face glistened and his muscles were swelled from swinging the sledgehammer. She slid her T-shirt over her head and stood waiting for him, her lips parted and her legs tense.

Stewie slung his own pack now and, for the time being, had stopped spiking trees. Fat black thunderheads, pregnant with rain, nosed across the late-afternoon sky. They were hiking at a fast pace toward the peak, holding hands, with the hope of getting there and pitching camp before the rain started. Stewie said they would hike out of the forest tomorrow and he would call the ranger station. Then they would get in the SUV and head southeast, toward the Bridger-Teton Forest.

When they walked into the herd of cattle, Stewie felt a dark cloud of anger envelop him.

"Range maggots!" Stewie said, spitting. "If they're not letting the logging companies in to cut all the trees at taxpayer's expense, they're letting the local ranchers run their cows in here so they can eat all the grass and shit in all the streams."

"Can't we just go around them?" Annabel asked.

"It's not that, Annabel," he said patiently. "Of course we can go around them. It's just the principle of the thing. We have cattle fouling what is left of the natural ecosystem. Cows don't belong in the trees in the Bighorn Mountains. You have so much to learn, darling."

"I know," she said, determined.

"These ranchers out here run their cows on public land— our land—at the expense of not only us but the wildlife. They pay something like four dollars an acre when they should be paying ten times that, even though it would be best if they were completely gone."

"But we need meat, don't we?" she asked. "You're not a vegetarian, are you?"

"Did you forget that cheeseburger I had for lunch in Cameron?" he said. "No, I'm not a vegetarian, although sometimes I wish I had the will to be one."

"I tried it once and it made me lethargic," Annabel confessed.

"All these western cows produce about five percent of the beef we eat in this whole country," Stewie said. "All the rest comes from down South, in Texas, Florida, and Louisiana, where there's plenty of grass and plenty of private land to graze them on."

Stewie picked up a pinecone, threw it accurately through the trees, and struck a black bald heifer on the snout. The cow bolted, turned, and lumbered away. The small herd moved loudly, clumsily cracking branches and throwing up fist-sized pieces of black earth from their hooves.

"I wish I could chase them right back to the ranch they belong on," Stewie said, watching. "Right up the ass of the rancher who has lease rights for this part of the Bighorns."

One cow had not moved. It stood broadside and looked at them.

"What's wrong with that cow?" Stewie asked.

"Shoo!" Annabel shouted. "Shoo!"

Stewie stifled a smile at his new wife's shooing and slid out of his pack. The temperature had dropped twenty degrees in the last ten minutes and rain was inevitable. The sky had darkened and black coils of clouds enveloped the peak. The sudden low pressure had made the forest quieter, the sounds muffled and the smell of cows stronger.

Stewie Woods walked straight toward the heifer, with Annabel several steps behind.

"Something's wrong with that cow," Stewie said, trying to figure out what about it seemed out of place.

When Stewie was close enough he saw everything at once: the cow trying to run with the others but straining at the end of a tight nylon line; the heifer's wild white eyes; the misshapen profile of something strapped on it's back that was large and square and didn't belong; the thin reed of antenna that quivered from the package on the heifer's back.

"Annabel!" Stewie yelled, turning to reach out to her—but she had walked around him and was now squarely between him and the cow.

She absorbed the full, frontal blast when the heifer detonated, the explosion shattering the mountain stillness with the subtlety of a sledgehammer bludgeoning bone.

Four miles away, a fire lookout heard the guttural boom and ran to the railing with binoculars. Over a red-rimmed plume of smoke and dirt, he could see a Douglas fir launch like a rocket into the air, where it turned, hung suspended for a moment, then crashed into the forest below.

Shaking, he reached for his radio.

2

Eight miles out of Saddlestring, Wyoming, Game Warden Joe
Pickett was watching his wife Marybeth work their new
Tobiano paint horse, Toby, in the round pen when the call
came from the Twelve Sleep County Sheriff's office.

It was early evening, the time of night when the setting
sun ballooned and softened and defined the deep velvet
folds and piercing green trees of Wolf Mountain. The nor-
mally dull pastel colors of the weathered barn and the red-
rock canyon behind the house suddenly looked as if they
had been repainted in acrylics. Toby, a big dark bay gelding
swirled with brilliant white that ran up over his haunches
like thick spilled paint upside down, shone deep red in the
evening light and looked especially striking. So did Marybeth, in Joe's opinion, in her worn Wranglers, sleeveless
cotton shirt, and her blond hair in a ponytail. There was no
wind, and the only sound was the rhythmic thumping of
Toby's hooves in the round pen as Marybeth waved the
whip and encouraged the gelding to shift from a trot into a
slow lope.

The Saddlestring district was considered a "two-horse
district" by the Game and Fish Department, meaning that

the department would provide feed and tack for two mounts to be used for patrolling. Toby was their second horse.

Joe stood with his boot on the bottom rail and his arms folded over the top, his chin nestled between his forearms. He was still wearing his red cotton Game and Fish uniform shirt with the pronghorn antelope patch on the sleeve and his sweat-stained gray Stetson. He could feel the pounding of the earth as Toby passed in front of him in a circle. He watched Marybeth stay in position in the center of the pen, shuffling her feet so she stayed on Toby's back flank. She talked to her horse in a soothing voice, urging him to gallop—something he clearly didn't want to do.

Persistent, Marybeth stepped closer to Toby and commanded him to run. Marybeth still had a slight limp from when she had been shot nearly two years before, but she was nimble and quick. Toby pinned his ears back and twitched his tail but finally broke into a full-fledged gallop, raising the dust in the pen, his mane and tail snapping behind him like a flag in a stiff wind. After several rotations, Marybeth called "Whoa!" and Toby hit the brakes, skidding to a quick stop where he stood breathing hard, his muscles swelled, his back shiny with sweat, smacking and licking his lips as if he was eating peanut butter. Marybeth approached him and patted him down, telling him what a good boy he was, and blowing gently into his nostrils to soothe him.

"He's a stubborn guy—and lazy," she told Joe. "He did *not* want to lope fast. Did you notice how he pinned his ears back and threw his head around?"

Joe said *yup.*

"That's how he was telling me he was mad about it. When he's doing that he's either going to break out of the circle and do whatever he wants to, or stop, or do what I'm asking him to do. In this case he did what I asked and went into the fast lope. He's finally learning that things will be a lot easier for him when he does what I ask him."

"I know it works for me," Joe said and smiled.

Marybeth crinkled her nose at Joe, then turned back to Toby. "See how he licks his lips? That's a sign of obedience. He's conceding that I am the boss. That's a good sign."

Joe fought the urge to theatrically lick his lips when she looked over at him.

"Why did you blow in his nose like that?"

"Horses in the herd do that to each other to show affection. It's another way they bond with each other." Marybeth paused. "I know it sounds hokey, but blowing in his nose is kind of like giving him a hug. A horse hug."

"You seem to know what you're doing."

Joe had been around horses most of his life. He had now taken his buckskin mare Lizzie over most of the mountains in the Twelve Sleep Range of the Bighorns in his district. But what Marybeth was doing with her new horse Toby, what she was getting out of him, was a different kind of thing. Joe was duly impressed.

A shout behind him shook Joe from his thoughts. He turned toward the sound, and saw nine-year-old Sheridan, five-year-old Lucy, and their seven-year-old foster daughter April stream through the backyard gate and across the field. Sheridan held the cordless phone out in front of her like an Olympic torch, and the other two girls followed.

"Dad, it's for you," Sheridan called. "A man says it's very important."

Joe and Marybeth exchanged looks and Joe took the telephone. It was County Sheriff O. R. "Bud" Barnum.

There had been a big explosion in the Bighorn National Forest, Barnum told Joe. A fire lookout had called it in, and had reported that through his binoculars he could see fat dark forms littered throughout the trees. It looked like a "shitload" of animals were dead, which is why he was calling Joe. Dead game animals were Joe's concern. They assumed at this point that they were game animals, Barnum said, but they might be cows. A couple of local ranchers had grazing leases up there. Barnum asked if Joe could meet him at the Winchester exit off of the interstate in twenty minutes. That way, they could get to the scene before it was completely dark.

Joe handed the telephone back to Sheridan and looked over his shoulder at Marybeth.

"When will you be back?" she asked.

"Late," Joe told her. "There was an explosion in the mountains."

"You mean like a plane crash?"

"He didn't say that. The explosion was a few miles off of the Hazelton Road in the mountains, in elk country. Barnum thinks there may be some game animals down."

She looked at Joe for further explanation. He shrugged to indicate that was all he knew.

"I'll save you some dinner."

*Joe met the sheriff and Deputy McLanahan at the exit to Win-*chester and followed them through the small town. The three-vehicle fleet—two county GMC Blazers and Joe's dark green Game and Fish pickup—entered and exited the tiny town within minutes. Even though it was an hour and a half away from darkness, the only establishments open were the two bars with identical red neon Coors signs in their windows and a convenience store. Winchester's lone public artwork, located on the front lawn of the branch bank, was an outsized and gruesome metal sculpture of a wounded grizzly bear straining at the end of a thick chain, it's metal leg encased in a massive saw-toothed bear trap. Joe did not find the sculpture lovely, but it captured the mood, style, and inbred frontier culture of the area as well as anything else could have.

Deputy McLanahan led the way through the timber in the direction where the explosion had been reported, and Joe walked behind him alongside Sheriff Barnum. Joe and McLanahan had acknowledged each other with curt nods and said nothing. Their relationship had been rocky ever since McLanahan had sprayed the outfitters' camp with shotgun blasts two years before and Joe had received a wayward pellet under his eye. He still had a scar to show for it.

Barnum's hangdog face grimaced as he limped aside Joe through the underbrush. He complained about his hip. He complained about the distance from the road to the crime scene. He complained about McLanahan, and said to Joe sotto voce that he should have fired the deputy years before and would have if he weren't his nephew. Joe suspected, however, that Barnum also kept McLanahan around because McLanahan's quick-draw reputation had added—however untrue and unlikely—an air of toughness to the Sheriff's Department that didn't hurt at election time.

The sun had dropped below the top of the mountains and instantly turned them into craggy black silhouettes. The light dimmed in the forest, fusing the treetops and branches that were discernable just a moment before into a shadowy muddle. Joe reached back on his belt to make sure he had his flashlight. He let his arm brush his .357 Smith & Wesson revolver to confirm it was there. He didn't want Barnum to notice the movement since Barnum still chided him about the time he lost his gun to a poacher Joe was arresting.

There was an unnatural silence in the woods, with the exception of Barnum's grumbling. The absence of normal sounds—the chattering of squirrels sending a warning up the line, the panicked scrambling of deer, the airy winged drumbeat of flushed Spruce grouse—confirmed that something big had happened here. Something so big it had either cleared the wildlife out of the area or frightened them mute. Joe could feel that they were getting closer before he could see anything to confirm it. Whatever it was, it was just ahead.

McLanahan quickly stopped and there was a sharp intake of breath.

"Holy shit," McLanahan whispered in awe. *"Holy shit."*

The still-smoking crater was fifteen yards across. It was three-feet deep at its center. A half-dozen trees had been blown out of the ground and their shallow rootpans were exposed like black outstretched hands. Eight or nine black bald cattle were dead and still, strewn among the trunks of trees. The earth below the thick turf rim of the crater was dark and wet. Several large white roots, the size of leg bones, were pulled up from the ground by the explosion and now pointed at the sky. Cordite from the explosives, pine from broken branches, and upturned mulch had combined in the air to produce a sickeningly sweet and heavy smell.

Darkness enveloped them as they slowly circled the crater. Pools of light from their flashlights lit up twisted roots and lacy pale-yellow undergrowth.

Joe checked the cattle, moving among them away from the crater. Most had visible injuries as a result of fist-sized rocks being blown into them from the explosion. One heifer was impaled on the fallen tip of a dead pine tree. The rest of the herd, apparently unhurt, stood as silent shadows just beyond his flashlight. He could see dark heavy shapes and hear the sound of chewing, and a pair of eyes reflected back blue as a cow raised its head to look at him. They all had the same brand—a "V" on top and a "U" on the bottom divided by a single line. Joe recognized it as the Vee Bar U Ranch. These were Ed Finolla's cows.

McLanahan suddenly grunted in alarm and Joe raised his flashlight to see the deputy in a wild, self-slapping panic, dancing away from the rim of the crater and ripping his jacket off of himself as quickly as he could. He threw it violently to the ground in a heap and stood staring at it.

"What in the hell is wrong with you?" Barnum asked, annoyed.

"Something landed on my shoulder. Something heavy and wet," McLanahan said, his face contorted. "I thought it was somebody's hand grabbing me. It scared me half to death."

McLanahan had dropped his flashlight, so from across the crater Joe lowered his light onto the jacket and focused his Mag Light into a tight beam. McLanahan bent down into the light and gingerly unfolded the jacket; poised to jump back if whatever had fallen on him was still in his clothing. He threw back a fold and cursed. Joe couldn't see for sure what McLanahan was looking at other than an object that was dark and moist.

"What is it?" Barnum demanded.

"It looks like . . . well . . . it looks like a piece of *meat*." McLanahan looked up at Joe vacantly.

Slowly, Joe raised the beam of his flashlight, sweeping upward over McLanahan and following it up the trunk of a lodgepole pine and into the branches. What Joe saw, he would never forget . . .